Alexandria 2050

A Novel by Subhi Fahmawi

Translator: Siham A. Hammouda
Middle East Manager and Editor: Ahmed M. Shalaby
Cover Design: Kareem Metwalee

AEEH PRESS INC

Sobhi Fahmawi draws a smile on the lips.

Readers, may it bring joy to their hearts dyed with tragedies and make a spokesman for the oppressed people everywhere in the world.

He won the "Tayeb Salih Award" in 2014 for a play entitled "Hatem Al-Taie the Mummy."

His literary works are more than 36 works, including 11 novels.

"Izbat," "Love in the Age of Globalization," "Harmtan and Muharram," "The Story of a Canaanite Lover," "Alexandria 2050", "The Black Widow," "Ali Bab Al-Hawa," "Sarwal Balqis," "My Jewish Friend," "Qaa al-Balad," and "Akhenaten and Nefertiti the Canaanite."

He has eight collections of short stories: Harvest Season, Uncomplicated Man, Twenty Girls, The Mummy Man, Chili Pepper, Attitudes, Everything for Sale, and Guffaws.

-"When it came time of the birth of the child of beautiful Myrrha - who turned into a luxuriant tree- its bark cracked and delivered a baby boy Adonis. The nymphs quickly picked him up, bathed him in his mother's tears and laid him on the grass. Adonis was so beautiful looking like God of vegetation."

(The Romanian poet Ovidus)

- "Would that you could live on the fragrance of the earth, and like an air plant be sustained by the light…. Your blood and my blood is naught but the sap that feeds the tree of heaven…. "I too am a vineyard, and my fruit shall be gathered for the winepress."

(Gibrane Khalil Gibrane, The Prophet)

"The collapse of an old world is indeed imminent. Something is going to happen on a vast scale. The world wants to renew itself."

(Hermann Hessen, Demian)

"Nile fled away and hid his head in the desert, and there it still remains concealed .Where he used to discharge his waters through seven mouths into the sea, there seven dried channels alone remained." (Thomas Bulfinch, The Age of Fable)

DEDICATED TO
18 QUANAWAT ROAD,
BAKOS QUARTER,
ALEXANDRIA.

Table of contents

THE PRIVATE INTELLIGENCE NETWORK!

Time: 25-9-2051
Place: Akka

We are a production network specialized in spying on people from birth to death. And based on the fact that he who is at death's door would collapse on the bed within the last hours of his life remembering his past and bringing back his memories from cradle to grave that events would flow pressed in his imagination with impressive speed during which he would recall everything as if he lived it now, our job rests on the digital recording of all that is going on the mind of man in that crucial moment.

The Romantic era that chanted about breeze crossing a beloved's cheek was over. If we expose the scandals and floating secrets that contaminate breeze before our eyes, a sane man would lose his mind and a pregnant would abort her embryo. This if she remained reasonable enough to keep her embryo!

The breeze that used to cheer up the bosom, my friend, we see now in front of our eyes permeated with living crawling worm! We mean it is permeated with moans, screams, information, secrets, messages, military codes, sciences, dangerous documents, betrayals, songs, films, music as well as voices for which God has sent down no authority.

All meditations, thoughts, hidden secrets within you, your grudge against others and unfair rulers, unimaginable future schemes that they cooked in their brothels and the vibrations of everyone who farts at the end of the earth would penetrate your ears that receive everything that comes from this integrated computer chip!

We exposed you and recorded all that in the guarded tablet.

The scandals, worries, and torments are indeed inflicted on the receiver that they could drive him insane, but there is clearness in the vision. We took the cap of invisibility off secrets; hence the secret is no longer a secret. Also, there is a specialty in receiving because these devices analyze and classify political data into scientific and technical ones together with numberless specialties…!

You can say that we are a private intelligence apparatus specialized in privatization. As that of the public intelligence is incapable of obtaining the ABCs of information that our private institutions record on their sensitive discs, it relies on to declassify what is classified!

We are skilled at tracking thoughts going on in the mind of outlaws and opponents, sucking, recording, and exposing the fakeness of hypocrites. We succeeded in digging in their minds from inside without approaching them and recorded all that go through their heads including thoughts, greediness, conspiracies, and deviation from the general framework!

And we, who carried out these pleasant heinous acts, though they contravene human freedom, do not refrain from detecting the moves of governments directed against the dominant capital. Yes, we spy on governments in favor of individuals. As long as they pay, we say to them, "Yes." We are simply a licensed technical company for wiretapping that carries orders out without arguing!

And upon the request of Mr. Burhan, we had recorded the thoughts going through his father's head Mashhour Shahir Ashahry within the last hours of his life as he was convulsing in the throes of death here in Akka. For this reason, we placed headphones on the head of engineer, Mashhour, not to make him listen to verses from blessed Quran while he was dying, but rather to wiretap and suck what is going on in his mind in this critical moment.

The dying Mashhour Shahir Ashahry, who was lying on his deathbed in his private suite which his daughter Samar prepared for him since his return for retirement, relaxation and spending the rest of his life among his people in the city of Akka, was drawing his last breath between life and death left for him feeling as if the sky approached the earth, while he was caught between them breathing from the eye of a needle! He was trying to enjoy the last universal light beam detected by his senses giving up on him and refraining from serving him. But his mind —his last fortress- was still working with impressive speed.

The memories, thoughts, and past fantasies that we sucked from the mind of man and recorded on a digital disc are really amazing and you can hear easily and softly on your cell phone. So, go ahead, man, listen and read what we had recorded, written, edited and presented in the form of an impressive novel which we could document, tabulate, arrange typographically and translate into all spoken languages in the following integrated chip:

THE YELLOW TIME!

O my God! How beautiful you are, white swan floating on the azure sea!

O paradise lying on the sands of the gold beach! How luscious you are, fairest of the fair being drenched with an orange fragrance that in your love, breezes fell. How chase you are, with the sea washing your feet and splashing its water that roars in your pool, climbing your bared legs, massaging them day and night that you look in it like the witch of elves! You bosom that occupies sea waves, rises and falls and the sheets of your up-and-down waves fashion the body form of women of Alexandria of all shapes, sizes, and colors, those dressed but appear to be naked and those carrying in their hands the papyrus on which the names of Allah are written.

O playful sweetheart, how arrogant and mean you are! You are ignoring me, looking away from me with arrogance and pride. You don't dream or ask about me, and though I love you and knock on your door, I got the cold shoulder from you!"

"Our separation so abides, and flies, that thou, residing here, go'st yet with me, and I, hence fleeting, here remain with thee." This is what Antony told Cleopatra as he was kissing her and continuing his verses,

"When such a mutual pair

And such a twain can do't, in which I bind,

On pain of punishment, the world to weet

We stand up peerless."

"Thou knew'st too well

My heart was to thy rudder tied by th' strings,

And thou shouldst tow me after. O'er my spirit

Thy full supremacy thou knew'st, and that

Thy beck might from the bidding of the gods"

Antony was enjoying the love of Cleopatra surrendering to him, but I am yielding to your love seizing control of me, Alexandria!

Many years passed and I'm away from you! They say, "Out of sight, out of mind" and I swear to God that I did not abandon you, but time was hard! I have been all over the globe and no corner of a beautiful woman's body was left without my wagons moving along it, but the beautiful for me are not the beautiful of Nizar. They are the seven hundred world wonders .I traveled around the world starting from Norway waterfalls escaping from the hands of God to fall amid dark green forests with flora and algae odors and valleys hung in the sky. I was captivated by clouds flying at the bottom of the ocean, wandered in burnt sand deserts where snakes swam in their internal rivers and enjoyed the beauty of Arabian Andalusian gardens taken hostage by the French who changed its name in the same way they change a girl's maiden name after her marriage to French gardens. I chased condiments, perfumes, and spices in the velvet road, along which Muslim Arabs walked toward Indo-China, and evaporated with the waterfalls of Equator with lustful scents in the jungles of Africa. Then I grew into a mango tree, the young breasts of which were close to Egypt delta, mother of the world, and Tsunami of the Far East tossed me to the Great Wall of China. I celebrated with Vietnamese liberated from depleted uranium, and then found myself attending the next party on the sand of the Arab world depleted of its black gold oil. I was frozen to be a statue in Alaska glacier and I jumped from Berlin revolving TV tower to Eiffel tower standing in the sky like a man staring at leaning tower of Pisa, and from liberty statue breaking loose from its bonds to world trade centers and those who are ill-intentioned!

I moved among all these wonders and other ones, but I find none like you, Alexandria, in this country! And I beseech you not to blame me because I am one hundred years old and started to show signs of dementia. Is this the age of dementia? I don't think so, for my grandmother had live one hundred and twenty years and she used to chop roasted broad bean with her teeth that were never treated by a doctor! which means that I am still in control of my mental faculties. Still, when I am alone with my mirror and stare at her eyes, I sigh and admit to myself lurking in her, "Hey, you, mellowed old man, you become senile!"

You, old man, have never realized that you will be back to Alexandria in 2050 after more than 80 years, since the first time you came to study at university. You returned fervently to see your son Burhan, longing to hug him and breathe his smell, worried about the medical examinations of your green grandson, Canaan, at Shanghai – Alexandria Hospital which he mentioned to you, saying, 'This is the European- Arab-African Department of International Medical Shanghai City for the celiac disease most consulting and surgical operations of which are conducted online via computers. Even Chinese needles in it are inserted under the guidance of the center!"

Hundred years and years of lost life as if you came to this world from a door and went out from another! You did not realize that you will live to see this green time! They used to say,

"There will come a yellow time for people, when yellow winds would blow and paint the entire universe with a yellow color that streets, houses, trees, and faces in it become yellow. Pale Gog and Magog would also attack turning everything into yellow color! You could understand all of this even in a fantasy world, yet that your grandson could be the pioneer of real green time has never crossed your mind.

Here is the hydrogen aircraft (Airbus 636) carrying you from Dubai. You can see from its small window the blue seas and pale deserts, racing white clouds in the air and steams covering the space surrounding it, to rise quickly crossing the gravity of the earth toward the cramped space. New aircraft are escaping the gravity of the earth like the launch of a satellite to cross the distance between Dubai and Alexandria International Airport in just half an hour as its automatic pilot said.

And the plane, with food, steams of its passengers, different scented beverage, sweet perfumes mingled with fart odor withering quickly thanks to efficient suction devices, was drawing you closer to Alexandria while its computer screens film and display for you in a live broadcast scene of delta area attacked by the effluent sea that floods a land which was once arable and green, and was almost approaching the dam lake which they have recently built above the branching of the Nile tails that were shallow, so they encircled them to make use of every drop that mingled with seawater in vain!

The plane proceeds with the bravery of a valiant person above the lake area approaching Abukir beach, an envious, spiteful, slothful who had no friends but that kind-hearted man Abusir with whom he kept the company in alienation and when earning for a living .The latter helped him, took pity on him, fed and sheltered him, but glorified be God " no good deed goes unpunished!" as Abusir suffered so much because of him not for once but many times— for thousand years and years— but his greed killed him. Then Abusir brought back the body of his cursed companion Abukir with him and buried it with its rottenness in this place. And after a long life the well-respected man, Abusir died and was buried next to Abukir.

Yet, history recorded but evil and did not preserve the generosity of Abusir, but rather the wickedness of Abukir and his ugliness. Therefore it eternalized him by naming the beautiful beach after his name, and nowadays no one in Alexandria keeps the sweet memory or knows anything about the kind man Abusir. Most of them love the wicked Abukir! Even you mortal, do you hate Abukir? Of course not, for you love her and wish that she will be back to breathe her gentle oriental air carrying with it the scent of the delicious fruit of guava farms and drown, drown in her shy calm sea.

It is astonishing how Man doesn't eternalize kind people! And if you don't like my ramblings, have a close look at history and you will find out that the most eminent characters being immortalized are murderers and ravagers starting from the cursed Satan that was more famous than all angels –it is a farce!- because the most appalling history murders were rewarded Nobel Prize for their violent killing and brutality . Which prize was they rewarded? It was Nobel Peace Prize! By God if it was Nobel Prize for war, for example awarding them a prize called Zios prize, the deity of war, it would have been possible, but that it was rewarded to those killers for "peace", is absurd!

Al Mamura beaches and Montaza Palace appear on your screen linked with Alexandria city in one architecture, and they were in your childhood days apart, separated by farmland. On the other side, Mariout Lake and salt evaporation pond, which used to sprinkle salt in the eyes, appear on your screen as if they never existed! They said they drained it, and here you can see that it is covered with architectural projects, colored with gardens, cheerful with parks, and glittering with their bewitching crystal towers! From afar you can see the vast wide space of demographic deformation of rusted squeezed tinned houses scattered in the ends of lake area seemingly belong to the remnants of farmers and workers eaten away and molded with the debris of globalization city together with those spitted and alienated by the capital freedom that banished them to far isolated deserts as if you were in front of architectural panorama with discordant pictures!

As for the spoiled city lying scantily clad, with all its dimensions on the beach sand, you felt the urge to thrust your face in its folds, descend into it , smell the wetness of its body flowing eastward and running away westward like the wings of a huge roc linking east with west!

The computerized host of the four-winged hydrogen-powered aircraft announces its near landing while you stretch out your hand to take a nerve tonic pill and swallow a pill of the elixir of life. In the meantime, people get ready for arrival and safety belt are released automatically without our consent to begird us, we, the passengers, while the safety airbag is swelling embracing our bodies to protect them from all sides. The aircraft equipped with means of safety lands softly and smoothly at the ground of Alexandria International Airport .You, then, feel safe being stuck to our mother the earth .O God, how beautiful this new airport is!

The first time you arrived at Alexandria through Cairo Airport was in autumn 1966, when you were seventeen years old. The plane, you boarded for the first time, was DC3, a two-engine aircraft that ascended with its shaking passengers above and between clouds, but you paid no heed to the vibrations of the plane taking off from Kalandia Airport in Al-Quds. You had never dreamed about boarding a plane as you heard only about those planes coming home, worn out by the victories of the Second World War ending up useless, therefore they were offered to those who did not fear God. Hence in 1948 they were enjoying bombarding caravans of displaced Palestinians who were carrying their children in their mouth escaping the lava of brute occupier like cats moving their kids away from a dangerous place. And amid casualties, there was a mother of a baby whom a shot of a sniper dimmed. She was gunned down on the sidewalk. Blood clots were bleeding from her wounded bosom by a bullet and flies were roaring above her bleeding corpse while her suckling remained stuck to her with his hands clinging to her breasts that became cool as he was still suckling, suckling for the last time!

The aircraft, stained with blood victims, played with them hide–and–seek, and then would surprise them from behind a mountain and bullied them. Later they bombed them as they were running away in the valleys to increases their fears. They hurried to get rid of them by driving them out of the green borders of Palestine toward the Arab deserts with moving sands!

LOVE IN CRUEL WIND!

This luxurious hydrogen-powered aircraft, made of lightweight paperboard as hard as metals, and whose secret lies in the paper including the same carbon atom present in hard iron —in one way or another- is different from that adventurous heavy metallic plane (DC3) where at that time a European lady was sitting next to you reading her book. She noticed how bewildered and worried you were. And when standing up to leave that plane, you shook her hand goodbye; hence you smelled on your hand her sensual woman's perfume!

(Don't work hard.) She said smilingly, "Do not work hard for no matter what you do, you will never become number one in the world, that is why you should give yourself a break, stop worrying and start living!"

You didn't know why she was telling you this! Was it because she loved you that she wished you long life, peaceful labor, and enjoyable happy life? Or was it to hold you back from contribution and keep you an Arab left behind by technology moving crazy fast? I wish you had listened to her words and had given your life a break from the misery of this fast worn out age! I wish you could have played and rejoiced despite annoyances.

But how would you rejoice if you are the son of bygone Palestinian Nakba? How would you rejoice if you were born in a tent, donated by great, merciful, savage, civilized, democratic authorities, which was blowing the blaze of scorching summer heat and dripping ongoing winter drizzle?

How would you rejoice if you had a childhood dipped in gluey mud in which you were molded at cold winter nights, and played in when it rained with tender bare feet? You tried to get rid of mud by pulling your drowning leg slowly from here to stick there, that your foot would be wounded by a broken bottle buried in the mud of the sidewalk or a rusted iron nail would penetrate its soft flesh or your swollen feet would go blue from severe cold. And despite that, they kept wandering in the world of pains, while the yellow ooze letting off your red nose with sick rottenness scent found but flies to contain, so you wiped with your arm.

How would you rejoice and the torture of gastric juices of your stomach made your mother Zakia push toward you a plate on which there was a green tomato pickled with ammonia odor on the top of which a white layer of fungus of pickles which you ate ardently and insatiately with a loaf of bread she borrowed from your neighbor Umm Mousa promising her to pay her back when she would bake.

How would you rejoice if you spent a shattered miserable childhood walking determined in the path of water carriers collecting water in heavy buckets from the bottom of the valley, and then carried them laboriously, besides being assumed the responsibility in the mountain to irrigate plants of tomatoes, onion, eggplant, and moroheiya (Jew's mallow) that your father planted in a jointly-owned land and subjected his children to arduous work in it to feed you and keep you safe?

You walked in "the street of fog" while carrying heavy water. It was not "the heavy water" that the stray empire used to make small nuclear bombs similar to childlike toys that it threw on the street so that naughty children like you would pick them, and hence they would explode in their faces to accuse then those who survived of terrorism. The weight of the two irrigating water buckets was heavier, and you could not carry them, but you made a virtue of necessity. You were then walking with a feeling that your soft shoulders were dislocated and the muscles of your baby arms were torn apart that you could not stand it anymore!

How would you rejoice if you spent the beginning of your adolescence in the company of a white donkey as big as a mule on which you carried –upon your father's strict orders- farming requirements, plowed the earth, and ground the piles of wheat on the threshing floor and thus storing up a year supply of food so that you wouldn't need the loaves of your neighbor Umm Musa or Umm Isaiah or even Umm Mohammad!

With the call to fajr prayer, your father woke you up forcefully. You rose as if you were alone in this life, Adam without Eve! Was Adam tired when he descended to the earth with Eve or was he a mature wise man who was aware of his rights and duties? Was it true that Adam and Eve descended to the earth in a spaceship, one of those they talked about, coming from another planet, and because of a technical hitch in their vehicle, they were stuck on earth and could not return to their far planet? Hence, they stayed on this planet blameworthy and insolvent and their grandchildren remained up to now bored, complicated, depressed, gloomy and sad no matter what they possess because of their alienation from their remote mother country?

You got up as if you were Adam coming from a remote planet! Was Palestine another planet far from earth, and you were coming from it all alone? Did your spaceship crash here to be treated as a stranger…?

You got up at dawn and headed toward the corral where you saw your burro urinating on his dung, the fermented ammonia smells of which penetrated into your nose then into the bronchi of your lungs when biding him good morning. You took the strong faithful animal out and accompanied him toward the hard labor path! Because you were with no companion, you found yourself talking and complaining to him about your worries, while he was looking at you understanding your situation, and together you laughed at this insane fairytale life as you couldn't find anyone but him sympathizing with you and with

Palestinian people! You hold his bridle and walked next to him with a defeated soul with all confidence and determination! Have you ever felt a defeated soul walking with confidence and determination?

You walked in the company of your burro as being the greatest companion, talking to him, and confiding to him your imprisoned love. He sneezed in your face (Abrrrrr!) sprinkling you with the spray of his foamy saliva with the smell of fermented hay in his mouth. If it was a human being, you would have been angry and roared in rage but his spray was clean! At least he did not pollute his mouth by backbiting and for this; his sneeze was that of a good fellow! He talked to you about his concerns and you got angry because of his suffering, but you fought with him when he deviated from the way, and then shared his happiness if he saw a beautiful jennet passing by and went back from where he came to express his love and infatuation with her! And if your father saw you letting him break loose, he would look daggers at you, so you hold his bridle and kept him away from sin and recklessness asking him smilingly, "Don't you feel ashamed about yourself, you being a donkey as big as a mule?"

You couldn't understand that day, why you rejoiced over love even if it was between a donkey and a jennet. Perhaps, because you did not feel it between people for people did not love each other. They ruined the earth and spilled blood, whereas your kind donkey did not spill blood, but rather loved his jennet! You were watching him as he was trespassing obstacles as if he was in a race competition to reach her shelter. He embraced her fervently and rubbed his neck against hers. She was smiling as he was enjoying himself for moments cheering her up, while she was relaxing in front of him drawling! The one who said a donkey doesn't t know love is...

From that day on, you grew scared of the path of girls."The path of girls is thorny" Your grandmother Aneesa told you, whereas your mother Zakia didn't talk or say a word, (They are willfully` deaf, dumb and blind so they have no understanding.) Indeed Zakia was intelligent and understood love and life. You realized that when she once told you a popular saying in ignorance. Your father did not hear her, then, because if he did, he would cross her out from life records and considered her a history! She said then, "The one who wants to kiss me knows where my cheek is." I understood that she knew love and kissing. But she didn't know that a kiss moved from cheek to lips and other spots that we were not allowed to mention! She had knowledge but not the right because they officially appointed the Mufti and no one was authorized to give a formal legal opinion but Mufti who shattered us with crumbling his fatwa!

Zakia did not interfere because she did not eat porridge as much as she was beaten! Your father used to hit her for every slight mistake she did! So she- under rigorous instructions- became automatically programmed —she would wake up at dawn, knead the dough, and extinguish the fuming lamp to save its coal oil though the price of oil was not expensive those days.

The price of oil was fifty cents per barrel. God is great! The price of a big barrel of oil was half a dollar? Our Arab oil traders are indeed tough in trade and like their ancestors, they are traders of One Thousand and One Nights who used to sail the seas, wrestle genii, and tame the roc in the sky. And although they always lost their way, and the route in oceans was cut off before them, they came back home victorious with pieces of jewelry and diamonds they gathered from the bottom of the sea. They returned home after they had spread our Islam by trade and love in the land of East and West and not by the dirty war that the stray emperor waged against our Islam. And with their sincerity, integrity, and purity, Indonesians and Malaysians converted into Islam that urges to feed the poor and contrary to savage capitalism statement, it states, "The world belongs to God!" What difference is there between them and our great "oil traders!" who would sell us cheaply and sometimes our great oil pipe is opened to fill their hearts with seas of black oil for free without counters so that 'victorious men' would overflow. That's not what Arab voice from Cairo Radio said. It rather said, "Arab oil is for Arab, or we will burn it!"

"O Arabs raise your heads!" But no one raised his head! Even you, refugee, surrounded from all sides, did not raise your head in front of your "patriotic" village classmates in Al-Fadiliyah High School in Tulkarm as they were heading toward Taurus restaurant overlooking the city travels square to have lunch. "Today we will eat baked Kofta with tomatoes."

"Tahini kofta is more delicious," Another objected. "It has a soul-reviving smell especially when it is taken out of the oven very hot!"

And after many dialogues and deliberations, they entered the Taurus restaurant, agreeing that the half of the dish would be Tahini and the other half would be with potatoes. As for you, obscure, you had nothing to do but to wear the cap of invisibility and run away from them sneaking behind restaurants and shopping stores like a person who was tracing the scent emitted from kitchen exhaust fans, whose blades were covered with black greases as they were releasing their poisonous fumes and steams in the streets. You pulled out your loaf of bread that your mother folded and shoved between your books into your cardboard bag as you were reaching the remnants of a vendor standing on a street corner with his Falafel's frying pan shaking on a rusty metal stand with its tar-black oil which was boiling for ages. You bought three Falafel balls for one half piaster, smashed them up on the loaf of bread and then wrapped it like this…Before you sat on the edge of the sidewalk, you picked stray cardboard in the dust of the street and put under you not out of respect to you dear butt, but to not stain your trousers with the waste of burned greasy oil spilled on the sidewalk. You sat and mauled it with the passion of hunger and not with the gluttony of desire, reeking of Falafel oil that was boiling in the boiler and splashing on the ground!

How would you rejoice if your father used to give you two piasters every day-your pocket money- when going from the camp to school to pay one half piaster to Tablu bus for the going and returning trip? However, you used to save the piaster and walk a distance of four kilometers on your weak feet, and then would back again just to save what enabled you to buy Arabi magazine or Literature Magazine at the end of the month and see a movie featured by Abdel Halim Hafith and Zubaida Tharwat. You discovered love with suspension, then. You were eavesdropping on the talks of your civilized fellow students as they were flirting with beautiful girls and telling stories about love and passion, while you were alone thinking how disgusting you were, being a refugee living without love! And again, you ended up with an emotional problem.

You saw that girl student walking in front of you under heavy rain from the camp to her school in Tulkarm, while your black umbrella was shielding you from the rain. You started to think about that poor girl walking without an umbrella and a coat. She was not even wearing a sweater to protect her body wrapped with her green school uniform!

The freezing rain penetrated her thin body like bullets, but she carried on her walk swinging like a disciplined soldier walking forward inside a minefield under rigorous military orders! You didn't know even her name, and despite that you found yourself approaching and offering her to walk next to you under the umbrella.

The girl winced and walked away scared, continuing her walk in heavy rain!

You felt her stubbornness, but you took pity on her, and thus you gave her your umbrella while you remained unsheltered from cruel rain. You sacrificed yourself for her sake despite her refusal to approach you. You felt that the girl did not want to push you away, but she was afraid of a merciless community. If someone reported and said, "So-and-so was walking in the company of Mashhour in the way of Tulkarm." it would be a disaster! That's because people who were out of work kept themselves busy with gossip …The news would spread like wildfire and the scandal would ruin the girl. (Poverty and chastity are better than poverty and scandal!) The girl took the umbrella because she was dying from severe cold and water was interfering in her inner affairs and poured on her betrayed body cold and frost that you couldn't help making her feel your affection and mercy. You were looking for compassion and human love that no one gave you, so you tried to savor, embody, and give them to the street.

And like Arab-Andalusian seamen who challenged the perils of the storms of the Atlantic ocean looking for a western sea route to

India, and despite reaching the shores of the land of the Maya to be known later as Saint Augustine, and building palaces like Zoraida Palace and set up mosques along the shore, they failed to gain recognition from twisted history books of their shrewd adventures of discovering the new world.

And this is who you are. Though your body cells were freezing, you sacrificed your umbrella. The student drenched by cold rain did not confess her love to you; therefore, you realized that love had no room in this cruel wind!

A SNAKE OR A BELL!

Would the green generation of Canaan succeed in twisting the arms of man's evils against his fellowman? Is it a dream or an absolute reality?

You compare this stunning Alexandrian airport with that of Cairo where you deplaned for the first time. You read that day what was written on its gate, "Enter ye Egypt (all) in safety if it please Allah." You felt relieved for what you had read, then. And after a long queue in front of the security barrier, you had your passport stamped, and then carried your brown cardboard suitcase with you not knowing the way out of the airport or where to find a taxi to take you to Cairo City.

You went out that day wandering in the crowd, so one of the taxi drivers suggested that you should get in his small black car that was round like a turtle. The driver turned the ignition key, but it didn't work. He went out of the car and tried to push it with all the weak power he got, but the vehicle did not move! A policeman noticed its stillness in the station, and volunteered to push the vehicle while we were in and thus its ignition worked! What was this? A policeman helped you with pushing your car! I was used to the saying," A policeman is troublemaker!"

But this police officer was at the service of the public! You felt ashamed of the generous man and you didn't know how to pay him back! You heard that apple was rare in Egypt famous for mango, guava, and delicious orange, so you stuck your hand out of the little car window and handed him a red apple. The police officer felt happy, smelt its fragrant scent, and thanked you. The car then set off for a hotel whose name slipped your mind! Its name might be the Cairo Hotel.

And before you relaxed in your fresh room, you opened your suitcase; you found that it was not yours. It was the same brown cardboard suitcase with brass metal corners from outside and it was noticeable that most passengers' suitcases were of this type. It seemed that no one with you in the plane used Samsonite or Samsung suitcase... Even Uncle Sam himself was hidden from Egypt those days! But the cardboard suitcase was not the same from inside because the clothes and stuff in it weren't yours! What would you do about this mistake? You had nothing to do but to call the hotel reception. You picked up the phone carefully and told the receptionist about your problem. He told you, "I will transfer your call to the hotel reception."

You called the airport baggage clerk who understood your problem and promised you with a prompt solution. Just in an hour, the owner of the switched suitcase brought yours and took his and things went smoothly against all odds.

You looked at the view from the high balcony of your hotel room and you were amazed at these Cairo apartment buildings of different height and size, watching this myriad of pedestrians that you did not expect to be abundant as such. A seventeen-year-old boy moved from a camp and from kerosene lamp that barely lighted what was surrounding it and from a dreary moonless night to Cairo at once! You stretched your hand in the dark night of the camp, but you could not see it!

The electrical grid lines did not cut off and the generator was not out of order either to feel hopeless because there was no electrical grid in the camp to cut off! And while walking in narrow winding roads between obscure rocks, you came across this snake with horns or that rattlesnake that electrified you instead of electricity, as it was slithering after a mouse running away scared. Then they would disappear under a high prickly pear shrub surrounding every refugee's house! A prickly status for self-defense!

No refugee had a car to demand to make a road or just clearing one without paving it to reach his house because rocky narrow roads in the camp were bypass roads, and since then they have been changing, expanding in every part of the country like hepatic fibrosis disease that all Palestine was infected with, in which snakes with horns and rattlesnakes were roistering!

(She wrapped you, she did not wrap you. Your grandma fed you shit. Your fat grandma was broke.) This is how they used to sing for us, we refugees, to rejoice over our childhood!

You moved from that darkness straight away to electricity that turned night into day, a Nile like the sea, and an extraordinary city; Cairo City, the voice of the Arabs!

My father used to gather us under the blanket and open the radio on Voice of the Arabs from Cairo so that no one would hear us. We listened to the speech of Jamal Abdel Nasser secretly and rejoiced over his victories in Bur said! My father, elated, would scream, then.

"Oh, my God! Egypt defeated the attack of Great Britain and with it France and Israel! At last our turn came to achieve victories after eras of successive setbacks! "

My father who was feeling dispirited by the dreariness of Nakba all the time, used to rejoiced and exulted when looking at the photo of the great Arab leader in Photographer Magazine and the Last Hour Magazine displayed outside Saffarini Library in Tulkarm. We flipped through it, but we did not buy it as we could not afford it. He, illiterate, looked passionately at the leader that was standing with greatness, pride and glamour like all leaders of God's creatures next to Khrushchev above the High Dam saying to you, "look! Look! Wouldn't we witness a day when we rejoice and feel that we have a leader of whom we feel proud as he is standing shoulder to shoulder with world leaders and not...!"

You used to feel happy when Abdel Halim sang, "We said we are going to build the High Dam, and here we built the High Dam. O colonization, we had built it with our hands, the High Dam!"

And as far as you are concerned, without Abdel Nasser allowing Arab students to study in Egypt without differentiating them from their Egyptian students, you, as a refugee, would not have been able to enter universities at all. When you, later, educated your son Burhan in Germany you spent a fortune until he graduated and became a genetic engineer. Afterward, they cannily hired him to deprive him of returning home and serving his country. But what country would he serve? Are there any hereditary engineering laboratories in the big Arab world from the ....ocean to ...Golf?! Such a purposeless graduate would be hired by Arabs as a fifth-grade school teacher in Al-Ras village in Eastern West Bank, but you don't know east from west! Get lost!

THE PATH OF GIRLS IS THORNY!

As the hydrogen-powered aircraft is landing gracefully and quietly at Alexandria Modern Airport, you see from above a great number of paper planes spreading across the spacious airport. In our childhood, paper planes used to be mere papers fastened with threads that we played with and flew in the air, whereas now the giant planes become paper but as hard as copper... However, you are not thinking of the airport or of the way of strengthening carbon atom in paper to be as solid as carbon atom in copper or of the lightweight of paper of which modern aircraft are made instead of metals to legalize the consumption of conventional galvanized steel that is not available anymore in the world, neither are you interested in what they are inventing to lighten the weight of vehicles with aircraft at the top of the list so that their lightweight would result in the simplicity of manufacturing, increase the speed of the airplane and save energy as much as you are eagerly thinking of meeting Burhan and the little green Canaan.

Is this greening operation going to succeed, hence the green animal would seize control of this savage bestial universe? Are you witnessing a new transitory period after the primitive Man who once had been civilized, moved to the phase of the second Man, and here he is assuming the form of a green being after his civilization became savage and his earth was destroyed, and thus you are witnessing the phase of the third green Man?

When Burhan was young, you used to read for him The Prophet, a book written by Gibran Khalil Gibran, and you still remember some of his expressions, "Would that you could live on the fragrance of the earth, and like air, plant be sustained by the light." You were mesmerized by the expression "Your blood and my blood is naught but the sap that feeds the tree of heaven…." and you dwelled on the expression 'I too am a vineyard, and my fruit shall be gathered for the winepress…" You love Gibran who washes you with grape juice, saying, "That you might seek one another through vineyards, and come with the fragrance of the earth in your garments." Then he concluded by saying, "But these things are not yet to be."

It seems that the idea has been occupying the mind of Burhan since childhood and its time has come now, so he produces his green son, Canaan.

There is no doubt that your grandchild is enjoying his father's care and that the giant firms are chasing him to raise him with the best available means and introduce him to this universe turning into greenness.

You compare your misery with his care when you were his age because when paying school fees, the accountant used to say, "Do not take any fees from them because relief agency pays the fees of those… Is there a refugee among you to give him school books for free?"

He called loudly in front of all students queuing up in the school's courtyard in the morning, but you did not raise your head to not disgrace yourself, though Voice of the Arabs from Cairo shouted every morning like the rooster of One Thousand and One Nights, "O Arabs raise your head!" you were wondering on that day," Is it because they are refugees, Arabs didn't raise their heads? Did Arabs escape oppressing sand with their tents to space dust because they are refugees? Did Arabs run in the maize of the tents of Maysun al-kulaibi who said, "The tent on which free winds are beating" because they are refugees?

You are an oppressed refugee yielding to the shade of humiliation of relief agency that took your country from you, and then chased you to give you your daily bread, while those who claimed the heritage of Joseph threw you into a dark well! No one took pity on you but that one who banished you from your country, and then turned you into one of the tigers of Zakaria Thamer in the tenth day.

You were disdainful of this dirty game that the cat was playing with the mouse because after it had attacked it and enjoyed its sadistic playing, it let it slip out of its hands...amazing dramatic moves... a black distraction... You didn't know why the cat left it though it was at its disposal, while the poor creature run on the floor escaping its inescapable destiny before the criminal chased it down, picked it up again, and bit it allowing it to enjoy the last glimmer of life light before being eaten and swallowed. Similarly, charity organizations chased you, while you ran away terrified!

In the 20s and 40s of the 20th century, there were neither televisions nor newspaper reporters that could photograph the torture and killing of Palestinians resisting being uprooted from their cities and villages, and expose the colonizers who made them walk barefoot on the hard poisonous thorns of prickly pear leaves to remanufacture, refill and package them to be exported outside the country!

"We will make you sleep in your Palestine on beds of cactus spikes!" said the colonizer to those who were not killed, still clinging to their country soil. "Why are torturing yourselves? Migrate to countries of the Arabs (Arab countries are my home lands!) and give this small Palestine to the miserable escaping Hitler's oppression!"

The empires, allied against us, were those which resorted to eliminate a glorious state and create a new one in its place on the surface of the earth, and it was you who paid the price of all this hereditary modification because Arab Palestinians were replaced by strangers from all over the world by mighty power! They say that it's God who promised to give them a Canaanite land which is not theirs, a Canaanite language which is not theirs, a Canaanite temple which is not theirs, and a Canaanite star which is not theirs, why not? They are God's folk (*2), while we are relief agency's!

You walked with your head down and you didn't look at anyone! You didn't even think of flirting with one of the girls attending Rabiia Addawiya High School adjoining ours. They were beautiful, coquettish girls wearing short skirts showing an inch or two of their knees that they unveiled the temptation of the plumpness of their thighs brimful of luscious adolescent femininity! You didn't raise your head, not in opposition to Voice of the Arabs, but rather because you were not qualified to see the anesthetics of breasts that were overflowing with generosity, warmth, and affection arousing the feelings of children and grownups. You were even deprived of smelling that forbidden feminine scent, being confined within the limits of the smell of Falafel balls that were fried in a cauldron boiling with tar oil.

How would you taste the anesthetics of divinely-molded bodies of pink girls with glabrous skin walking among people? You didn't raise your head because you couldn't afford a perfumed damask rose that you could give to a girl from Rabia Al-Adawiya School, so you buried your head in the scent of Al -Arabi magazine - you poor thing -and you were felt shocked because you saw on its cover one of the beauties of this school. Her face was gorgeous. It was a childlike innocence with ripe femininity and an incredible charm of woman! Where did this pure angel come from? You read what was written below, "Tulkarm, the City that Sleeps at Sunset!"

You kept trying to give your love and passion to a feminine thing, but you could only find beautiful models photographed in natural colors on billboards advertising for perfume or soap or Nivea Cream or whatever, so you hung them on your bedroom walls. You were too cowardly to stand with a girl not because "girls' path is thorny" as your grandmother Aneesa told you, but because you were expecting your girl to ask you, "Which Tulkarm neighborhood do you live in?" You would feel, therefore, ashamed to tell her, "I'm from the camp." Hence, you found but a book to bury your head in, and that's why your relationship with the book became stronger as you understood the meaning of it as being the best companion.

It was arranged for us to read a piece of Caesar and Cleopatra play by Shakespeare for school reading. You remember Julius Caesar moaning in sadness, "Even you Brutus!" After that, he said, "Am the scabby sheep?" And this was our tall school friend Rasmy Minaret, who was used to stretching his head with his long neck that teacher Salim Al-Baziq called him, "O you minaret!" and since then his word had become a nickname!

Rasmy Minaret was standing in front of us, while we were gathering in summer heat behind his house, staying up late as he was enacting the theatrical role, gesticulating, bending his legs and pointing with his index finger, saying," Even you Brutus. Ah! Am I a scabby sheep that our neighbor Abu Salim painted with burnt tar oil?"

He was improvising the words Ah!, our neighbor Abu Salim, and burnt oil tar which made us laugh, we, the children of the camp, who had no stage but that one behind the window of the house of Rasmy Minaret which the relief agency built.

If Shakespeare had heard us saying ah! he would have sued us for tarnishing the intellectual property and would have asked for ten billion for that horrible mistake! And why wouldn't they pay? They had too much oil which would make Shakespeareans blackmail and fine them for the fall of a dead hawk from the sky and accuse "the Arab terrorists" of killing it. And those in authorities, "generous", would pay easily and smoothly the ten billion, obeying their masters, while their children were sleeping inside their tinplate houses hungry!

You walked in the city streets while keeping your head away from the heads of its residents wondering,

"Am I a scabby sheep?"

     (*) the holy book (10God gave you good great cities you didn't build, houses filled with all kinds of good things you did not provide, wells you did not dig, and vineyards and olive groves you did not plant--then when you eat and are satisfied. "Deuteronomy 5, 6/page 216". (Translation and examination by Private Intelligence Agency)

ONE THOUSAND AND ONE NIGHTS' PLANE

The hydrogen-powered quadruplane stops at Alexandria International Airport. You ask your seat computer for an explanation of that. The talking screen answers you, "The four wings were designed to provide a better balance and better protection in case a problem happened with the hydrogen burner of one of the wings, and its idea was originally taken from one of the giant birds in the amazing One Thousand and One Nights novel." You ask her jokingly, "Is this one of the amazing planes of One Thousand and One Nights? The computer woman giggles saying, "No matter how much we progress, we will never be able to realize the wonderful fantasies of One Thousand and One Nights. Did you read it?"

You and the comers disembark the plane and head toward the baggage claim area where you would receive your suitcase. *Are we going to meet at the appointed time, Borhan?* you thought. You set your watch to European flight schedules. Burhan is punctual for his appointments and work, and that's why, he is respected and hired by a college laboratory. When he started work, he told you in an intense voice," Father, I started working as a lab assistant. I clean test tubes and wipe tables." You answered him, "Work was not a shame especially if you had the goal of finishing your study ahead of you." You sensed his happiness flowing in your veins through phone head as he was saying," But I started to get involved in tubes and prepare settings intended to work at and when things went well, I began helping technicians with preparing the substance, the area of research."

And when they noticed his intelligence, they appointed him as a laboratory research assistant. He then seized his chance to study a Master's! Fifteen years had passed slowly since we left until Burhan earned his doctorate from German Hessen University. When Hessen Engineering Institute announced its need for researchers, he applied for joining the institute and they accepted him.

"I started to immerse into my work, father. And because of my feelings of alienation and discrimination, I spent day and night doing successive researches to prove to them that I'm capable of competing with them and even outdoing many of my colleagues in the institute! The results of my laboratory researches stunned my teachers!"

After five years of hard work, they hired a research assistant to help him. She holds a Master's degree in genetics.

"The girl is docile, helpful, innocent and highly impulsive." he said about her. "She, whole–heartedly, gives what she possesses including her researches, her doctoral study, good behavior, her stunning beauty and her uniqueness from other girls." And when he seized your satisfaction, he added cheerfully, "I started to go with her to the restaurant watching her chasing with her fork and knife the last rice grain. She ate it and cleaned her plate. I told her, then, "Why do you clean your plate of the last grain of rice? Is this all about cutting spending?" She answered me smiling, "We can in Germany import millions of tons of food, while nations are deprived of rice. Also, we shouldn't throw food in the dustbin so that other people find excess food to eat! "

You felt happy for Burhan, so you strengthened his roots by saying, "Our religion says, 'Waste not want not.' But is there anyone willing to revitalize our economy!"

"She recycles all garages in the garden," he added, "and she throws only rare waste in the garbage bin because plastics are put in a bin and glass is put in another one. I felt that I'm learning from her. I accepted her invitation to her apartment and after getting to know each other better I started to sleep over at her apartment."

Hence, you warned him severely, "Hold your horses, son! The path of girls is thorny!"

He answered you laughing, "That concept was popular back in your day, father. Today, girls are more careful than boys. Do not forget that they mature before guys and understand sex before them, and a woman who is working as a researcher in a laboratory is aware of her dignity, knows her path, knows deadly illnesses and plagues and does not go astray, that's why I accepted her invitation as my best friend after I was sure that no woman can make me happy as she does.
"

After she gained PhD, the gentleman gave her a wonderful party to which he invited his friends, close colleagues, and of course me, his late mother Omaima, his sister Samar, his uncle Ghaleb and his uncle 's wife Tamam.

Before going on holiday and leaving my engineering works in Dubai and all interrelated projects associated with me, I had assigned the signing of the exactness of the implementation of every foundation or post or roof to my assistant engineer Gerges Mitri who had to take his responsibility for that as he realized the appalling risks that might arise due to a civil wrong related to calculation of lengths or weights or..

We attended a cheerful party. Happiness was overwhelming the bride, the groom, my daughter and her mother Omaima who embarrassed us in front of the German as she was ululating (lo lo lo lo liiii!). The German bride's family and all attendants rejoiced at her presence and surrounded her. She taught the bride's mother how to ululate. The intelligent German woman started to move her tongue right and left and ululated (lo lo lo li), while we were laughing!

She started teaching eager German guests how to dance Palestinian Dabka twirling her handkerchief as she was leading them in the steps of the Dabka.

The late Omaima understood the convergence of North civilization and that of the South and she meant cross-fertilization of civilizations not the clash of civilizations that evil people philosophized to explode.

Meeting you, Omaima, for the first time in my brother's house Ghaleb was like someone discovering a treasure in a frequently visited place.

"I introduce you to my neighbor's daughter, Miss Omaima." Tamam told me that, and I understood that she was up to something, then. "She is from your hometown Akka. She is not my fellow townsperson. She is not from El Nassira" –she put her hand on her chest– "to not think I'm currying favor with her! She is a very polite and intelligent damsel. Her father got her an employment contract after she graduated from Damascus University and she started working in Arayahin School adjoining your firm."

You were a shy girl, Omaima, with your happy eyes looking away when my brother's wife was introducing you to me. She didn't mention anything about your beauty since you were in front of my eyes, a deer in a lush garden!

Your visiting Tamam with your mother was frequent, and sometimes you were on your own. And since I was living in my brother's house, I started to sit with you for a while especially if I chanced upon you there. You were gracious, so I loved your way of expressing, explaining, justifying, asking, and arguing. And I understood from my conversation with you that you were specialized in business management.

I had hired my brother as one of the team members monitoring the implementation of my civil projects. Then we moved to live together into a wider, more spacious, beautiful apartment.

Afterward, we had fallen for each other; we started to prepare for marriage. We looked for a separate flat and entered it as the happiest newly-wed couple and after that; I transferred you to my firm to be my director of communication and public relations.

I remember your giving your gracious speech in a magnificent dinner party that allowed us to meet families of the contractors of Dubai waterfront project on the topmost floor of Burj Khalifa when you told the audience, "Our religion states, 'A penny saved is a penny earned.' and in another chapter, it warned them, 'They who hoard up gold and silver and spend it not in the way of Allah, unto them give tidings of a painful doom.' And you hoarded a lot of money praise be to God, so if you donate the cost of this expensive dinner to the orphans of Jenin camp whom tanks crashed their houses and killed their parents…"

Hence, my Emirati partner, Mr. Monther Mohammad, stood and pledged to build an integrated medical clinic in the camp, so that its operating costs and requirements including materials and medications would be at his expense. And after him, donations flowed and this initiative united the feelings of the audience toward the case of your betrayed people!

You discussed with me the necessity of going back to Akka as we were walking along the beautiful lawns in Jumeirah Beach Park and enjoying watching fountains and colors of flower fields. You played with your kids Burhan and Samar and sometimes you chased them down as they were running from you under the trees embracing the sea.

Tamam wanted to visit the zoo, so you took our children and spent the day there, while I and my brother Ghaleb went to play golf in Abu Dhabi and then would meet at night. Burhan and Samar were jumping while they were telling me with amazement what they had seen. I cried bitterly as I was remembering. My tears run down wetting my mustaches that I tried to shave but you insisted on leaving them bouncing grey on my face.

Just for remembrance, I left its thick hair missing your pure face! Why did you leave me and go far away? They say that woman lives seven years longer than man, so how come that you died too soon leaving me all alone with all this life's trouble on my shoulder! If I had known that cell phone causes cancer I would have never let you stick it to your ear and talk on it all the time about managing the business. My father used to say, "Many hands make light work." But now you carry the whole burden on your shoulders, heavy, while you are an old man suffering from Osteoporosis! By the way, you forgot to take Osteoporosis medication, hyper intensive drug, insulin inhaler, and the rest twenty pills that... But there is no need to do so because you are dying on Akka bed and vanishing from its bewitching horizons little by little.

Omaima could not wait for more than a month to ask Burhan about children. He told her surprised, "Our marriage, mother, did not give us room to give birth to children as Arab people do. We rather become more involved in our work!" You, therefore, took the phone from his mother's hand to change the subject and asked him about his job. He said proudly, "Our genetic research has developed, father. After the first scientists had succeeded in inserting a plant cell into that of animals and produced from them the first cell of a green animal, we took up the baton of developing researches conducted on it.

AN ORPHANED SUIT!

The moving walkway takes you from the hydrogen-powered airplane into Alexandria International Airport building whose design looks like a space city broke loose from a remote galaxy and fell behind Alexandria City... No traveler could lose his way in this city for direction signals are pinned everywhere and the elderly and children are riding in free electric cars taking them to the passageway they want.

Back in your day, there was no passageway to reach Alexandria in front of you but the iron door hunkered down the heart of Cairo. You bought the cheapest ticket and walked toward the train that was heading for Alexandria watching this enormous crowd of people, then

A porter walked toward you and tore you out of your bewilderment at the noise of Ramesses -and without permission- he took your cardboard suitcase to put it in the wagon. You felt scared to lose the bag in that crowd, so you snatched it from his hand, but he grabbed its handle when he noticed that you were wearing a new black formal suit. He didn't know that your father, celebrating your earning high school diploma and your admission to the university, stepped out from his meanness and took you by your hand to the store of Adel Alghathban, the most famous tailor that made suits in Tulkarm, who took your measures and then made it of English velvet fabric and chose red satin for its lining. Ghathban told you, then, "I have never made a suit for someone with such a slim waist and big chest!"

The porter didn't know that it was your orphaned suit and that you were wearing your white t-shirt and a red necktie that you couldn't remember where you bought, of course not from the relief agency's bundles of second-hand clothes. For this reason, you didn't put it with your money in the suitcase for fear of losing the valise with its suit and money because your mother Zakiya had closed and sewed its tiny inner pocket hiding in it the expenditures of a full university year that you brother Ghaleb, escaping the torments and darkness of refugees' life, had sent you from Dubai.

The porter, watching you bewildered and worried about your belongings, told you as handing you his credentials, "Do not worry; I'm a clerk in the station! Here is my official copper piece of eight. Leave the valise! I'm going to carry it and I will charge you just five piasters for that. It won't cost you so much!" You made sure that he was a civil servant or a man providing a reference, and then surrendered the suitcase to his hands while following him with your worried gazes.

"Put your trust in God," he told you as he walking so fast with it, while you were running behind him amid the crowd. You remembered the statement of actor Amin Alhinidi, "He was made a fool of!" But you put your trust in God and boarded the train wagon.

The porter put the suitcase on the shelf and made you aware that his mission was accomplished. You gave him five piasters. You said, "Here you are." He thanked God, then left.

You felt amid that cramped crowd in the wagon that you were out of place, for there was neither an empty corridor to walk through nor an empty chair to sit on. There wasn't even a place where to stand!

These women farmers were putting their huge baskets, filled with their belongings, the sides of which were joined with white and black sackcloth and a piece of grey fabric to cover them, and this man farmer with his loose grey dress was placing his swollen belly between his legs and sitting absent-mindedly as if he ate a sack of broad beans before getting on the train with his head leaning right. Another farmer was tilting his head left and that woman as fat as a meat cow (Knock on wood!) was fastening the feet of her three white geese, putting them together ,and then placing them on her big basket overflowing in the corridor, while the white bewildered geese were moving their eyes right and left scrutinizing this long catacomb crowded with its luggage and residents!

You noticed that bags and suitcases were fatter than passengers. After the train moved, you discovered the discomforts of getting a cheap ride.

You saw in front of you a thin man sitting with his back curved and his chin touching his knees like an okapi folding knife, glorifying God with his right hand using a long rosary dangling to hit against his shoe, while his left hand was holding a portable radio close to his ear so that he could listen to the voice of Mohammad Abdel Wahab- despite the intersection of passengers' voices with those coming from the train itself - as he was singing, "O boat tell me where are you heading ....O boat tell me where are you coming from?... O boat, tell me... O booooat, tell me... And on the same seat, five children were piling upon him and upon his wife sitting next to the bags. She was wearing a large black dress filled up with her flesh flooding over their luggage that heaped up around them blocking the passage of the vehicle.

A guy your age was standing next to you, so you asked him and he answered you mockingly," It is the fast express train!" And when he knew you were foreign, he finished his mocking talk," This Train was fast in the Era of Ottoman state may Allah have mercy upon it. When the state died, the train felt depressed and started to cover the distance from Cairo to Alexandria in about five or rather six hours. It stops at every station except the one you want to reach!" His cynical way of speaking made you laugh and he, sensing your liking him, added," But there is a modern train called the runner. Oh! If you board it, man, it will take you to your destination in two hours!"

You discovered amid that smothering crowd - which was one of the facets of resurrection day - that people were kind to one another and warm-hearted. But what really pleased you was the view of vast farms (paradises of everlasting beauty!), greenery farms from which sprang lofty palm trees among the fields of corn, wheat, clover, broad beans, and sugar cane, looking like infinite minarets of mosques in the vast horizon! You used to see palm tree farms only in Egyptian white and black movies and here you were watching them in color and in person! It was the charm of green Egypt that they later turned into a desert!

You noticed that after finishing his previous song, the singer Mohammad Abdel Whahab was back to the ear of the man - okapi knife-with the song (How beautiful the life of a farmer is! He's content and his heart is at peace), but your Egyptian friend Mohammad Mohammad whom you would live with in Alexandria later, would say, "Mohammad Abdel Wahhab sang this song from Azzamalik. He didn't live with the farmer to see how mosquitoes - the army of the feudal - suck his blood, how bilharzias disease makes holes in his veins with the awl of foreman and how he is deprived of everything but death!"

The train pulled out of Cairo and stopped at Banha Station. Some disembarked with their luggage and others got on it with their luggage and thus emptying and filling process took place simultaneously. Street vendors from the station folk boarded the train, and one of them was carrying a basket and screaming as he was moving his legs gently and audaciously through the piles of bloated bags. His basket hit against the flesh of women spilled inside dark blue and black dresses. Men defenders then defended the territories of their women with enthusiasm and chivalry. "Simit, eggs, Gouda cheese," he yelled at his high voice intermingling with the voices of the train community. "Eggs and simit" A young street vendor followed him carrying on his shoulder a bucket full of water with colored bottles inside it.

"Cold soft drink!" He barged in as yelling at the top of his voice, "Cold soft drink… cold soft drink." Of course, it was neither soft drink nor cold! And when he walked past you, he wiped the bottom of his muddy bucket with the shoulder of the jacket, the sole suit that you were arrogant by wearing inside the wagon. But this bucket humiliated you and made you stand like that one who defecated and did not wipe his butt...!

The young man who was standing opposite you saw the muddy bucket's harassment to your shoulder and felt touched by its gluey sight. He laughed as witnessing your embarrassment and said to you, "You should have boarded at least the second class. There, you would have a seat number and would be treated with respect!" Now you understood that you boarded the third class and that people were used to each other and their hearts were forgiving and generous. As for your sole suit that you were going to wear for university …it was a big disaster!

But you were prepared for the worst during this journey as your father told you may God bless him, "Be careful about everything, son. Don't get upset if, God forbid, something bad happened to you. The reverent prophet's motto was always "Don't get angry". For this reason, you didn't feel angry. You rather remained standing during your journey, and watched greenness and fountain-like palm trees hanging in the sky, the matchless spacious Nile River and these colors made of greenness and red bougainvillea. Sometimes the Nile looked blue, sometimes pale grey and scabby with its wastes, studded with its buffalos going around their norias, the invisible clay houses in farms, ovens of women farmers who were enflaming its rising fire baking their bread, herds of girls collecting cotton from its fields and a cart pulled by a donkey overburdened by the heap of clover piling behind it.

And unlike the minarets of palms heading for sky, the sun came down in search of a nest where to sleep among cornfields! You watched the red-orange sun as it was racing the train, setting off in parallel, and then was left behind. It disappeared behind its long crocodile tail. It tried to race the vast horizon and when the sparkling golden orange sun hit against palm trunks, you feared it would burst and fell fainted!

The tangled throng of people inside the wagon forced some young men to sit at the upper inner metal grid shelves, which were designed to put the handbag on, and thus passengers changed into luggage laid on shelves. You saw a man watching his small monkey which in the wink of an eye jumped gracefully to seat itself politely in the mid of the young men sitting on the shelf as it was putting its finger in its mouth smiling, while its hazel eyes were rolling right and left watching comers and goers, brimming with happiness for having a free high seat.

You felt a pain in your legs spread wide because of the basket between them, so you moved your legs aside among luggage. You watched the two young men sitting on the shelf with their feet dangling above the heads of wagon's passengers that a man sitting under the mercy of their heavy shoes screamed at them, "Would you respect people sitting under your heavy shoes?" A woman who seemed worried about her son sleeping in her lap added, "If a shoe falls on my kid's head, he would die!" Another would say, "This is a shame by God! A fourth man took courage to lift his head toward them yelling, "O young men, you're certainly coming from a respected family and you are well-brought-up and it's not appropriate to put your shoes on our heads! At least take them off and keep them away from our heads! "After many condemnations and disapprovals, the two young men took off their thick shoes and put them on the shelf next to them. Their white socks then introduced themselves, stretched their necks black and muddy with rottenness, while their toes were sticking out of their worn socks.

They started airing their toes sticking with a grey paste of gluey rottenness and separating them from each other to breathe. A stinky smell spread killing the noses of the passengers sitting under the mercy of the upper shelf's inhabitants. An old man sleeping on his luggage sack woke up yelling at them, "Spare us this smell smothering us!" His wife that was sleeping on a basket covered with a piece of stitched fabric woke up, saying, "It's right, what's this stinky smell!"

"Wear your shoes and dangle them on our heads." Another person burst saying, "Your shoes falling on our heads is more merciful than the smell which is killing us!" Here one of the two guys occupying the upper shelf sprang saying, "You killed us with this story of feet, take off, no, put on! Well, take off! No, put on. Choose in this case of feet! Shall we put on our shoes or take them off?" The cheerful young man standing next to you told them then, "What about cutting your feet and throwing them out of the train? We will, therefore, get rid of their stinky smell? At least cats there will benefit from them instead of bothering us with them during our journey!" One of the men in the upper answered him with defense, "Really, man with silk socks! It is as if your smelly feet were musky!"

GIVE SOMETHING FOR GOD'S SAKE!

You move on these travelators inside the automated airport - according to signs- where you take your suitcase from its arrival station numbered on the screen. The robot takes your numbered suitcase on your portable device and puts it on the vehicle. You ride it and move with the controller to take you wherever you want in the airport.

You only have to welcome the two darlings; the son and the grandson. It is a matter of seconds and they would arrive if God wishes at the appointed time. You scrutinize this spacious airport's rooms, corridors, these shops that are still marked with Pharaonic style distinguishing them from the shops of other world airports, these automated security barriers, arrivals terminals and departing passengers' terminals equipped with all comforts.

You are still comparing it with the first day you arrived in Alexandria to join your promising university. After the long stop of an express train in numberless stations from which you could remember but Tanta station that's because the train stopped here for a quarter of an hour. The driver's helper said he was repairing the level crossing. What was the level crossing? Because you didn't know!

"You can refresh a little bit on the station sidewalk." The assistant volunteered to inform us. You descended, but you did not go too far because you were surprised at seeing many young men riding for free as they were jostling with each other, standing up as clinging to each other outside the wagons and piling on their roofs with amazing audacity as if they were luggage carried on the train! The station was hung over a bridge of a huge iron framework of the train that crossed through Said Badawi City .Give something for God's sake, O our master Badawi!" A host of passengers who considered Tanta station as their arrival terminal disembarked the train too.

It is a community, whose members stuck together, hated, supported, loved, and despised one another. They were friendly too! Each one of them was visiting Said Badawi for some reason! That's what the young man was standing near you in the train wagon and still standing next to you on the sidewalk to breathe fresh air outside the smell of the neighbors of the naughty monkey told you. He introduced himself to you, "My name is Mohammad Adawi."

"I'm honored to meet you. My name is Mashhour Shahir Ashahry."

Mohammad Adawi laughed, "Welcome sir. I was imagining you being famous for lifting your sword monthly!" He said teasingly as he was tapping on your shoulder, "What a beautiful name? Did you buy it or was it for free? "

Despite their poverty, third-class - passengers were funny. They were making fun of each other and saying jokes to entertain themselves and forget their sufferings in all their actions.

Mohammad Adawi noticed that you were standing at a loss, observing the crowd, and watching a town strange to you. He stood next to you, looking at people disembarking with their luggage from the station on a huge bridge from which wide rusted iron stairs dangled. The stairs descended between the giant iron bridges on the right side, then an iron landing, then on the left side, then... and the feet of people descending and ascending were scabbing the iron saying, "Path, path, path, path..! That's not the subject!

A bunch of men attracted your attention."They are Upper Egyptians," Mohammad Adawi informed you, laughing. "They came to visit the tomb of Said Badawi, to be blessed with his shrine and ask him about a cow that disappeared, a person who was killed and they don't know who the killer is or a missing girl and they want him to show them her whereabouts or a patient whom doctors fail to heal or didn't go to see a doctor in the first place." –He carried on with his derision as he was watching them–" and the healing doctor is the tomb shrine of our master Badawi who heals with his blessings every patient, gives back to every blind person his sight and every missing person to his family. He also helps you win over your enemy, blesses the life of every newly-wed couple, returns every divorced woman to her house, prolongs the life of every old person, impregnates every sterile woman and gets out genie from the body! –He turned to you as he was leaning on the barrier laughing–" yes, he is by Allah!"

You saw a bunch of them descending the iron stairs with white, grey and brown turbans on their heads perfumed with incense inspired from heaven's scents - and as Adawi was saying, "These turbans were not only for protection against the scorching sun but also for reverence, glory, honor of manhood, tribal glory and eminence. And the most important of all was being a store for their hidden money that they feared would be lost or stolen in the celebration of the birth of Said Badawi. And as you know there are many people in the celebration, that's why they put there on the top as no one could know the secrets of Arab seminars! "Look! Look!"

Adawi grabbed you from your shoulder and when he caught notice of the mud that dried on it he removed it, saying," Look at those naughty three boys that are bouncing on the huge iron framework of train station imitating that monkey that..." You watched the scene where the naughty boys were standing on the edge of the stairs which connected the upper station sidewalk with city streets looking at the visitors descending the stairs with eminence and scrutinizing their feelings as they were descending in tahlil and benediction asking for God's forgiveness with submissiveness in the presence of the city of the tomb of the great blessed Said. You noticed that each of the three children had a long thin crooked iron steel in the form of a pointed hook, so once the rich men went down, the naughty kids stretched their steel grapnel and each put a hook in a turban of a farmer of one of those humble strange guests seeking God's blessings.

"Look! Look!" Adawi would tell you.

Each one of them pulled his hook with its hunt as quick as lightening and disappeared running with the turbans and the money in them.

Each depended on his luck and God's generosity in that snatched turban! The strange men cried at once, wailed, got upset, threatened to revenge, to shoot and to kill! But, then they discovered that air was whooping their bald heads shaved to zero - what a pity that they were in a foreign land and that there were no tribes, no clans and no mayor to give them back their lost honor and money in the plundered summit!

The train whistled, so we got on our wagon quickly to not miss it and thus we would ended up without train especially you who could not distinguish Tanta from Malta, and without Adawi you wouldn't be able to know a thing!

Finally, the train stopped at Sidi Jabber Station. Your friendly friend told you then, "This is your station." You opened your mouth waking up yourself. That's what they explained to you, you should get off a station called Sidi Jabber. You bid him farewell with hugs and got off the train quickly embracing your... suitcase.

It was a humble clean station where there was no traffic crowd. On the wide sidewalk planted with bright green fig tree —the same trees of the sidewalks of Tulkarm City - you saw a big yellow board that read, "welcome to Alexandria", and reddish horses with carriages whose umbrellas were decorated with Alexandria embroideries and cravings. The smell of its manure, which was in disharmony with the beauty of the place, hit you. One of them was peeing in front of you while its driver was sitting lifting the stick of his whip on the driving seat behind it and next to him there was a handful clover that seemed to be a meal for the horse. He was waiting that God would send to him a great catch.

Here, in Alexandria, taxis distinguished with their black color decorated with yellow, seemed to take you to remote places. You rode one of them and the driver had no difficulty in switching the engine like what happened with that black tortoise at Cairo Airport.

"Where are you going, God willing?" the drive asked you, so you answered him feeling small," To a cheap hotel nearby!" The man then showed his Alexandrian experiences saying," I know a suitable hotel in Cleopatra Hammamat nearby! "

"Hammamat, Hammamat!" you answered him, helpless!

The man stretched his hand in front of your face that the fume thread of his wretched cigarette in his mouth annoyed you, and zeroed the metal taximeter fixed on your left.

The car opening its radio on Voice of the Arabs moved toward the sea beach while the radio program The Box of the Liar Abu Lama and Khawaja Khristo was presenting a story about dishonest pride starting with the voices of the chanter (chorus), "They stole the box, O Abu Lama!" Abu Lama would then reply to them," But the key is with me!" Then the chorus would chant," The box." The program presenter would say, then, "The box is a subsequent episode." The chorus chanted, "A chain." And the broadcaster would say," Prepared and presented by... "

You knew neither Abu Lama nor Khawaja Khristo, but you knew that he was a dishonest storyteller and in every daily episode, he presented a story about dishonest pride of his unexhausted untruthfulness.

It seemed as if the radio of Voice of the Arabs in this comedy program guided the Arab listeners and warned them not to make a hill out of a mole, made them laugh and entertained them without licenses, modern feminine coquetry, or obscenities. A modern radio in the fullest meaning of the word after which modern Arab TV Stations lost their seriousness becoming scandalous, bare twisted and cheap showering on us money of our muslimized oil to kill our legacy, culture, dignity, and Arabism with our hands in the time of globalization!

You felt happy as you were breathing Alexandria's pure wet air and watching the huge clean sea city style! The taxi stopped in front of a small hotel in the form of a cottage or a villa on Cleopatra Beach on top of which pale tiles located close to sea waves were invading the beach.

Wow! Oh my God! Oh my God! The sea! It was the sea! Oh, darling, my Mediterranean Sea! Why did they drive me away from you there? Why did they unfasten the ropes of small boats of fishers rocking under the weight of the cargo piled in Akka sea asking the protection of the walls of Ahmed Pasha the butcher, remove them from their iron posts, and open fire on them that bullets pierced through their old antique woods, shedding their blood? Red was mixed with blue; boats perished with their fishers and cut woods immersed with sea waves, then. They were eaten by an eared seal, and since then your grandfather hadn't come back!

The small brick hotel was sleeping along The Sea Corniche Street. You read the name of the street, "El Geish road" and you thought that the army passed by from here toward Bur Said! You who hadn't ever seen the sea noticed that the white sea was blue. Choppy waves came from Akka to welcome you here, in Alexandria! Was that your beautiful Akka Sea that you hadn't seen since you were born?

The mother weaned her child using a bitter plant. She rubbed it over her nipples whose veins dried up. As for you, they weaned you from your Akka's white sea with machine guns, cannons, and explosives before you were born and thus you remained a desert boy living without sea! And here you were, poor thing, turning around, heading toward it from the south. Then you hugged each other when met!

Imagine that Akka and Alexandria were breastfed by one sea and weaned by one sea! And Egypt and Palestine were brothers through breastfeeding and brothers in language, religion, customs, traditions, geography, history, common interests, country, love, Isaiah of Palestine, and his grandchildren Mohammad, Omar, and Ali.... Isaiah who used to say, "Whoever slaps you on your right cheek, turn the other also to him." He would continue by saying, then, "Take up your cross!" He didn't conclude by saying, "Let him who is without sin cast the first stone." that's because he was always repeating his statement "love, love!" But, all they did was stealing the cross of pains and sufferings, transferred it to the west, and said this is our God. They made him carry a submachine gun, and tied him to Apache Helicopter to kill his people in the Far East and the Middle East and sprinkle opium on China's people, and atomic bombs on Hiroshima and Nagasaki. Hence, he forgot the milk he was breastfed! They denied him the right to the promising return to Palestine unless they set up their empire on the corps of the Arab World... He asked them as he was bleeding on his cross tied to the FFF aircraft, "what if your empire is barren does not give birth to children?"

"Then you will never get off!" they answered him with spite. "We will never give you a visa to enter your country!" O spirit of tormented humanity, how great, kind and helpless you are! You were not asking for an empire nor trillions of oil but rather asking from God to provide you with the bread of your day from Alexandria that buried Alexander of Macedonia and all Caesars of Rome who failed to form an empire on our land looking out the remnants of crusaders unable to form their empire on our land. And you saw Napoleon failing in Akka and failing in Alexandria, unable to form the great Middle East Empire over our bodies! Glory be to God! All losers in their countries wanted to set up their empires on your body that refused to be violated, O great Arab world!

It was the first enjoyable trip in your glorified history. Oh, God! The sea was wide. Ahhh how beautiful it was! White waves whose foam was chased down by other white waves along a blue sea! Subsequent chains of herds of white geese progressing toward the shore in a white bridal procession along a blue sea!

And though the time was evening, you didn't wait for dinner or stayed up late, but rather you fell asleep without rocking. Splish splash splish splash, you slept at the amazing sound of sea waves! It was the first time you sleep near the sea, but the sound of choppy roaring waves through the night kept violating your hotel bedroom and then flooded you in your bed, washed you with their overwhelming foam and dragged you with them along the shore sand to the sea! You felt that your bed was a stray boat in the sea. The sound of waves, filling hearing and sight, controlled all senses and washed your stiff nerves throughout the night. Hence you were drowning, drowning!

The next morning, you discovered that the sounds of sea waves had massaged your muscles, stroked your body and refreshed your mind intermingling with the bitter trip of life. You woke up active, relaxed, and healed from the hardship and suffering of traveling with eyes brimming over with happiness thinking of going to engineering university.

"It is near from here," the hotel worker told you. "Ask about the station of the tram of Cleopatra Hammamat , take the tram from the station and then get off at university station for the faculty is near here. You got off with your fellow students who got off at the station and took a shortcut leading to it."

Before going to university, you entered a small restaurant here on the corner. For the first time, you had fava beans in cottonseed oil for breakfast. You found that it tasted weird, something you could not get used to it - for you are the son of the land of Hummus and olive oil that the relief agency turned into butter oil and thus refugees refused to consume-and next to it a small plate on which there were two balls of Taamiya, tomatoes, and onion slices. It was OK. It was good food and "whatever will satisfy hunger is good food" because you didn't eat anything last night. You ate and praised Allah, and then headed to your promising university!

It was the first time you got on El-Raml Tram, and here too the tram was separated in two classes; the first class for two piasters and the second class for one piaster! But what was this separation for since all would arrive at the same time and to the same station? What applied to train, applied to electric tram and buses? Each bus had a separation between first class and second one. Something, you were not familiar with in Tablu Bus that transported the passengers of the camp from and to Tulkarm in one class for one half piaster for a student and a piaster for others. It was a differentiation of time not of place. You had discussed with your companion Mohammad Adawi the matter of train classes. He told you laughing as usual, "Degrees exist even in paradise. Some pious believers are closer to the prophet than others and some end up in the highest place of paradise. There is also a separation between people, so why it shouldn't be the same thing in life?" You understood the idea of hierarchy. Due to the hardships of your first trip from Cairo in…class, you desired to be here in the highest place and have a subscription for a year to the first-class on the tram and get a student discount card.

Upon your first entry to university building which you would later know that its design was taken from the features of the palace of Pharaoh queen Hatshepsut, you were entranced by the aesthetics of the place. So, you carefully explored its buildings, amphitheaters, ways, the seats of its gardens, and cafeterias. And a month after your attendance, you took notice of the diggings of the foundations of the new apartment building. They said they were building it to be separate from the civil engineering building.

Almost two weeks after the start of digging, you were surprised at witnessing the collapse of the soil front parts of the excavation and the disappearance of eight workers under the rubble where the ground was sandy. You didn't forget that its name was the Sand Region though it was far a bit from the shore. They weren't using any mechanical excavators to give the poor a chance to provide for their families and to absorb labor unemployment.

You saw them digging a foundation in the sandy earth deeper than ten meters as if it was the place where a savage metro crashed in the center of the university and thus the rubble of sidewalls collapsed and crashed over them burying them. The workers who were left and hadn't been buried yet screamed, and thus about twenty workers jumped on the rubble to remove the sand off their dead colleagues without graves which added salt to injury because with their philosphication, they killed who hadn't died yet!

After some dredging, screams, and tangled movements, they lifted them from there, still bodies, one by one! And after rising wails, whipping, crying and terror and everything had been over, the fire engine and ambulances showed up with siren wailing and horning saying, "We're here!" The workers became alert and insulted the firefighters as they were agonizing and weeping over their dead colleagues.

DRESSED BUT NAKED

I read on the computer screen of your hydrogen-powered aircraft that after they had been annoyed by the traffic of Cairo International Airport, the crowd of people around it and the inability to expand it to meet the needs, they built Alexandria International Airport in 1945 to take its place to soothe the pressure exerted on the capital and to spread tourism across the country, so that it would not suffocate in Cairo. Hence Egyptian tourism has become concentrated in the north and the south more than in the pyramids of the Great Sphinx of Giza that was smothered by demographic invasion crawling from all sides!

They discovered that it was the most important airport in the heart of the Arab World linking united Europe with Africa depleted of its contents, with rich East and exhausted West. And that Yun Zhu , the Chinese firm, purchased the land of the airport and its surrounding in the North of Beheira Governorate and built it on a space of one hundred kilometers square that was covered by salt evaporation pond of Mariout Lake, was considered very intelligent!

The Chinese bought the whole area and dredged it, and thus the remnants of the greenish local lake disappeared and an international spacious airport took its place. And according to internet data, it was a wonderful Chinese commercial transaction in that the airport suffices the passage of one hundred million travelers yearly!

Notice how much tourist work is required to serve this tremendous number of passersby who will pay with Chinese Yuan or Arab dinar!

Travelers are moving in all directions in groups and alone, men and children with their decorated t-shirts and their short or long trousers. Some women wear black milayat, each is covering an obscure skeleton and others are half-naked as they wear but threads swinging on their chests and butts to cover. I mean they can barely cover anything! You didn't exchange your money at the airport because your account number on your mobile device can pay in Arab dinar or Chinese Yuan as you wish.

You don't see any human beings hired in this airport because the automated barrier representing security scrutinizes your identity card stored in your cellar device that remains in your pocket without opening it.

Each of us used to have a passport, an identity card, a bank account card, a family card, private car cards as well as subscriptions to the club, the union, the association, assurances and hotels along with endless certificates, but now everything is written on this portable device, internationally recorded at all official agencies and on the internet. Your information is exposed to all public centers and circles, gentleman! After the automatic secret check of your luggage contents, as the devices can smell everything even the smell of your underwear to differentiate it from the smell of drugs or any smuggled materials without bothering to open your suitcase, the barrier opens in front of you after a digital examination without anyone bumping onto you. You moved on the travelator toward the claim baggage coming from Frankfurt to meet Burhan and green Canaan there. The moving walkway reminded you of the line of Imru' al-Qais:

"Stop, oh my friends, let us pause to weep over the memory of one beloved,

They cry to me "Do not die of grief, bear this sorrow patiently."

Does this amazing prince mean us as we are standing on this moving walkway!? Did he realize that I would perish from sadness as I'm patiently waiting for my son and my grandson? Did he realize that now we are standing on our ride, this beautiful crawling carpet that takes the place of genuine Arab horses - that are still racing and beat all world horses, but they were not developed by us to reach the civilization of this carpet!

Since Egypt joined the Arab United States, the Arab nations have been reassured about their future that kept each Arab leader in his position, but it launched the opening of economy and frontiers in the same way as the European Union started because Arabs, who didn't know where to reinvest their oil milliards, which wherever they go, were subjected to confiscation under any pretext; sometimes under the claim of terrorism, and sometimes under the name of money laundering. Sometimes their money was seized due to suspicion of leaking fighters against occupying their country, and sometimes it was seized because of financial abuse of charity. How ironic! They became responsible for managing our Zakat funds! And that was achieved sometimes through diplomatic circumvention, and sometimes through Arab generosity, and many times by forces that...

Now, Arab manufacturers, have giant factories in Egypt, Sudan, Morocco, and the Levant. Also, Arab traders started to import and export their complementary goods to any Arab city without taxes or customs and without stopping at frontiers especially after the fast modern trains were launched through network lines linking the parts of the Arab World from Mauritania to Bahrain then Kirkuk and Aleppo, together with Turkey which is linked in the first place with Europe......

PARADISE UNDER THE FEET OF ORANGE

Here Burhan and Canaan come to pick up their luggage from the claim baggage area at Frankfurt airport. Your meeting with your son and green grandchild makes your soul happy! "Hug me Burhan! Hug me, dear Canaan! O, Canaan! You become tall and strong when you are but ten years old! May God protect you! You grow mellow green like beautiful shady plants! Knock on wood!"

You feel shy to make any remark about your green grandchild Canaan holding a green small dog and his wearing transparent clothes decently designed to embrace sunshine to carry out the process of photosynthesis and to protect him against weather factors as if he was in his sea suit. You saw him as naked as he was born when a child and you said he was still....but his being as tall as you is another story! Yet, sea Alexandrians would not be taken aback by your nakedness even if you were in a swimming suit! Besides these days people are used to seeing women who are half-naked and Canaan wouldn't surprise them whether he is dressed in his nakedness or undressed. Still, you see him turning heads with his green body color as well as his green dog accompanying him!

This green section of society hasn't yet prevailed in the street! You ask Canaan about his feeling when half-naked with this diaphanous dress, and he clings to your tenderness telling you, "I read The Prophet, the book by Gibran you used to read to my father when he was my age. The one in which Gibran says, "Your clothes conceal much of your beauty, yet they hide not the unbeautiful. Would that you could meet the sun and the wind with more of your skin and less of your raiment. The earth delights to feel your bare feet and the winds long to play with your hair."

Then you ask him about his feeling toward his green plant color and he answers you, "Gibran says, 'Like a giant oak tree covered with apple blossoms is the vast man in you.' Don't you see that I'm following in Gibran's footsteps with my nakedness and greenness, grandpa?"

You are thrilled by his definition of Arab green nakedness, while the boy continues by saying, "My father told us a lot about you. He mentioned you a lot when we were with mum Albina and my sister tawadud enjoying listening to music or when visiting a museum or an art gallery and we would stop at a statue or a painting or when he read to me an Arabic poem and would say, 'My father said, and my father said…' Your son unveiled all of your beautiful stories and revealed all of your buried secrets to us, grandpa. He also implanted in our minds all your useful instructions. And for this, we love you especially my sister Tawadud who longs to see you, grandpa!"

"How glamorous my green svelte grandchild is!" you told Burhan as you are taking your vitamin pills made for the elderly and then drinking water from your small bottle that is always with you. "His hair is green grass, standing stiff, dense, fresh, and shiny and there are glowing and softness of orange leaves and their greenness in his face!"

"Of course father!" Burhan answers you taking pride in his son. "Since his father is a cell from my body and his mother is a cell from an orange leaf why wouldn't he be as green as an orange?"

Canaan asks you as he was moving his dog whose gazes are pinned to his friend Canaan and his green ears are sagging with the green grass covering his small body from his right side to his left, saying, "Do you love orange color grandpa?"

You sigh as you answer him, "O, grandson! How delicious Shamouti orange of Akka is! Paradise used to be under orange feet!"

The robot takes their suitcases to two electric vehicles, each boarded his and we comply with the instructions of the dear airport staff. Those robots smile at us, but if you break airport rules you would see them frowning at you and block your way preventing you from moving with their obligatory barriers.

Their distinctive feature is that they don't talk a lot like human beings. Yet, this relaxing silence is dreary sometimes, especially when you feel you are alone in a world crowded with people! And thus your meeting with your son and grandson makes you feel the return of water to the parched land with thirst... Burhan tells you as we are going outside," You talked to me about Jaffa orange multiple times that I loved it so much, but I was not practically sure of my feeling until I visited my sister Samar upon returning from Frankfurt. I wish I could stay there even as a Jaffa orange picker so that I could smell the orange scent of the home country, and that's why I decided to mix this Canaan with its green orange color and refreshing smell.

But we were tardily aware of extending the life of our green product, so we produced my daughter Tawadud from the cell of her mother with a cell from an olive leaf and we produced some animals by mixing a yellow tree leaf so that she would live longer in the same way as Palestinian olive and oak do. We are working on extending the life of Man and animal to reach the age of Noah who is said to edge thousand year..." You are amazed at this information that you flirt with Canaan, saying, "I congratulate girls who will love you!"

He shyly, says," I am humbled, my grandpa! "

"And where is Tawadud?"

Burhan answers you saying," Now and after nine years, Tawadud has become an artist. She draws on her computer the most beautiful paintings and plays the most beautiful tunes on her piano. We are trying to make her more educated, smarter, and more beautiful than her excellent predecessor Tawadud, Haroun Alrashid's odalisque. Added to that, she speaks Arabic fluently and pursues learning literature, arts, and historical development as well as correct human behavior. So, you find her mother lightening her path with knowledge and new education, 'love your colleagues, complete them and do not compete. Help people and cooperate with them. Love nature, serve plants, play with animals, and help them enjoy life and get rid of pain. Play music for plants and animals. Be beautiful, you see the universe beautiful.' "

The green boy drinks vegetarian water mixed with nutrients from his own bottle -as his father told me once- then he gives his green dog to drink and then said, "At school, they direct us to learn sciences, arts, and love. Our teachers insist on us exploring the space for the purpose of learning not invading the space in the sense of attack. They urge us to be friends with animals, not to hunt them and to learn about know nations, not to invade them."

So you tell him as you are going out of the gate of the building, "We read in Quran, 'And made you into nations and tribes, that ye may know each other (not that ye may despise (each other). Verily the most honored of you in the sight of Allah is (he who is) the most righteous of you.'"

THE EAST AND THE WEST!

At the gate of the airport building, hydrogen-powered spaceships are landing to load passengers in turn, and then take off. We drive our electric spaceships laden with our luggage and we reach the vehicle that would take us. A smiling female robot walks toward us and puts our luggage in the vehicle. Canaan jumps gracefully to the vehicle's box holding his dog, with thick green hair, followed by Burhan whom the female robot holds his hand, and then helps him sit quietly next to them. With one pressure at a button on her robot hand, she closes the cubby door behind us as if we sat in a spacecraft!

The space car lifts off to take us to the hotel that Burhan booked. This vehicle reminds you of the space train on which you traveled to the moon, and while we were losing earth gravity you feel fear and alienation and that the separation from our mother earth was a loss beyond compare!

You were like a baby taken away from his mother! The emptiness of the moon's surface was dreary and grey and the atmosphere dusty and scary! During that trip for which each one of us paid more than three millions of Chinese Yuan, we saw but sands ‹flatlands, highlands and meteor craters, a crater of which has a diameter of tens or hundreds kilometers.

It was a scabby moon where there was no plant, no water, and no air that allowed you to breathe! A cluster of colonies of adventurers, scientists, explorers, and students were trained to explore the space! I hated the scorching temperature during daytime and frozen at night, and without our space suits maintaining moderate temperature and oxygen flowing from our devices, we would die in minutes. Since then you decided that you would not go on such space trips again during which passengers rejoiced over returning to gravity area of our Mother Earth.

You ask Canaan about his space trips and he answers you as he is putting his green grass head on your shoulder," Every year the school sends us for a space trip, grandpa. And the next trip will be on Mir International Spacecraft! We want to learn about the universe in which we were created. Who knows? We might discover another alternative planet where coming generations would live if... In the last visit, we swam in the space individually for far distances, and then made it to our spaceship unharmed... it was a scary, safe, and enjoyable experience at the same time! "

"May God be the protector, Burhan" –you pat on his shoulder tenderly– "you are still in good trim and tough. You are not like your weak old father! »

"You are still in good health father, praise be to Allah!"

"Why don't you come and live with us here in Hessen, grandfather? Hence, we can see you every day?" Burhan backs his son up, "Your popularity among us is wide, father. You are in high demand! What do you think of public wish?

You answer him as you are touching your bones that hurt, "Once we were born and descended to the ground, our unfaithful feet ran and sent each one of us to a different way. So, we wandered off and got lost in the crowd and these unfaithful legs kept running while hiding from us the fact that they are taking us to a maze leading to our Grave!"

Burhan then says, "Don't be such a pessimist father!"

You change the subject and ask him, "How is Albina doing? How do you spend your time there?"

"Time passes quickly, father. I and Albina work for long hours at Hessen Institute for Hereditary Engineering and we go out just once or twice a year. We go on holiday to Frankfurt or any other European city, unless there is a seminar about hereditary engineering in China, or wherever it is held!"

"You have been working on your scientific research for 40 years? Even my meeting with you here is a kind of tracking your hereditary experiments!"

"He who enters the hereditary world loves it, gets involved in it, and does not leave it unless he dies!"

«Take a break from your dark laboratories and let us meet in Samar's house in Akka. There, the nightly chat is more pleasant with Samar."

"I wish we could return to live next to my sister Samar and her children in Akka, but I can't leave my work for I am a mole that moves with liveliness inside the tunnel of the Genetic Institute. In the nineteenth century the children of the neighborhood of Pasteur used to strike stones as he was going out of his house screaming in his face, "Madman, Madman!" And here the madman had discovered incredible things and was the first to insist on the necessity of isolating patients with communicable diseases!"

You correct his information by saying, "The sacred hadith states, 'If you hear of an outbreak of plague in a land, do not enter it; but if the plague breaks out in a place while you are in it, do not leave that place.' For this reason, we believe in the necessity of continuing scientific research and rejoice at its positive results."

The aircraft sets off floating in space. The female robot is flying it and talking to us, and if one of us asks her about something she answers briefly. You take out your medicine box and swallow a pill for joints that ache because of traveling. Then you ask her about the place where we are and the place we are heading to. She answers you with discipline and in a soft voice but void of spirit and vividness of woman ferventness, "My name is Chee. We are now in the Mariout Area, sir, and we are heading north toward the sea. "

"But where does this flowing water come from? Where are the Mariout Lake and neighboring salt evaporation pond? She turns her smiling robot face toward us, saying, "There was a lake called Mariout, but they dried it and built different projects in its place. Yet, as you can see water flows again because of the rise in sea level. If you look closely, you will find out that the El Beheira Governorate is threatened by being washed over by sea water because of the increasing temperature. The sea transgressed us and extended to cover vast spaces of the shore and coastal areas that disappeared off Egyptian map, and water flows here and there. We are now studying solutions to these environmental challenges! "

"I remember that there was the Mahmoudia Canal here. Where is it now?"

"The Mahmoudia Canal? I've never heard of that, sir! Let me check my files." Chee thinks deeply and then speaks with her electronic knowledge, "Wait, sir, I'm going to answer you straight away. There was a canal called the Mahmoudia Canal. On 8 May 1807, Mohammad Ali ordered the building of a canal to carry Nile water to Alexandria and to be a waterway for commercial boats, and for the citizens of every region through which the canal passed had a share of land to dig. The order was given to citizens to work with axes and cutters and there was a choir walking with every area scout with drum and clarinet. The Mahmoudia Canal and City were named after the Ottoman Sultan Mahmoud Khan, Astana Sultan because Egypt was an Ottoman province, then. After that, the colonizer divided the Arab World, and Egypt was, therefore, lost like other Arab countries and now comes back to be the leader of the Arab states union."

Chee laughs and comments, "Beautiful rustic views. Aren't they sir? I wish I lived in those days to see the choir walking slowly on the edge of the canal! I love country music! I wish I was one of those!"

You noticed that she speaks fluent Arabic, saying, "But the conflict in the Upper Nile over the use of farming water by the farmers of globalization sucked water and nothing is left but faded landmarks. Hence the canal was replaced by a water pipe extending from El Beheira Dam that has been built recently above the bifurcation of the shallow Nile tributaries to prevent fresh water from reaching the sea-mouth flowing to Delta. The canal was filled and leveled with the ground and a large road was paved above it linking Alexandria to Cairo as if nothing happened! - Here-in seaside facet-scarcity of water is reaching the point of terror!"

"What are these wide streets," says Burhan as he is looking from high at Alexandria landmarks. "There are Sprinkler irrigation system along the sides of roads and lofty glass buildings that come into view from afar as if they were a slice of hamburger! I never imagined that Alexandria would be as beautiful as such!"

Chee says, "The water of agricultural sprinklers is refined wastewater. The sewers of Alexandria were descending in big pipes to the sea bottom ruining marine ecology there and covering Cleopatra City sinking beneath the eastern harbor with a dense layer of feces. But today after the Chinese Tianjin Firm had bought the privilege of managing Alexandria City and all its rights to receipt and disbursement, selling and buying it, it built a wastewater treatment plant and it started to clean and pump it for irrigation and made compost of its solid debris, and hence the environment becomes clean as you can see. Then they sold Cleopatra City which was drowning under the sea to Emirati Arab Firm that populated it and set up in it the lighthouse of modern Alexandria to take the place of its predecessor, the wonder of the ancient world. Recently, they have opened it to visitors."

It seems that the robot knows the city's secrets so she takes part in the conversation to make us feel her liveliness and that she is not an idol flying our spacecraft. She says, "Selling the agricultural province of Al Tahrir in Beheira to a foreign" strategic" investor for one hundred billion Chinese Yuan - to pay back some foreign debts - caused alarming public demonstrations and protests. Also, selling property rights of Suez Canal Community to a strategic investor for ninety-nine years was the cause of economic collapse which caused Central banks to fail and led to a public turmoil that tipped scales. So, Egypt was forced to join the Union of Arab States for its conviction that nations that want to survive not perish, like the era of pharaohs annihilated by Cleopatra, should ally with great regions like the European Union, the Chinese Union, and the Latin American Union, unlike the African loss that was depleted by foreign "strategic" investors. The Arab union came into existence to stand tall among world giants and to protect us against enemies and those lurking in our weakness!"

You marvel at what you see so you tell them, "there were here houses of Al Hadrah Region made of clay in rustic style inhabited by farmers clinging to the city like a dry coconut shell gluing to its white pulp. I remember a farmer who was plowing this land planted today with lofty buildings in the spring of 1969 while we were carrying out a scientific study for the foundations of Alb Hadrah Hospital. When I greeted the plowman, he fervently invited me to drink tea with him. The tea kettle was boiling on a fire started with farm firewood under a lofty palm tree. He poured me dark tea as dense as cane molasses in his frosted glass cup! They used to grow grains and legumes, extra-long-staple cotton, citrus trees, Guava, and mango here as well as breeding buffalo and bees, so they sold the townies their milk, honey, cheeses, butter, and pink veal. "

"What's pink veal grandfather?" – Canaan stretches his green grass head– "Is it an Egyptian flower?"

You answer him smiling, "Veal, dear, is the flesh of a young calf. It's the spoiled child of Egyptian cows and its flesh is pink."

The green, scared, asks, "Did they slaughter children of cows, grandfather?"

"They used to, and they are still slaughtering them, my beautiful grandson!"

Canaan drinks a bit of water from his bottle then says, "They are criminals, heartless! I object to this killing! Why don't they spoil their cows at least in the same way as Indians spoil them?"

His father answers him, "When the green color of yours is generalized son, they will produce a green calf that cannot be slaughtered like this dog of yours!"

Canaan puts the water straw in the mouth of his little dog and carries on with his green revolution saying, "I'm surprised at the fact that Man attacks, violates animals' properties, drinks their milk, destroys their beehives and steals from them honey. Nature should stay free without mauling. Our life should not be built on the death of others! We mustn't kill, slaughter, and assault life! We must live and let other living beings live like us. These beings are complementary pearls on the surface of this rare earth in the universal existence, so how can we kill them!"

His father answers him, "Try to convince your grandfather about this green revolution!"

You understand what they are saying, but the new concept is just a science that you didn't prepare yourself to follow.

You are expired, being so old. Let them try, you thought.

And to enlighten them about the past of the city you continue by saying, "The inhabitants of this region used to perform medium works between farmers and city dwellers because the countryside cowhides were the source of beautiful Alexandria shoe factories. Their fava beans ended up in Alexandria as the breakfast of prince, the lunch of the poor and the dinner of donkeys; their extra-long-staple cotton enhanced in their Egyptian nuclear ray laboratories was the source of distinctive underwear in the world; cotton oil was the source of the oil of fava beans dish and all food and the milk of their cows was the source of all townies' dairy products."

Canaan, disgusted, asks, "Why do they make shoes out of cowhides not from the debris of plants and their dead leaves? I refuse to wear those killed leather shoes!"

The green dog barks quietly in objection making us feel that it is supporting the viewpoint of his friend Canaan. His father laughs at this loyal friend. You take notice that you are floating in the space of the vehicle flying in the air and facing the ones coming from the opposite direction. So you ask the woman, "Where are we, Chee?"

"We are now, sir, five kilometers away from the grand Guangzhou Hotel. We will be there in a minute. Here is the hotel looking upon us with its famous tower!"

"Shares of unknown origin!" Burhan says. "Before you know it, billions of shares are transferred from Western investors to Chinese or Indians. The center of civilization moved now from the West to the East. After they used to call us the Middle East and the Far East, because they had the grindstone while the East used to revolve in their orbit, the Chinese began now to refer to Europeans of Midwest and the next continent as the Far West."

"Look, the hotel is extending on all Riyatha Region and El-Ibrahimiya Region and digs its giant feet into sea beach" –you draw his attention to what you are seeing– "it seems that the inhabitants of Alexandria have become strange guests to those global firms owning everything in the city and its suburbs!"

We approach the Chinese hotel that is facing us with its two lofty towers. Burhan says, "Though before booking, I saw on the internet all its entrances, hall and suits, I've never thought it would be of such beauty and magnificence!"

The air vehicle lands at the entrance of the hotel. We see that the atmosphere is clouded. The sky is grey, the fog is invading apartment buildings and hitting the ground as the northwest wind is getting ready for rain along the Alexandria coast.

You swallow the immunity hormone pill, and then say, "A hotel along a vast area! Where are the quarters and streets of El-Ibrahimiya which were modern back then? Nothing was left but houses about to collapse."

THE PYRAMID HOTEL

In front of the reception, Burhan gives the robot woman the booking number. She makes sure that it matches, bows and welcomes us warmly then says, "Please wait here in the room for a while until we get the suite ready for you." We sit in the hotel hall on the blown air chairs and you see on the right corner a big statue of a Chinese yellow dragon putting a model globe under its feet! You are panicked by the statue that you ask Burhan, "Is great China planning to put the earth under its feet like all former empires did or will it achieve human equality regarding rights and duties for all nations?"

He leaves his small dog walking with arrogance swaggering, with his dense green wool among chairs and on the Chinese carpet. Tourists and hotel residents convening in the main hall take pleasure from playing with it from distance, while Canaan sits on the edge of your balloon chair clinging to you, saying, "This blue beach that we saw from sky mesmerized me, grandpa! In Hessen, we live without sea. Many beautiful lakes scattered here and there, but we can find such a warm endless sea, only when we go to Hamburg and cold Baltic waters. These Alexandrian views are breathtaking!" –he laughs–"you Jump from here and your foot treads upon Athena, on the other side of the sea!"

You answers him while caressing his grassy hair, "How smart and cultivated you are, dear Canaan! The sight of the sea mesmerized me too, for I have never seen this aerial view before because we were seeing it from the earth, and we were not flying in Alexandria sky. The height of beach houses and buildings in 1966 ranged from one floor to fifteen. However, these one-hundred-floor-glass buildings with arrogant loftiness and adjoining dreary ruins are the globality of civilization!

You think silently as you are watching the remnants of El-Ibrahimiya, apartment buildings and houses collapsing and being destroyed like remnants of old boats seized in harbor corners waiting for someone who would put an end to them and to old people who refused to yield to the change, which was eating away everything around them, and thus it becomes a must to change them!

And in the yard that appears outside the glass of the hotel, you see a robot servant walking in the company of an old man carrying a box under his armpit. You see robots leaving and entering the apartment buildings, and three naughty children in rags playing in the dirty ruin jumping in their spring shoes with tremendous speed like kangaroo animals. You imagine if we had like these shoes that raced the tram of old days that we would have used to take us from and to university. We would have crossed the distance jumping like a kangaroo, and hence we would arrive within minutes. The era of speed has affected everything, even walking on the streets have changed into jumping!

Worry appears in Canaan's green eyes, as he was asking, "Are we going to the hospital tonight, dad?"

"Don't worry, my dear" Burhan answers him with a reassuring smile. "We'll be there tomorrow as scheduled, God willing, so we could take a rest from the hardships of traveling and enjoy the company of your grandpa."

The kid touches his shaved hair that looks like a yellow ripe pumpkin. You enjoy sharing his feeling with his grandfather.

"No one is dearer than a child but the grandchild" –you surround his green waist with your arm– "You father represents my extension and achieves in life what I couldn't, as for you, you make me feel the pleasure of your father's success in changing this universe with this beautiful green product of my grandchildren."

He sits cross-legged in front of you on the floor with his shoes made of the remnants of plants leaves saying, "I'm happy to be a pioneer of green generation on the surface of the earth. It is not only my green color which is distinctive but also forms, content, and human goals which have changed because the world after generalizing the green Man would not see black, or white or yellow race. All this color discrimination will end and there would be neither fanaticism nor racial oppression. All people would be equal like the teeth of a comb. It's a wonderful future, grandpa!"

You like the glow of his health and symmetry of his green body that his transparent clothes reveal, saying, "The sacred hadith says, "Muslims are equal like the teeth of a comb."

"That's true" –Burhan intrudes the conversation– "even though some kill each other. Our theory states that people are equal like the teeth of a comb not only Muslims; an absolute human theory that is not directed against anyone."

OPEN SESAME!

A robot woman who looks like an innocent girl with Chinese femininity walks toward us and tells us that the suite is ready, so we head to the elevator. Each one of us point with his cellar phone to his suitcase that crawls like a snake toward the hotel elevator which opens instantly and we enter it in the company of the lady. The numbers of elevator jump every ten floors at once that they appear in front of you 10,20,30,40, and in a few minutes, we are on the ninetieth floor where our private suites are. Burhan opens the door with the code written on the mobile while Canaan tells you as his father enters the opened suite," Grandpa, our house door in Germany opens with voice not code, so if one of us says,(open) in front of the door, it opens automatically. Your voice is your unique print as no one could imitate its vibrations."

Hence, you told him about the story of keys, "In the time of primitive Man, doors used to be closed with rocks and in the days of our Canaanite ancestors, the key was made of wood and it was about arm's length. And when we were young the doors were handled with manual keys that were reduced to be as small as a fingertip. After that, they were turned into digital cards that we would thrust in the door crack and it opened. However, in the time of Aladdin, it was said to the door (open sesame) and thus the grotto opened. And that order to open doesn't differ from yours. They are voice vibrations. It means that you are in Germany implementing the techniques of One

Thousand and One Nights in science fiction literature and foresight that were ahead of all ages in terms of progress. And now in Emirates, a person presses with his fingerprint on his doorknob and it opens automatically."

The robot gets in with us while the suitcase goes to its place. The woman welcomes us and explains to us how to use the suite's facilities, turn on the wall TV and how to use the healthy air apparatus* through controlling it with the mobile of each one of us."Welcome into your home, gentlemen." she told us, bowing respectfully. "My name is Chen 7. If you want to know something, just say my name on the portable device and I will answer yes, sir, in a second. We grant your wishes no matter what. Shame is not part of our vocabulary! Everything is valued with money as the Arabic proverb so simply states, 'He who has money the daughter of Sultan will be his bride.'"

Each one of us rests in his private room while Canaan's dog has a beautiful small bed for dogs. In the meantime, you spent the time talking to yourself remembering the beautiful days in Egypt, for when you entered the station of Bab Alhadid trains in Cairo for the first time, bound for Alexandria amid an unprecedented crowd that you hadn't seen in your life, you thought there were public demonstrations or a crowded reception for the president or an important person. And amongst the crowd, stood a giant statue of a person you don't know. So you asked the driver who answered as he was coughing because of environmental pollution, "God be exalted, they live great on the bodies of their citizens, die great in their tombs and are immortalized in life and hereafter! I remember my mother screaming nervously in our faces out of helplessness that day, Yes he's our God. I beseech great God to forgive me. What would he give us in the hereafter? Does he have time to grant every Muslim what would satisfy his mood, please and gladden him!? He would tell people, 'Will each of you go back to the work you used to do in life!" the poor driver added in his husky voice," It would be a catastrophe if something like that happens for king Farouk will return as a king and a driver like me would be a driver!"

You answered him mockingly, "Do not be surprised, for this is Rameses II who used to be great upon the necks of his people, is standing today in glamour and grandeur in Bab Alhadid greater than all people."

And it was true, for in 2006 they moved him outside the crowd of Bab Alhadid after they had realized he was about to suffocate because of environmental pollution. They were not worried about citizens who were dying on streets every day because of pollution or bothered themselves to transfer them to a larger space or even to handle pollution radically!

In 1977, I visited the former Soviet Union and I saw in Leningrad the tomb of Peter the Great with that glamour and magnificence, and the brown embellished granite marble. The communist guide told you that day, "This is the tomb of Peter the Great." I, hence asked him surprised, "Why do you say (The Great) if the communist revolution broke out against him and you said that he was against his people's freedom?" The communist guide then said, "It is our great history!" Here Peter the Great came back great again and Leningrad City was peeling its skin to be the city of Saint Boutros again! Would great Lenin come back again to Leningrad in the future as a great man?

*We Read in the dairies of the be blessed Mashhour that manufacturers do not care about polluting the air because pollution gives them the chance to package healthy air and sell it like bottled water designed for those who can buy it and release it inside their closed rooms!

ANFUSHI TILAPIA

In a narrow alley of this district, I lived for the first time behind a building that is still keeping its number 12/815 Army Road where Umm Arabi used to rent an empty apartment in the aforementioned alley in the area of Cleopatra Hammamat consisting of three rooms that she furnished and rented to university students. When you came in to see the room, I introduced you to other occupants: Mohamad Najjar from Gaza, Mohammad Mohammad Mohamad from Al Mansoura and you were the third of them from Akka.

Umm Arabi was an Anfushi woman in her sixties, one of the folks of Ras El Tin wearing milayat laf and putting on her nose a veil of black threads in the shape of fishers' net with a small cylindrical wooden ring looking like the bait of fishing hook on it. It seemed that the veil represented customs, traditions, and traits of the face of a woman from the delta, a local woman. The net showed her mouth and chin on which she drew the tattoo of local women as if it was the head of a tilapia that the net muzzled, fished and prevented from passing through.

They were old local attractive aesthetics, costumes that Versace failed to design. The fashion of the country and what country?! It's Anfushi Alexandria that was in olden days more important than the road of Sulayman Basha in Cairo. Alexandria is the capital of the foregone Era, of Khawaja and Greeks, and of import and export harbor where simple Bahri farmers used to meet with tricky city traders. It is the capital of trade foyers full of legal goods, brothels in which contrabands were distributed and crumbled, and where service offices of customers from the West would hide.

It is the country from which the rebellious Saad Zaghloul was banished to Malta Island, the gathering place for the members of foreign intelligence, lovers' resort, the pit for gays and lesbians, movie theaters, playhouses, alleys of nightclubs, nests of cabarets and prostitutes, capital of king Farouk who planted his palaces in Ras El Tin, El Montazah, Al Mamurah, and everywhere, the country of Said Darwish, the residence of Bayram Attounsi and don't forget that it is the birthplace of Jamal Abdel Nasser. Yet, the Nasser Era nationalized all these castles as well as their gardens and turned them into public parks for the people.

We used to go for a walk in the bewitching park gardens, and then go into the palace built in the style of Andalusian Garnada palace exploring its floors that we climbed without knowing on which floor we were because the design of the palace was amazing for there was a magic way that led to floors without stairs. And the chief tried as much as possible to arabize Alexandria, clean it from inhuman pollutants, and plant El Raml Region and even Bakos with apartment buildings designated to middle-class children and erased Anfushi aesthetics and Ras El Tin! For this reason, Umm Arabi headed toward El-Raml Region, rented an empty apartment, and paid a fortune as its key money.

Umm Arabi took you inside her small apartment, saying," If you go out of your room, switch off the lights and if you go out of the bathroom or the kitchen, switch off the lights." she said that with firmness and discipline."Don't get home late. If you are late after eight pm, do not come back home. You should stay over at the house of the people you are visiting!"

From that day on, you disciplined yourself to turn off the lights but you were not self- controlled when dealing with her beautiful daughter Nadia!

On your first night in your new place, you heard drums and celebration songs. You looked out the apartment balcony and you didn't know whether it was an engagement party or a wedding celebration, or a birthday party! You saw from your balcony the crowd of people singing and dancing on the sandy soil of the alley and in the midst of them a dancer shaking her waist, barefooted among the crowds, wriggling like a big fish just taken out from the sea and they were frying on a blazing fire. She was shaking and twirling in a dress with slits on both sides while she was moving the two long slits revealing goods in the color of golden coffee. You saw as you were looking out from the upper floor her wheatish thighs rebellious to chastity, a stunning scene for a young man who hadn't seen in his entire life but a woman's face.

You found the celebrators, men and women surrounding her, mingling, swaying in tune with dancing that moved even the laundry hanging over their heads. And it seemed that the damned man saw her underwear that's because you heard and saw an outlaw repeating his words to her whenever he took notice of the most dangerous hidden thing, "Let it breathe! Let it breathe!" Hence, the disciplined and the shy women burst into laughing arousing the curiosity of the quarter's residents watching from the balconies. Amid the crowd, you saw a young thin man wearing the clothes and a hat of Bahri fishermen standing up, swaying his hands, head, feet, and butt among the crowd, yelling with whatever song and talking nonsense.

The dancer then would answer him with flirtatious singing: "As for the fruiterer,

> His love is mighty,
> He feels jealous when other guys talk to me,
>
> Day and night,
> He fed me cucumber,
>
> Made me smoke a cigar,
> And filled my house with

Kids and grown-ups
Who turned my life

Into a living hell! "

During the party, you were allured by the sight of the crowd of women and men, the quarter's inhabitants swaying in the wedding gathering, the passers-by who stopped and marveled at what they saw that they together sang what the lioness was saying in the form of a singing chorus and responded to the dancer who was shaking herself in dancing in a bewitching manner putting on her head candelabra within hand's reach. The clown kept responding to her singing with nonsense of this kind you didn't understand at all. Umm Arabi heard the sounds of the wedding, so she looked out from the balcony, unexcited. So, you asked her about the party and what the singer was saying.

"Nonsense!"

She answered you, smiling this time that her chin tattooed with dark blue dots took the shape of a bird's stomach as a kind of the aesthetics of Anfushi woman, "People want to rejoice, so they do anything. (A three-ring circus.) This is the wedding of an old newly-wed couple. The groom Attriss works as a fisherman. He fishes ten fishes a day that he sells for two riyals or three and wants to marry the laundry woman Akila. So, what wedding do you expect them to have more than renting a sandy hall in this narrow alley for free with few losers, sitting in the quarter waiting for joy or grief. You will found the same people spending their time in a funeral striking their faces with their hands out of grief till satisfaction."

Then she finished her point of view saying, "O God! O, God! Go check your books and study a lesson that will benefit Muslims, and stay away from nonsense!"

You went into your room and forgot about your study and those who studied!

The most important person who sometimes visited the apartment was her eighteen-year-old daughter Nadia as she sometimes came in the company of her mother from Ras El Tin, and sometimes on her own. A young man from the neighborhood looking like a mule named Mohamad Nooh would visit her swaying, then. They stood whispering in the closed kitchen this time, and you didn't understand what they were doing there! The saucy girl was wheatish with narrow black eyes, of good height and her face was sculpted with seawater. Her hair, cut into bob, had a thick hairstyle. You saw her fat but not overweight. And when she was alone she would go into the only bathroom in the apartment and after a one-hour bath or God knew what she was doing, she would come out singing one of Shadya's songs, (The moon is hidden, O cousin, take me home...)

You went in the bathroom in the apartment after she went out and you were stunned by her colored soft fine underwear and her pink bras thrown on the bathroom sink, and sometimes on the slab floor of it. You didn't know if she left them for display as if she was said, "We're here! Or it was customary for a girl to leave such clothes in the bathroom of the apartment of young men to be washed later.

Sometimes the girl sat on her own in the kitchen boiling a cup of coffee or a cup of tea, unhurried. She put a metal comb on the fire of the kerosene stove, lifted it burned, combed her hair, and then twirled it in a bun. You smelt the smothering scent of grilled hair from inside your room and it stirred your curiosity. You went in the bathroom to watch something new to you; clearing her hair and twirling it with a grilled metal comb. You didn't understand the secret of your attraction to the girl!

The truth was that you loved the scent of the young female who was standing in the kitchen, but you still did not know how to talk with females. You were just surprised at her grilling her hair and you did not interfere in something else. You prepared a cup of tea, and then, stunned, you went back to your room.

This was less bad than your stupidity and your behavior toward Nadia. Your misbehavior toward her was no equal to disrespect. It seemed that the beauty loved you from first sight as you were going into your apartment. You took pride in your youth with your tallness, brawny chest, slim waist, white face and wide blue eyes, therefore you didn't greet anyone!

You didn't examine your image in the mirror to see how arrogant, complicated, idiot, and awkward you were. The rules of your grandmother Aneesa might be the cause, for it was she who told you, "The path of girls is thorny!" And your mother Zakiya consolidated her advice with her saying," Do not let girls of Estankiriya deceive you!" You laughed at her mistake and corrected her saying," Alexandria, mother, not Estankiriya!

"So, Umm Ghaleb repeated her words," Estankiriya, Estankiriya! How should I know? "

Your grandmother Aneesa added in warning, "A girl makes fool of a young man and empties his pocket thoroughly! Then she makes him sit on the slab floor! And once his pockets are empty she damps him!" You used to hear nonsense of this kind before you had come to Alexandria of beautiful Cleopatra because grandma Aneesa neither knew the difference between Cleopatra and a kilo of Okra nor that Bombay, Julius Caesar, Antony and Augustus Caesar, though great, drowned in the body of a beautiful woman. So, what money would you spend compared with Antony who spent his life between the legs of an Alexandrian enchantress?

Did you have in the first place any money in your pocket to spend on this delicious girl? You were penniless, blindfolded, with gelded lips, blind and witless! You noticed that Nadia, the girl from Ras El Tin, her mother's indulgent and only child, was watching your youth, and handsomeness having a crush over you and thinking you were her night's Kaïs. And the more your arrogance and indifference increased, the stronger her desire to get closer to you became.

Umm Arabi told you as she was stirring coffee she was making on the kitchen stove, "Behold that Nadia is my only child, Mashhour, for after the marriage of my son Arabi and his being independent of us especially after his father who was a famous fisherman across Bahri drowned..." You were taken aback by the news, so you asked her, "Did your husband drown and died in the sea!?"

"Yes, he drowned and died in the sea!" You asked her being moved as if the accident happened yesterday," And how did that happen?" She then answered quietly and indifferently as if she talked about the fisherman Attriss who married Akkila the laundry woman yesterday, "He was fishing. We don't know the details. It seemed that he was fighting the eared seal. He pulled and it pulled! So he fell and drowned after a dizzying fight with its waves! After that Arabi was handed over fishing job from him. It is a job that children inherit from parents, and from grandparents. "

"What do you mean by grandparents? How did Arabi's grandfather die?"

The Anfushi woman looked at you as she was still stirring her coffee, and then said, "Drowning in the sea."

Surprised, you asked her, "Your husband drowned in the sea, so did his father before him? Do you mean that both of them were fishermen that the son inherited from his father the job of drowning in the sea? Still, you allowed your son to inherit the same job? It is the job of death, then? "

She sighed sadly, saying, "What shall we do?" Her coffee boiled over. Its foam spilled over the burner and extinguished it, while the old woman lifted the coffee pot and added, "This is the norm of life! We, the inhabitants of Bahri, have a job devoted to the sea, we are dependent on the sea, our living is from the sea, our life and friendship are with the sea and our end is in the sea exactly like the most beautiful brides that the pharaohs used to throw as a gift to the Nile. They were the brides of the Nile but here we are the sea brides!"

"Since your end is in the sea, don't you fear for your son's life as you had watched his father and his grandfather dying from drowning ...?"

The Anfushi woman adjusted the net fishing her long nose and tattooed chin, and then the tilapia fish spoke from the inside of her net, " What about you?, where do your family and relatives die?"

"They die on the bed!", you said, then.

"And where do your neighbors and acquaintances die?"

You answered her, surprised at her question, "On the bed of course!" Then the foreteller said, "So you don't fear from sleeping on the bed and panic at night?" You stepped back as you were answering her, "It's true! Your words are logical and insightful Umm Arabi! I thought that you are a reasonable woman but not a philosopher too! I should have worried about sleeping on the bed!"

I could not understand you, O sea jostled with your waves coming from afar! (A wave is chasing a wave wanting to catch up with it.) Are you so generous that you give everyone resorting to you food from your infinite bounties, and therefore they sleep on your beaches safe and reassured? Or are you so savage and unfaithful, that you attack creatures, maul and crumble them, and then hide them in your stomach, and like a tiger you would lick them with your tongue cleaning everything surrounding you, and therefore you can display publicly your body, chase, pure and transparent? Are you so innocent, naive, and indifferent that you live eternally?

Or are you mean, deep and spiteful that you didn't let anyone remain around you but you, all alone? Are you an Arab dictator that doesn't move from his seat and lives forever? Or are you a cure that they put on the wound to heal? I love you, O sea! I fear you, O sea! I will miss you, O sea; I bid you farewell, O sea because I'm not going to see you anymore! I hate you, O sea because you will stab me in the back as you did with those who preceded me and get rid of my corpse, and then forget me while you stay forever!

After the death of her husband for whom no funeral was held, but rather flocks of fish and sea shark gathered and devoured him there quietly, his fellow fishermen looked for skin or even bones, but they couldn't find anything to bury. Fish had cut him into slices, divided them , and then distributed them to their friends as an act of revenge for their victims that the fishermen's net harvested every day, and to distribute his blood to fish clans, and thus it would be difficult to avenge him.

After his blood disappeared and his trace vanished, the sheik of fish ruling high seas called out," You did very well. Attack is the best form of defense. Put them in your belly before they put you in their bellies. Be as mischievous as they are. Belly for a belly and the bottom is more obscure!" No one understood what was going on, and each was swimming in its sea!

The mannish Anfushi woman did not remain passive, but rather collected her savings and all the money that Arabi's father left her and started furnishing her apartment that she began to rent to university students, then. It was a good source of income for such a family consisting of two members. That was what she explained to you one meeting inside the kitchen that was no more than two meters in which she put for herself a bench big enough for two persons to sit on or for just one person to lay down on his side with his legs curled underneath him that was if the woman and her daughter wanted to rest in her house kitchen whose rooms she rented to three students.

Umm Arabi stood with you in the kitchen teaching you how to brew coffee or tea as she was telling you the story of her life. The sixty-year-old woman knew that you were a naive boy who didn't know how to make a cup of coffee or how to fry an egg, so she played the role of mother to teach you the ABC's of alienation!

"Put water in the pot, light the gas stove and let it simmer, and then take a small coffee spoon, put it in water and then put a small spoon or what pleases you of sugar and stir the coffee, water and sugar on a low flame. Keep stirring as long as the water in the pot gets hotter on the fire. Once the coffee boils over, pour it like this in a Turkish coffee cup with foam. And may it bring health to your heart! "

The old Umm Arabi almost treated you with kindness like one of her kids and teased you comfortably. When winter came, you felt cold, so you told the old woman with your Palestinian accent, "It is cold, Ahha!" You didn't understand that the word Ahha in Alexandria community was a sexual, sexy and embarrassing term while it was an innocent Shami expression especially for those who were feeling cold!

And once your roommate, the student from El Mansoura ,Mohammad Mohammad heard you, he told you, "The parents of a country girl in the province of Alsharquiya killed her upon hearing her saying the word ahha."

However, the old woman answered boldly when hearing you saying ahha . She said, "Go and fuck her, then!" You were surprised at the rude word, but you felt that it came from an experienced woman, so you swallowed it and accepted it from her. From that day on, you refrained from saying the word ahha even if you were at the edge of dying from cold!

THE GREAT SPHINX

After disappearing for a while in his room on the ninetieth floor of the hotel, Burhan intrudes into your seclusion.

You tell him yearningly, "Where have you been, man?"

He sits next to you on the bed, saying, "I was taking a hot bath!"

This Burhan doesn't know anything but talking about environment and heredity. He looks at you and told you, "Could you imagine that all Arab World lacks an institute active in hereditary engineering, father! So, you tell him trying to escape a huge embarrassment, "They set up an institute specializing in hereditary engineering in Abu-Dhabi two years ago to produce enhanced breeds of purely-bred Arab horses to spread them and market them on a large scale in the world, but I don't know whether it would be green horses like you wish or..!"

"The world of genetic engineering is a sort of insanity, passion, and a sort of creating a new life, father. The human life that we dream about! The ancient pharaoh scientists thought of hereditary engineering and crowned their thought with the statue of the Great Sphinx that embodies their hereditary project consisting in combing the head of a thinker with a body of a brave lion; intelligence with power! The statue might be the motto of the intelligent and powerful ruler and the purpose might be purely scientific to be the man enlightened with lion power. And this is what we achieved on the ground. But we don't want to combine man with a lion, but rather combine a lion with plants and man with plants and every animal with plants so that the life of a vegetarian animal would not depend on the instinct of fight for survival, but rather on survival because love and enjoyment of the universe would appear.

Tell me, father as a great engineer in terms of importance and prestige; aren't you too tired with living costs, enduring seventy years of continuous work in civil dry soulless engineering projects? You feel this wasted life but you could do nothing but to rise, and pee in the toilet and press the flash that comes down in the form of pressed milky steam. Then, you turn on the pressed steam facet to wash your hands. All of them are tools that use rationing water. An environmental issue that we are used to in Emirate, but that it happens in Beheira, Alexandria is shocking as you see with your own eyes its parts, which were once green, with their dried branches, pastures changing into desert and grieved sand and fields which the flow of Nile waters cocooned on itself and did not couple or fertilize anymore!"

You feel thirst drying your throat and you get worried again as you were answering him, "I am considered a retired for twenty years and as I told you once job is a hardship. For this reason, you can't find me enveloping in garments, but rather I arise and warn people against angering God. After I took part in projects of establishing about fifty buildings of heights from twenty to ninety floors, bypass roads, and bridges, our engineering office now is involved in designing the shores of Dubai Seaside Facet. After this global warming that resulted in the rise in the sea level which washed over thousands of low islands in Indonesia, the Philippines, and the Caribbean and flooded the Delta-Egypt green paradise and food basket- along with some low Emirati islands that drowned and disappeared, the danger started to threaten all coasts, and the golf tsunami hurricanes have become our main concern!

"And to face these challenges, our library provides consulting in strategic and environmental engineering projects as well as supervision on carrying them out. And now, I'm not doing any more regular job but I'm rather an owner of the half of Mashhour's Engineering- Consulting Firm that has become famous in all Emirates.

"We, Palestinians, who are deprived of a country, try to express our national complexes through hard work, and creativity compensates partially for the bitterness of displacement. I went to Cairo from the camp and from Dubai I sent you to Germany, and here you are making miracles and contributing to changing life on earth, and here is Canaan is thinking of humanizing rather than invading the space like he said. These ambitious achievements compensate us a little bit for deprivation!"

Burhan said optimistically, "Here, in Akka and Jaffa racial discrimination era is over after implementing the absolute right of Palestinians' right to return. The anti-Semitism came to an end with the recognition that Arab Muslims and Christians and former Jews are Semites and equal in rights and duties without any racial or religious discrimination, and our country was accepted as an integral part of United Arab states, and after this union, it becomes a free oasis of security for all divine religions and secular principles without any distinction which was a historical achievement accredited to those Arabs who were in the last centuries incompetent."

"It seems that I grow older than I can handle. For this reason, I will go back to Akka. I missed it so much. I must do anything and go back to live with your sister Samar, her children and grandchildren. There, I will build a public library house and offer it with all its contents to Akka city and put aside in the bank what can provide for its employers' salaries permanently after my death including a prize value called Mashhour Engineering Prize to be rewarded to the best engineering project that would contribute to rebuilding the desecrated villages and cities that occupation destroyed. The time has come to relax there in full view of old fishing boats sparkling along the shore lips."

"I wish I could go with you to Akka, father. But it was you who taught me to be serious in my life, so I plant and reap. And now, frankly, I never leave my job unless there is an absolute emergency like these check-ups of Canaan that hospital will perform tomorrow. I'm tied to my firm with a bond much stronger than the chastity belt which Europeans used to lock on the bottoms of their wives while they were adventuring on world seas or across the globe. I'm clinging to my firm with contracts, lawyers, and documents. And for this reason, excuse me and try to understand my situation, father.

"Is it to this point you can't leave your work?"

He puts one leg over the other, and then says, "Even if I think, my hereditary successes become what tie me to the institute. And truth be told, our firm is showering us with huge wages. The financial management would tell you,' Spend as much as you want. Buy whatever you want without limits, but disclosing the secrets of work is a red line! He switches his crossed legs and continues by saying, "We, researchers, accepted this game, and hence our main concern becomes to compete to get the earth into resuscitation room for we might bring back health and balance to it. Could you imagine that when they blockaded environmental pollution and replaced oil machinery with others using plant fuel, the effects were worse!"

"Of course they were worse, because biofuel uses plants in place of oil, and therefore instead of cultivating to feed the hungry, they start cultivating to feed mothers of machines, and that's why food prices rise. Here is the loaf of bread costs one Arab dinar. The poor are being killed in a plague of global famine and the consumption of water leads to the thirst of the earth!"

"And here too the loaf of bread reached two Euros! Biofuel killed earth inhabitants with hunger! And for this reason, hydrogen-powered machines that emit water steam took control instead of oil wastes and fuel debris. Consequently, the weather cleared, vision improved and people are relieved, but the surprise stemmed from the clarity of the weather and the brightness of sunshine which led to a rise in the temperature more than before. The earth is melting by heat and our plight is that we agreed to be the healing doctor, son."

"During our last journey on the United Arab flight, the passengers were drinking wastewater sprout from burning hydrogen with oxygen believing that it was the best water to drink!"

"The same thing happened to us on the united European flight for the host was bragging that he made for each one of us a cup of coffee or tea with water of hydrogen-powered aircraft's incinerator."

Burhan switches his crossed legs as he's asking you, "How do you treat the rise in sea water?"

"We are designing a separation wall like the separation wall which they built at the beginning of the century to smoother Palestinian people inside one of the biggest ghetto in history. And here we designed a wall separating people from sea life." So he tells you, "Isn't fair to deprive Emirati of their sea like they deprived Palestinians of their homeland? You, scared, answer him," We are doing this to protect the shores of the city from drowning because the wall separates the shores and organizes the contact with the sea."

"You, my father, are like he who measures the sea with his hat! Could anyone bridle the mouth of a horse? If the horrifying Berlin wall collapsed with blows of the German and Palestinian ghetto separation wall fell in front of resistance fighters' blows, would the wall of the sea of Emirates remain resistant to the angry waves of the earth, then? Tell me how much such a project would cost if it is extended to all parts of the Emirates."

"It would cost hundreds of billions of Arab dinars."

"You mean what they got as a price for oil will be spent on fighting the results of burning it? The arrogant civilization of the West leads to a life of ease by burning oil in their cars and factories. The misleading advertisements tell you," Fill your giant car with cheap oil and set off to your love! And after the era of oil, they used woods, and then planted instead of them beautiful apartment buildings that discharged under them stool and sewers polluting the environment and emitting space gazes and toxic that annihilate life on earth!"

"We, engineers who carry on our shoulders sea waves, have but this solution!"

"The solution doesn't lie in concrete because nature is more powerful than Man no matter what he does to conquer it, father!"

"The earth belongs to God. He causes to inherit it whom he wills of his righteous servants." you answer him hopelessly.

"You said it yourself! He stands and leaves as he is saying," Traditional Man proved that he is not righteous! So, how would you know that God wants to bequeath it to his green servants who are righteous?"

THE BEETLES

Burhan excuses himself and retreats to his bower to get some rest, while you go in to take a hot compact steam bath to get rid of the hardship of traveling. Amid your steam, the final exams of the first year at university crossed your mind. Your fellow student, the beetle Ragheb Ashrigi from Roshdi Area, called you that time, "Please help us. Neither Sarhan nor I have a book on the subject of socialism. We don't know anything about socialism, or capitalism, or even Al-Azhar!" he said that laughing!

You couldn't turn him down especially that he turned to you for help. You carried your book and went to the address. You rang the bell of the apartment on the thirteenth floor and Sarhan opened the door for you.

"Welcome, fellow student Mashhour. Come in."

You asked him, "Where is Ghaleb?"

He answered you, "He is there inside."

You came in and shook his hand as he was sitting on a squashy sofa. You found him busy watching the Magazine of Britain's Beetles (Beatles Magazine) as being himself a beetle from their group. The British Beatles fad was at its highest in the sixties and all gilded youth imitated them and on the top of them was Ragheb Ashrigui.

And as he mentioned to you once when we were in the amphitheater, he was born in Beirut where his father worked as a Moroccan diplomat and his mother was Damascene. The family of the diplomat moved with his job being transferred to London where Ghaleb studied. Of course, you didn't ask him about the reason behind his coming to study in Alexandria. It might be for independence reasons, or his parents intended to strengthen his self -reliance or the boy might be expelled from his English University or admission to one of the British universities was impossible for one reason or another! All that you knew was his long velvet black hair falling on his cheeks and covering his neck and his long sideburns that were covering his ears and reaching his neck, unlike his fellow student Sarhan whom you noticed his hair was covering just his ears, while his sideburns were trimmed at the end of his chin.

You sat and opened the book. Then Ashrigui told you, "Did you hear the last joke?" You loved jokes as they helped he who was depressed snap out of loneliness, and made him laugh according to the theory, "Draw a smile on your face, smile enters your heart." And since you had a complex about history and geography, you told him, "Go ahead."

He said laughing, "There was a barrel saying to a barrel, 'Why no one is seeing you around? The other barrel told him, 'No one is empty!'" We laughed together and Sarhan gave another joke," Two people are sentenced to death. One is a bore, and the other is a cold fish. They asked the bore, 'What do you want?' He told them, 'I want to see my mother.' Then they asked the cold fish, 'What do you want?' He told them, 'I wish this man wouldn't see his mother!'"

We laughed at the silly joke. Then Ragheb replied to him with another one, "A chief gave a stupid man in the army the most expensive bomb in the world and told him to throw it on enemies from the top of a mountain between the two armies. The man climbed the mountain and for the first time he thought and said, 'This bomb is very expensive, so our country deserves the most.' So, he threw it on his army!" You didn't laugh at that joke because it was old and unfunny. You told them," Is this a time for jokes, buddies?

And while they were laughing, the doorbell rang. Sarhan stood up and opened the door. You looked at the arriver. She was a woman in her twenties!

Praise be to God that a woman entered the house, so that these two beetles would feel shy around her and these silly jokes would stop, you thought, *especially at the night before the final exam, because If you fail, boy, you would be lost as you cannot handle failure!*

Honestly, the woman's femininity was striking; her white body was plump and her face - May God be the protector - looked like the full moon in its rise, not to mention her innocent eyes, her hair cascading on her back and her dress revealing her knees.

"Who's this woman?" You asked Ragheb who answered you smiling, "This is the wife of one of our friends. Her name is Afaf. "

"A wife of one of your friends! Why would a friend's wife visit you on her own?"

He scratched his neck acting dumb, saying," It is just a friendly visit."

The woman sat on the couch between Ragheb and Sarhan facing you, and then crossed her legs revealing two seductive thighs, no; they were rather luscious whose femininity turned you on as if she was sitting on your lap. Ragheb said to her, then "The nightgown is hung behind the door."

The chase woman stood up and grabbed a transparent woman nightgown hung on a hooker behind the door of the living room. It was weird! Whose this transparent woman's nightgown always standing up waiting behind the door of the living room of two single men, students in a respectable university, was?

The female went out of the room, went maybe to the bathroom, and then came back after she had changed her formal clothes. Next, she sat between them with her short transparent nightgown that was giving off the warmth of her hot body. She was an innocent and beautiful person and you had never sat facing a woman of this kind. Still, you were mesmerized by her beautiful femininity! The girl pulled out her comb from her large brown leather bag and talked with innocence while combing her hair, "My sister Mahassen invited me yesterday to Molokhiya with rabbit. It was very delicious!" –she fell silent–"my mother is so sick," she added. But no one of the drugged men sitting next to her answered her or asked about her mother or even was touched by the news! The only one who was saddened by her mother's sickness was this stupid you.

"We don't know what we should do with the bank that mortgaged my father's apartment," the beautiful continued her report, "It sent him a threat to sell it in an auction! He is burdened with expenditures, my dear! He's retired and his health is deteriorating!"

Ragheb was tidying his hair with his hands, while Sarhan was watching Beatles Magazine without sympathizing with this friend's wife. None of them discussed with her the subject. Not even a word!

"They can sell it!" the sad woman added. "Even so, it can hardly pay for our debts! Today my father is looking for a remote and cheap apartment in the popular district of Bakous to rent before selling our apartment. For this reason, he couldn't accept the invitation."

You took Ragheb away from the wounded woman and asked him, "Who is this woman?"

He answered laughing, "This? I told you. This is Afaf!"

"I don't understand those...! Tell me what's the matter?"

He answered you smiling," Honestly this woman is our friend. If you want to sleep with her, here you go!"

Here you go? Is it an invitation to dinner to invite me using the word here you go?"

"I'm telling you to take which means take! And I mean what I say. I mean it."

You told him solemnly, "But I don't deal with such women."

The boy laughed and asked you, "You mean you did not sleep with such women or you have never slept with a woman?"

You replied nervously, "I didn't sleep with such or with never...! The beetle laughed loud and Sarhan came to find out what was wrong, so Ragheb told him," Could you imagine that our brother Mashhour is still a virgin and has never slept with a woman!"

Sarhan was surprised and laughed a lot, saying, "Is it true? I ask you by God to tell me if you are still a virgin!"

"How could you adjure me by God, man? Don't you fear God that you adjure me by him in these issues?" The two beetles laughed together, then.

"We're sharing her with you because you are a guest," Sarhan told you. "You endured the trouble of coming with your book on socialism, so we want to teach you socialism through our friend Afaf!"

Ragheb supported him by saying, "You were generous to us by letting us flip through your book and we will be generous to you by letting you flip through the body of this beautiful. What do you say?"

You didn't want to expose yourself and appear like a stupid retarded in the beetles' market to that extent, so you told them," OK, let one of you start, and then it will be my turn."

The woman went in the room with Sarhan and closed the door behind them. You sat alone in the living room, while Ghaleb went to the kitchen to bring some food and tea.

You heard moans, bedrocks, and her sexy voice provoking all your body armies chained with the iron chains of your grandmother Aneesa, strict instructions of your father and behind him the bleat of your mother who could do nothing but to carry the seals of the king and approve the transactions under his name!

You thought of tomorrow's exam which bewildered you that you could see nothing but it. It was an obligation to pass the exam because the thirty guineas that your brother Ghaleb sent you would stop for good if he knew that you failed once. That's because his salary was just twice as much as the money sent to you and you didn't know how much Ghaleb was suffering to fight life to earn a piaster strenuously, so that he would provide for himself and his family in the camp, save money for a bright precious future and marry and support a dashed family! Your situation was hard Mashhour as you were resisting yourself in this dark night study! Was it obligatory to be loyal and helpful to these beetles missing life and hereafter to study with them the subject of socialism? And even if they studied it with you, would they understand socialism?

They did not disappear for so long, while you were biting your hands out of regret. The female went out of the room with disheveled hair, red cheeks, and bewildered gazes as she was heading straight for the bathroom. She was now cheap and diminishing in your eyes and her glory was fading away as she was going as if she was beautiful Venus statue falling apart and its pieces were dashed under feet. Sarhan came and sat next to you smiling stupidly, and then stood up and went to the kitchen.

After a few minutes, Afaf came back from the bathroom. She had washed her pelvis, wetting her transparent nightgown that unveiled her chastity and showed that she was without a pant hiding her nakedness that shower water exposed. She sat in front of you on the triple bench, while you were watching this sensual panorama! It seemed that she did it deliberately or she didn't care about drying the remaining shower water that her transparent nightgown revealed everything in the pelvic area. Your eyes were staring at a live broadcast nearby, sharper than those of an unhooded hawk getting ready to attack the meat of a featherless bird in front of it!

The lioness started to trim her fingernails with a thin nail-file and talked to you simply as if nothing happened. "What's your name?

You answered her with the gibberish of a surprised person,"
Mashhour. "

"What do you study, Mashhour?" she indulged you when
talking to you as if you were a kid in front of her. You answered her,
while you were still scrutinizing her with your gazes like someone who
was scrutinizing a scorching sun with his hands," engineering. "

"Are you in the same year as Sarhan and Ragheb?" she asked
you as she put her nail-file on her bag and stared into your eyes.

You answered her, "That's the problem!"

She understood that you were making fun of the two beetles,
so she continued her questions and went back to trim her nails,"
Where are you from Mashhour?

You answered her briefly, "From Palestine."

"Where is this Palestine? Are you Eastern or North African
student? In other words are you from the East or the West?

Believe me I can't distinguish east from west anymore!"

You were nervous and aroused, as she was asking you and you
were answering her as if you were in jail, a detainee under investigation.
You were not comfortable with her presence or sympathetic with her.
Honestly, you were sexually aroused to the point that if a fly perched
on your nose and you had a gun you would pull the trigger!

But your gun is suppressed by chastity belt and your
grandmother Aneesa standing at your door watching you as she was
supporting her old cheek with her right hand to see how you were
going to behave in this situation new to you! Your thoughts were dirty
as if you swam now with farmers' children in the water of the El
Mahmoudia Canal with its horrifying eggs of bilharzia!

The female was talking to you and you were distracted from
her by her. Your eyes were like the apertures of a video camera lens

trying to capture both sound and image. At the same time, you were thinking angrily about her talk.

Is it possible that this... has a father, a mother, a brother and a sister eating Molokhia with rabbits like people? We used to have a clay house special for rabbits and my father used to separate males from females and did not allow any one of them to get closer to females except according to rules while here rabbits mingled without rules!

Is it possible that these... women were that silly and simple? You didn't see any vices on the face of this woman! Her father would buy his apartment, her poor mother was sick, she was sympathetic with her mum and there was in her humanity and mercy! But how, why, when, and where... but, and so... perhaps, what a mess! You couldn't understand anything anymore!

Sarhan and Ragheb came back carrying a plate of food on which there were honey, eggs, and Pastirma. "Come and eat, man." They sat and started eating. The whore mentioned the name of God the All-Merciful! You were not looking at food, but rather at her lips mentioning the name of God! which meant she was a believer and feared God! So, she was not from the devil's people! Therefore, there was no right to burn her with astral oil! But what's your business? She took a path and you took another!

"Go ahead, man!" Ragheb told you as he was chewing sausages wrapped with bread, "Go with the lady."

You answered him bewildered, "you go before me, and I'll be the last."

Ragheb entered with her, while Sarhan excused himself and went to the neighbors' apartment to call someone on the telephone. He said that their telephone was out of order, while you stayed...! With your mind roaring!

Is that what Ragheb used to doing the night before the exam? The night separating the wheat from the chaff! So, how would you behave since you were the third of them?

With a courage that you didn't see before in yourself, you took your book with your right hand and went out of the apartment running away fast. You pressed the button of the elevator door which indicated it was on the ground floor. The damned elevator took too much time to reach the thirteenth floor! Someone might catch you as you were waiting for the great escape! And with the speed of a running cat, you rushed to get down the stairs...

The twelfth floor..the tenth...the ninth...the second...the first! And there you jumped toward a yellow taxi stationary near the sidewalk and with the eagerness of a perplexed person, you asked him to set off from Roshdi to Cleopatra! The time now was ten past five pm and Mohammad Mohammad was studying for tomorrow's exam. He saw you breathing hard! He felt worried about you. "Why are you out of your breath Mashhour?" he asked you eagerly. You sighed, saying, "Nothing!" His worry then worsened, "Tell me, did something bad happen to you?"

You reassured him by stopping your gasping. "No!"

"You made me worry man! Please let me know if you are fine!"

You have no choice, so you explained to him the problem, the gist of what happened. Mohammad was surprised. He said, "Are you crazy?" He sensed your stupidity as he was asking you, "How could you go the night before the exam to such trivial students, brother? Did you forget that tomorrow is the final exam?"

Just a few minutes later the phone rang, so you asked him to pick the phone up, "If the call is for me, tell them I'm sleeping, so that they would not annoy us with another telephone call!"

Really, you went to sleep to rest your nerves from the games of Ali El-Zeibaq and this Afaf...! After hours of sleep, you woke up at two am and started to go through the papers of the book on socialism and when the daylight broke, you were about to finish the book. Before going to university, you reread the underlined information many times that you learned by heart. In the exam room, you answered correctly and you succeeded. As for the marks of Sarhan and Ragheb...!

Your steam bath in this glass hotel hung in the sky was mingled with the memories of Sarhan, Ragheb, and Afaf. You dry your body with a white towel as soft as cotton, brimful of the steam bath ambience. You wipe the large blurry mirror to see your reflection in it, and then shave your chin after you warmed and moisturized its white hair. Afterward, you go out to take a nap after the hardships of traveling.

A WEAK WOMAN

You feel a little bit better after this vibrating steam bath that vibrated and massaged the cells of your old body with compact steam, thus relaxing to take a nap. Then, Alexandria take you to your childhood and to Umm Arabi who was a mother, teacher, and governess, but who seemed heartless that night when scream and wail rose to be followed by breaking of hard things. Metal pots were rolling and annoying sounds were coming from the upper floors of the building.

You paid attention to scream and wail that pushed your curiosity toward the apartment door! You found yourself searching with the nose of the Syrian officer "Abu Kalabsha" where a woman was thrown on the stairs of the building. She stood thus swinging at neighbors' doors, knocking on them one after the other to be turned down by every door, and then walked downcast and bewildered till she reached the first floor, the door of Umm Arabi .You expected her to be helpful to her neighbor because a neighbor means protection and it's the right of a neighbor over his neighbor even if he is unjust!

The beautiful stood at our door. The clock was pointing to two am and the woman's tears were falling from her eyes without sobbing. You asked Umm Arabi about her and she informed you that she was our neighbor living on the fourth floor of the building. The woman looked in her twenties, rich in her feminine treasures, humiliated without wail, heart-broken, and exhausted as if she was a worn-out Andalusian scarf. She explained her story to Umm Arabi in few words, and then begged her to let her sleep over at her house this night. She had no acquaintance in Alexandria as she was one of the residents of Cairo's quarters, and her husband swore that he would divorce her if she spent the night at his house as a punishment...! It was certain that the Anfushi woman would not turn her down and that helping her was taken for granted and investigation would be only about the meanness of the crazy husband who drove her to the mouth of the choppy sea waves! But you were surprised at Umm Arabi refusing to invite her in. After standing for a while in front of her door in the hope that her heart would soften or change her mind or find her a solution , the poor woman was forced to go out to the street; El Geish Road! And those who passed in El Geish Road after midnight are but.?

The captive stood for so long on the beach sidewalk, turning her face right away from that homeless man and left away from that drunkard and back away from that curious person, and then...! She was swatting flies away from her face. The ferocious stinging horseflies accustomed to suck blood from horses and donkeys' butts seemed tonight to attack the beautiful pink face of this deer. The flies became as big as a wasp and as strong as a flacon, and then grew as big as a flacon that carried a sheep itself and flew far away!

The weak woman held on till her limbs were frozen by cold night sea breeze coming from the gates of snowy Alps mountains. Hence, she gave in and collapsed on the bench of the sidewalk of the Corniche Street covered with sea spray!

***

A strange poet boat falling apart with insane sea waves keeping slapping it. Its fondling and slapping against harbor rocks were repeated in a rebellious night till they tore it asunder and it shrank like an octopus spreading out its arms hit repeatedly with force against beach rock till it gave in to the fatal blow and thus they put it in their octopus fishing basket!

***

It was two hours past midnight now. And after having patience and pondering on the way of thinking of that villain husband, he might awake from his drunkenness or a new conscience might grow in him or he might give up his insanity or he might come aware of his mistake and take her back to her house and ask forgiveness from God, but...

Cars came, cars set off and cars pulled over near her, and then wheels scratched the asphalt road after the lady ignored them. She was a lady but no longer! For she could not decide her destiny to be a lady!

The oppressed woman was so patient that she abjured her husband and entire life. At three after midnight, the desperate woman started to overcome her shyness, forget about feminine qualities, turn a blind eye to the meaning of honor, and break the barriers of customs and traditions. She abjured what was permitted and believed in the forbidden! And why shouldn't she? She didn't find in one of these concepts a piaster to spend! In the end, she was forced to say Ahhh. Therefore, the victim collapsed and agreed to get into the car of any man! Any man!

Here was Al Mahlabi coming from the bar. He stopped his car next to her and opened the door for her to get in. He was an expert in picking his living! He could recognize the woman without honor. He was like a shark. He did not attack before tasting blood scent. He looked into her azure eyes seeing her as a fish tossed on the sandy beach. The Tilapia that the sea tossed didn't wait for an invitation, but rather leaned on her pains and raised her broken self and moved with her free will to collapse on the seat next to the man with large mustaches like the wings of a raptorial flacon! The flacon took her and flew!

On the road, he told her his name and tried to wipe her left cheek with his palm saturated with pipe smoke and strong alcohols! No one saw him in this obscure night taking her to his flat and being very hospitable to her offering her intoxicating beverage she didn't know their brands, saying, "These are drinks of happiness made especially to warm someone who is cold and make you forget problems."

The woman, worn-out, poured it like that in her belly in two sips. "And this strong glass will make you forget your family," The dizzy woman spilled it in a deep abyss! "And the third glass is concentrated. It reveals your beautiful nakedness." She couldn't remember that she drank it, then!

The immodest woman relaxed, lay down on his bed and then melt like sweet feast. Al Mahlabi took her in his arms to the large bathroom inside his bedroom of single man, took off her chastity, bathed her and rubbed her, and then massaged all her sides. After that, he welcomed the sprinkles of a hot shower to rid himself of road cold, smoking odor and rottenness of the night club, and then he went out with her wrapped in a cotton bathroom robe that sucked her sea humidity, threw her on the bed to keep the naked woman warm in his arms all night!

After realizing his appalling mistake, her husband looked for her, ran in the streets and everywhere but could not find her. And when you asked Umm Arabi about her, she told you," The woman did not return to her house for when her pig husband dropped by to ask about her and look for her, he admitted while standing on the building stairs that he was unjust to her. I told him, 'You don't deserve a gem like her. You hit her for every mistake she does, while she endured and endured till her patience ran out. May God punish you, man?' The pig then left with his tail between his legs."

Trapped, the woman was forced to remain as a maid in the house of her new captor who started to take her with him every night to the night club of Al Mahlabi. Since that night, she discovered that he was the owner of the club, so he was her guest on the first night, and on the second night he introduced her to her colleagues in the job and after the third night, she was the right of the guest over the guest. He baptized her and appointed her as a barmaid and an oriental dancer. Then he made her go with his important clients after the end of parties to be paid a lot of money because of her!

That's what your Ismaili fellow student Yusuf, who was living in an underground apartment of the building, told you. He got all this information from his girlfriend Umm Fatouma who visited houses and transferred news like rats transferring Typhus diseases among people! And for this reason, you asked Umm Arabi, "Why didn't you give that woman a shelter that dark night?"

She answered you embarrassed, "Where would I put this girl if I, the landlady, sleep in the kitchen whenever I visit you? Would I let her sleep in the arms of one of the guys living in my apartment which will ruin my reputation and that of my apartment, thus deteriorating my business? And if I accepted to protect her, I would get in trouble with a low husband who doesn't understand the meaning of swearing an oath regarding his wife at midnight. There is as proverb that states that the one who swears is a pig. She is a stranger living far away from her family and he is her family, her protection and honor because she has no children till now to be her shield as she is still a new bride who hasn't yet completed a year in his house!"

ADAMANHOURI RESTAURANT

Worry overwhelms you as you are attempting to take a nap in this Guangzhou Hotel finding yourself thinking about the medical examinations of your grandson Canaan wondering.

Is Burhan walking in the right direction and would his green laboratories succeed in removing Man's claws!? Is it possible to remove vice from children of Adam?

You try to forget that, so you return to your old university mornings. Back then, before you went to university, you used to go to Adamanhouri Restaurant located on the street corner. There, you had fava beans that cost you five piasters, drank a big glass of dark strong tea for a piaster and you added a tariff to the check as a tip for Alhaja Aliya. But you stopped giving a tip after you understood that she was the restaurant owner, her being the wife of Alhaji Khalil Adamanhouri. And on your way, you headed to the store of Cleopatra sugarcane juice. You drank a giant glass for a piaster. Afterward, you arrived at Cleopatra Station and the tram took you to university station from which you walked to Engineering University. You met with your fellow students in amphitheater number one that could be filled to a capacity of more than one thousand female and male students.

In the evening, you went back to Adamanhouri Restaurant. Alhaji Khalil would welcome you with warm intimacy, "What do you want for dinner? Cheese? Pastirma and egg? Sausage? eggplant?"

As for Falafel, fava beans, and tea, serving them did not stop in the morning, or in the afternoon or in the evening!

During dinner, cheap perfume scents penetrated your nose. You noticed that it was coming from the two or three women in their thirties. They often visited this restaurant and sat with a man around a small round table located in a near corner because the space of the restaurant was narrow. You watched the women laughing impudently with the man who seemed to have one leg. You were certain about that when he and one of the women stood up as he was leaning on his right cane wrapped at the bottom with a plastic black patch. They headed outside whispering while she was tut-tutting and waving the end of her black melaya dangling like wings loosening on the side of the short colorful dress that could hardly cover the half of her rounded thighs.

You saw her bare clean armpits, while she was gesticulating with her hands right and left and arguing with the man with the cane who was wearing grey cloak on an Arabic long striped dress and one black shoe in his left foot. It seemed that his dress was designed to hide his cut leg. You saw one of the two sitters saying to him, "O go, honey, we will wait till you come back safe?" The other woman assured him by saying, "If you don't find us here, wait till we come back. We will go there with you tonight."

Where here and there? You didn't know!

The next morning, while you were having your breakfast, you asked Alhaja Aliyah, who used to work at least in the morning as she would prepare fava beans and other dishes and serve clients, whereas Alhaji Khalil would came most of the time in the evening and stay late after midnight, "Who are these women occupying the corner of the restaurant every night and laughed with that...," You feel ashamed to say the type of his handicap because one should not gloat the misfortune of a handicapped and that's why we would say when talking about a one-eyed man, his eye is holy and we would refer to a blind person as a clear-eyed one.

"Alhaja answered laughing," That's Hassan and in his company are girls..., you know.

You didn't understand what she was hinting at, did you? So you asked her with the naivety of an idiot," What do you mean by that, Alhaja?"

"I mean that they are some beautiful girls whom he let wander about freely." she said that while she was smashing onion and putting it in a frying pan whose steams burning with scents rose that all small restaurant's visitors could smell...

Is that possible that a man with these attributes ran such business? Let them wander freely! You hate such women. Are they sheep, so he would let them wander about freely? Even sheep wander about freely in the open space and eat but pure grass! How does this...man let them wander about freely? (This time you said it without shame), and where did he let them wander about? Is that possible that this restaurant is a brothel? And if so, how come that they serve breakfast and dinner and do not declare it as an open center for prostitutes?

Many questions were gathering like clouds that were raining acids on your head. And here you were intrepid to tell Hajja Aliyah, "How come that you give shelter to whores of this kind while you know their path, you, God-fearing Haja?"

"Hhhhh", Alhaja laughed as she was putting on your small table fava beans dish with cotton oil and next to it a small plate on which there was a half lime, a quarter of an onion, three pieces of pickles of cucumber, turnip, and pepper. She said, "No, I'm an open-minded Haja!"

You kept quiet for this cannot defeat you, but what would shock you immensely was seeing this limp Hassan on Friday who would recite this talk..

Here you were sitting in the second row between worshipers in Sidi Jaber Al Ansari Mosque listening to the sermon given by the imam of the mosque. The imam was screaming saying," He that shall be drawn away from the fire and brought into paradise will indeed have gained a triumph."

All of a sudden you were surprised at seeing Hassan, the limp, sitting in the first row among worshipers putting his stick in front of his imam to bear witness to him on the day of resurrection!

God the greatest! How could that... enter God's house? What would this Hassan say to himself between God's hands? How did he dare to stand in the presence of God impure as such?

You saw the mosque crowded with worshipers on whose faces seemed submissiveness and repentance, and the imam of the mosque was gesticulating and pointing his forefinger, teaching people, reminding, tempting, and threatening them, "Who are heedless of their prayers, who show off."

You watched the worshiper as they were answering, "Aaaaaameeeeeen, O Lord of mankind", while the pimp was sitting with submissiveness raising his hands to Allah asking forgiveness, repenting like prostitutes.

"How does a prostitute repent?"

Abu Gerges whom you would live in his apartment would answer you ecstatically by saying, "When a prostitute repents, she turns into a procuress!"

You asked him mockingly, "Ok, What a pimp, then, would become when he repents, Abu Gerges?" He answered laughing as usual, "He goes to hell!"

You came back from university and went into your room. You were taken aback by seeing the beautiful Nadia sleeping innocently, safely and peacefully on your bed and pretending to be covered with your blanket while the cover revealed her wheatish fresh plump legs and showed the extremely-arousing-lust things between them like Yasunari Kawabati's Japanese women in his novel Sleeping Beauties that Gabriel Garcia Marquez wished to be its writer.

What if Marquez stood face to thigh - you mean face to face - in front of one of the girls of the sleeping beauties' club! It was true that those were bare feet and naked while this one was covered and partly unveiled. Still, this Nadia was sexier than his sleeping beauties in your eyes!

What would an ignorant and arrogant teenager living with this house's family do in front of this scene? It was true that you wished to get closer to her and melt in her folds. Undoubtedly you desired her as the scent of her used underwear next to the bathroom sink aroused you when you took it with your hands, looked at it thoroughly, and then smelled it. Therefore, you knew that it was...and within you, a virgin sexual energy that could destroy walls. Would you get closer to her, kiss the cheeks full of freshness and softness, or smell her perfumed, fresh, soft neck, or kiss her auburn curved lips flaming with the color of fiery rose's petals or reach your hand to the warmth of her chest bulged with softness and freshness of delicious butter and which confused you as hiding two nipples in soft satin bras that your boiling sexual hunger drooled, so you tried to bridle in front of the girl relaxing on the bed!

Would you explore the rest of her covered body, slipped in beside her, and then would grip her waist and grope her belly and...? Then what would be the consequence of this..?

Would the beauty wake up and scream for help claiming that you sexually assaulted the chase woman, indiscreet. You would, therefore, get involved in battles about honor and rape and sit in prison blamed and destitute among prisoners. Next, you would be excluded from university and return to your family in the same way as a defeated leader would return from war battle as Al-Manfalouti once said?

Or would you drown in her love in the same way as Antony drowned in the love of Cleopatra losing himself and the woman empress, destroyed her people, and made her the last of the pharaohs? Would you lose your educational empire, burn your books in the same way as Caesar burned the books of the Library of Alexandria as he was fighting Antony and Cleopatra, and thus you would conquer her love, but fail university exams, and then you would together to give in disappointment and failure? There had to be wisdom in handling this situation!

When you visited them to bid them goodbye after you had graduated from university and after four years of absence, she was still unfriendly toward you. She confessed her extreme surprise at your behavior with her the day she slept in your room, then. She told you mockingly as if she took revenge on you, "I was like a kitten with closed eyes and you were heartless when you told me as I was rising from your bed yawning,

"Who allowed you to sleep in my room? I rented this room with my money, so if you sleep here again and see you like this I will throw you out of the window!"

You stood in front of her silent and ashamed because you never forgot that situation and you were still living every gesture or a whisper that Nadia breathed and remembering those dramatic stressful moments because Umm Arabi was standing at the kitchen door looking at you surprised at the stupidity of your behavior with a delicate innocent girl, a visitor that thought of having a rest in your room for a while!

Your imagination got carried away as you were remembering your days at engineering university. The only student in engineering university that wore a very long skirt was called Tahani Al-kafrawi and her name was famous just because she was the only one among students who wore long clothes hiding wrists and about one inch below the knees. As for other girls, they were wearing miniskirts. The skirt was about one inch or two inches long, and therefore it might or might not cover the plump, thin, tall, short, blonde, colored, wheatish, white thighs that were moving in the courtyard of universities. Some skirts did not hide anything especially when the student sat in the university canteen or a place where she found herself forced to cross one leg over the other!

Speaking about miniskirts, I and Mohammad Mohammad were once climbing the stairs of a building to visit one of his acquaintances from Al Mansura who was living on the fourth floor while a girl was climbing down from upstairs. We saw as we were looking up from the bottom of the stairs a soft red color under her mini blue skirt. We met as we were going up and she was climbing down. So, Mohammad told her rudely, "Don't worry! We didn't see anything!"

We were taken aback by the innocent-looking girl's answer as she was standing beside us on the stairs screaming win a nervous voice with her eyes wide open, "Why? Do you want to see?!" So we felt scared of causing a scandal and hurried in going up as you were saying to him, "God damn you! You could have got us in big trouble!"

He said frightened, "I did not expect the girl to be shameless!"

The student Tahany Alkafrawi endured day in, day out a lot of mockery and embarrassing comments from her fellow students especially those who didn't know her and were not intimidated by confrontation. Once the poor thing entered the university campus, one of the non-graduates surprised her by saying as he was walking fast, "O beautiful, do you feel cold today?"

And in university courtyard where she was walking by herself with dreamy romance on the Bermuda grass lawn seeing the flower beds arranged in geometric shapes, she came face to face with ...! What did come across her? You forgot what you were talking about! It seemed that you became senile! Oldness destroyed your memory! What were you saying?

Oh, Tahani Al-Kafrawi... a rude student came face to face with her harassing her by saying," Why are they wearing blankets?" His fellow student commented, "They hold back heat." A third student would say, "Oh yes, the skirt is woolen, but it's summer wool of high quality!" A seventh student would say, "This is a poultice in high summer. It warms the chest!"

Tahani Al- Kafrawi entered the canteen. A student saw her clothes and told her as he was leaving, "Are they distributing clothes for free?" His fellow student answered him, "She is wearing the dress of her farmer mother!"

An Alexandrian student asked, "Is it an engineering university or a manor for farmers?"

The shy student Tahani had a complex! And in the second year, you missed her because she dropped out of university that stabbed her in the back and gave up on study and what they were studying! It was said that her father made her wear a long dress and she was stuck in a fright triangle between her parent's pressure, that of university students and her personal feelings! In the end, she gave in and was forced to go home and ended up marrying a good man who contained and tamed her. You felt sad for Tahani Al-kafrawi who paid the cost of... the cost of what? The poor thing was lost without any cost!

On the wide road leading to the drawing-room, Mohammad Mohammad told you as a comment on the fall of university diggings that were still the matter of the moment students were talking about," If eight casualties were lifted from the rubble, how many thousands of casualties did disappear underneath the rubble of Swiss Canal that Great Britain took over tirelessly, then? How many millions of casualties did end up victims of pyramids, temples, cemeteries, and Pharaoh Statues to achieve the survival of the pharaoh regime?

Mohammad Mohammad was in pain as he was saying, "These simple kind people make sacrifices to shape the features of the civilization of Egypt Arabism. Notice that they dug the home land with their souls, fought, and died under its soil! Could you imagine that every day a bunch of workers was killed when building the high dam besides at factories, farms, the Suez Project and when establishing universities, schools and hospitals? O Mashhour! We are building a home country!

"The world was in a total mess, while I and you were laughing here and there! And for your record, we couldn't laugh and rejoice without those sacrificing their souls so that Egypt would remain free, Arabian!"

Mohammad Mohammad heard the speech of Abdel Nasser on workers' day and was shaken with pride as he was saying," When Abdel Nasser became a president, his father asked him to remain in his job as a worker in postal service of Ras El Tin and didn't behave arrogantly toward his humble colleagues!"

O Mohammad Mohammad, where are you? You used to say, "Each one of us must have an attitude?" Each one of us these days started to look for a seat.

ALEXANDRIAN CHAOS OF SENSES

The pedestrians on the roads of twenty-first Alexandria are rare. While flying above its streets, you come across but these glass buildings greeting each other sky-high, whose Sub-vitreous walls are glittering in daytime absorbing sunray and saving it. Then at night you find these walls returning the sunlight they stored and thus illuminating the city turning its night into day without costing Electricity Company anything!

Back in the day, people used to hustle here and there. The tram would warn pedestrians to stay away from its way clanking its bell, as the ticket collector was peeking out from the door saying to a woman, "Are you getting on or shall I whistle?" And a woman, who was covering her small body with milaya laf from top to toe, bumped into the tram, and then moved back away from its iron wheels that bit her right toes and snatched them. The bleeding toes would then fall between the railway tracks because she felt optimistic when entering the railway with her right foot. People would gather round her like birds of a feather flock together!

The salesman standing on the street corner swore that you took your purchases of vegetables and fruits even if you didn't have enough money. "Tomorrow, you will pay, man. I'm in no hurry" And all of a sudden, they announced the death of student Monther Al-Khurasany and his girlfriend May Musalam for they found them dead due to suffocation with a gas leak from the water heater as they were taking a bath. In the meantime, the painter Saif Waily who had beetle-black hair announced the opening of the summer exhibition in Biennale Alexandria.

Mohamed Shalabi was selling simit, eggs, cheese, and Cleopatra cigarettes on the quay of Alexandria harbor for captains standing in the sky on the deck of their giant merchant ships. They would lower for him the basket with a rope from the sky in which he would put the stuff while saying to George at the summit of the ship, "Hey George pull the rope up ... Hey, pull the rope up, George!" But the business transaction did not proceed, so his fellow workers would approach him saying, "Can George speak Arabic?"

"Back off!" Therefore, he would call out to George in English, "Hey George, can you speak English?" George became friendly with he who spoke English and answered," Yes, yes! "

Hence, he would tell him in Arabic," Since you can, pull the rope up, then!"

And a dusty woman in rags sitting on the ground was peeling half of a watermelon with her teeth. It seemed to be rotten as she picked it near the dustbin. And Albanians Defrawi near the gate of Cleopatra tram station was heating bee honey and pouring it from a height like flowing oil so that the passers-by would drool and could not resist buying it. In the shop, they would tell you, "May your morning be cream, and vermicelli, and may your evening be cottage cheese, white cheese, pastrami, and eggs, and may your night be milk, God willing!

The Soviet Warships carrying nuclear heads were stationary in Alexandria Harbor for a friendly visit. A journalist asked the Soviet warship commander," We don't see any nuclear thing on the ship deck. How the missiles that we don't see on the deck would work, then?"

The Soviet captain answered him with reverence, "I hope they don't have to work so that you would not see them!"

And next to station bars, a small woman was sitting with her milaya lef in front of a tiny table selling lime, every twenty pieces for a piaster ,and near her a blind old man was sitting almost melting in the earth due to his severe thinness, humming and singing, "O you whose lips are cherry and cheeks are plums‹

Your hands are bananas of which the market run out quickly,

And about an Alexandria poet living near us upstairs,

The heart loves before sight sometimes,

If it sees from afar any dress."

Hence, the owner of milaya lef told him, "Well, stand up and look for a job that would be beneficial for Muslims better than the nonsense you're saying! Samia the servant was arguing with the tomato seller wandering with his cart about a tariff. The damned seller raised the price of a kilo from piaster and a half to two piasters. So, she screamed accusing him of harassment, and therefore people gathered .Without inquiring or asking about what happened, each of them had a different interpretation of the situation. Oh my God! May you not go through his ordeal! Oh, man, he was beaten like no other thief in a market!

People were crowding, and the naughty actress Shadya was fondling in the streets of Alexandria in the company of a huge movie crew while shooting Miramar movie based on the novel of Najib Mahfoud. While a woman was hitting her carpet hanging from the balcony of the tenth floor of the building, the bamboo carpet beater fell from her hand. She saw a servant girl, pulling her hair with a scarf fastened on her small forehead, standing on the street corner, so she asked her to hold the carpet beater till she go down the ten floors. The little girl in the street assured her that it was in safe hands. She reached the building gate in a few minutes looking here and there but found none. The innocent girl had disappeared a year ago and played the role of a fox guarding the hen–house

In the first morning after the New Year's Eve, you looked at the seaside Greek style streets of Alexandria that were overwhelmed by the tornado of the party of new year's eve that you saw all world Chinese faience plates, white and colorful and even old clay jars which were dropped deliberately from balconies and high windows of the building and broken to pieces on the ground before midnight on New Year's Eve.

They said they broke a jar behind the year that had passed hoping that the New Year would be free from destruction. We, Arabs, are used to breaking something behind the person leaving, and that's why the giants of Arabs refuse to leave us so that they would not be betrayed by breaking a jar behind them! The police officer was investigating the girl servant about the stealing case that she was accused of. He saw her eyebrows that had been plucked though she was too young for love, so he screamed at her with his question, "Do you pluck your eyebrows girl?!

So, she answered him with impertinence," That's none of your business! "

When Ramadan cannon blasted from afar, the traffic police sat under his umbrella breaking his fast with fava beans and eating Ajwa dates for dessert as he was pointing to order traffic, and the buffets of the most gracious God providing charity Iftar meals for the poor on tables laid in the street of the commercial supermarket for Tom, Dick, and Harry. And all were eating what was allotted to them by God as brothers. In the middle of the street stood the seller of licorice near that of tamarind and the third one of them was a seller of carob juice with their long-spouted brass pots calling out at their high voice and praising their drinks that people gathered around them.

And a lost fool was asking an idiot standing in front of him, "Do you know the apartment building on the right facing the one on the left? The high lofty building, man, the block of apartment without a staircase and even its elevator collapsed! The one under which there was a big Café without chairs and people in it don't drink tea in cups.

They said it had sandwiches but there was no bread for sandwiches and there was coffee but gas cylinder was empty! The street over there! For I got lost and... The idiot would tell him, "No, I don't know it."

At night the ticket collector said to his wife who fell from their springy bed while making love, "Will you get on, woman or I will whistle?"

Silly ideas as such clustered in your memory making you feel dizzy as they were springing from you rudely, ugly, and worthless! Oldness might have passed by, and hence you couldn't distinguish cheese from chalk!

You snooze and take your nap on the nineteenth floor. Hallucinations of old people overwhelm you, dreaming about you spiting these cranes which are moving in the sky with their robots carrying with them strong manufactured bridges, lightweight and unbreakable, along with semi glass architectural facades wrapping the hard frameworks of the towers of skyscrapers of Alexandria! Where did those farmers who survived and didn't die under the foundations' sand go?

They were hiring itinerant workers in construction works to absorb unemployment, so that they and their families would eat bread and Halva. However, today unemployment absorbs itinerant workers and transfers them to far areas, and then burns them with astral oil! You looked for them, and chased them down as they were running toward the south of salt pond evaporation clenching their clothes between their teeth that their private parts were visibly wizened. You followed them and they guided you to destruction, another city in deserts of Africa far from seashores, another world of rusted tinplate houses piled over each other and mud houses separated by roads. Actually, they were not roads but rather canals through which passed the rotten sewages and walked barefoot people, lean with crooked backs as they trampled miles and sometimes two miles to not get involved into forbidden acts.

You slowed down your running. You walked slowly, forgot yourself amid the crowd and thought that you were in roads and quarters, and narrow alleys of Palestinian Sabra and Shatila that were invaded by the tsunami of Lebanon. But you were not in Lebanon, but rather in strong Somali tinplate houses. No, you were not in the suburbs of Mogadishu empty except for flies.

You looked and stared at the foggy things in front of you in Darfur, the Arab groupings in western desert. Some places in Mauritania were declared distressed areas as you could find in the Moroccan desert the camps of Deir Al-Balah and Al-Maghazi that were named as such because many times the transient strange invaders had ground their children and mixed their flesh with concrete and thus their heads remained lifted among the ruins of concrete and iron bars, along with Al Shejaiya neighborhood, Jabalia in the south, the southern suburb in the north, Tel al-Zaatar and Nahr Al-Barid that became hot because of snows falling in the middle of summer, Ein al-Hilweh that they gouged out. Also, Al-Adhamiyah neighborhood that was turned into bones, fleshless. The latter was a masterpiece from its old Babylonian Assyria museums; the Arab history disemboweled, as they were extending Abu Gharaib prison to cover all Arab World, thus uniting it with Guantanamo so that the poisonous cobwebs would wrap the entire globe.

It might be a horrifying Somalization but of an Alexandrian type. The roads were so narrow that the right wall could join with the left one like the pages of a giant book and you, passing by as such, would be squeezed between them like the chewed meat that they put inside the pages of a chewy hot hamburger sandwich. The sandwich was hot, so were the streets, houses and hearts which were melting and dripping their souls little by little. Dust, fire and fume were wrapping the air and a donkey was stuck with its cargo of clover between the banks of the canal that was getting narrower and narrower that the crypt passage trapped it and it couldn't move forward or turn its head or turn round because the high walls between neighbors were so narrow that no one but a skinny person could pass through.

There were women sitting on the ground here and there facing each other with their naked breasts dried like milk bags squeezed from their content swaging. They washed them with the treated and purified sewage water that they gave them claiming that it was good for drinking and washing, while children were playing in sewages and throwing each other with their contents. And the farmers' bee boxes that used to produce the honey of Beheira disappeared to be replaced by swarms of flies and mosquitoes that stirred swarms of bees, flies which were eating decayed corpses inside the heaps of rubbish you didn't know whether they were of human beings or animals that prematurely expired and then dimmed on the road.

Men and women disappeared from alleys and entered their suffocating houses to hide the disgrace of their time, starving as they were vanishing like burned cow dung because job opportunity slipped away from them and their lands and farms which disappeared by a mighty power and thus they dragged them to places out of sight of tourists, foreign investors and strategic firms' owners for fear they would disgrace, and humiliate us and say that Alexandria Region was not qualified for investment. Therefore, they threw them out of the beautiful city where there would be no need for them after they had been replaced in the promising building region by construction cranes, bridges and intricate iron bars which do not get along with anyone and take orders only from computers that inform them about the angle of the building, the allowed weight and the fastest speed in accomplishment, the details of architectural, civil, mechanical, electronic, electric, water and communicative works, decors, designs, inner and outer last touches and even the beautiful gardens, vast roads around the building and car parking hidden on the top of the roofs of buildings. You would find this automated demon thrusting his pen in everything that has a relation with modern architecture and accomplishing it according to standard specifications!

You miss those Upper Egyptian farmers and workers from the inhabitants of Bahri who were sitting there on the ground next to the diggings of architecture building! Where did they go? They used to put bread on a spread cloth bundle and halva on a halva paper as we, students, watched it glistening with oil that was dripping, and dribbling under it like the sweat of their forehead which...and whenever a worker or a guard or even a university student would passed by, they said to him, "come and eat! Come!" They don't say to you "welcome" as the Alexandrian saying goes:" Being invited to a Barmecide feast." They instead say "come!"

It was a genuine generosity and a request for sharing food "come! And what was each one of them eating? What a pity! He might be eating can of sardines or you found him biting a slice of Michi cheese, butting an onion, and sometimes crushing Tamiya in the shape of two flat discs or a plate of fava beans without oil would suffice! The Egyptian farmer would tell you as he was praising God, "This is so beautiful!" Everything was very beautiful to them and they would not acknowledge but Egypt and would not surrender Egypt even a bit to anyone!

"Kunafa here in Alexandria is very beautiful!" Umm Arabi would tell you.

Kunafa Nabulsi is the best of Arabic sweets, aunt!" you arguably replied to her. "Say that in Alexandria there is so sweet sugar cane on Kunafa, but it is not as delicious as Kunafa Nabulsi! Admit that there's at least one thing which is not Egyptian to be the best because Kunafa Nabulsi is the best of all sweets in the world!"

She answered you determined, "No, Kunafa here in Egypt is very beautiful!"

Your friend Mohammad Mohammad heard you. This time he stood against you, saying, "You should know that Egypt is the mother of the world, Mashhour . O father of engineering, the pyramids have been the greatest architectural building in the world since five thousand years, and the great sphinx is the greatest old stone statue in the world. Also, the Egyptian mummies were embalmed by the greatest world medicine and the beacon of Alexandria is the greatest marine lighthouse building in history and one of the Seven Wonders of the World. Today we will open television building in Maspero Cairo and it is the biggest of its kind in the world and the Voice of the Arabs broadcasting from Cairo is one of the most powerful world radio stations listened to, utterly clear from Mauritania to Bahrain, and all that was achieved, while we are still in first year of university. How would be the situation like ten years or twenty years from now? And what a great man this Nasser is! He sets up every day a great project, opens every day a factory and fulfills every day a great accomplishment!" he said that, but he didn't expect that the opposing powers centers would wait for him to fail, sweep away his accomplishments, and kill him in his youth not waiting until he achieved his great dreams!

Mohammad was not aware of the greed of "strategic" firms across the globe that would buy the land and what on it including the factories, universities, and the building accomplished once in an aspiring phase! He didn't even imagine that they would buy the pyramids at a low price, that they would give back the farms that were nationalized once to their feudal and that they would walk in the same path of Abed Nasser but with a rubber!

ABU FATOUMA!

It is a lovely bright morning, and in your eyes the sea of Alexandria differs from other seas especially with you soaring, looking at it from the large glass front of the ninetieth floor! It seems that you are not able to cope with Alexandria 2050, and you determined to immerse into the role of the youth of the sixties of the twentieth century being infected by the illness of nostalgia to olden days. You stand at the gate of the sea from this lofty height, but you alight from it at the third floor where you rented your room in the apartment of Abu Gerges, to which you moved after the problem that took place in Umm Arabi's, the day when Mohammad Mohammad Mohammad squashed you in your room and challenged you to wrestling game. We were playing like kids and when the fight heated up you lifted him and tossed him on the bed and thus one of the wooden slats of bed frame carrying the mattress was broken! We felt guilty and didn't know how to react, so we hid the broken crime under the closet drawer.

When Umm Arabi came back from Ras El Tin and made the bed, she discovered the crime, so she faced you saying," If you told me that you had broken the slat, ..." You stood in front of her with downcast eyes like a guilty primary school student as she was reproaching you with the calmness of a detective, "But your hiding this in this manner gives me a reason to doubt you!"

You did not answer her at all, but you took the blame for the two mistakes; misbehaving with Nadia on one hand and breaking the slat bed in your room on the other hand! And when the woman told you, "I started to doubt you." You had the right to leave! You consulted with Mohammad Mohammad who told you, "The rent of the room here is ten guineas for each person. It is considered high, and we can't afford it anymore and since we get along with each other and become friends, I suggest that we should leave and look for a single room with two beds in the house of a family and thus we pay less money than this?"

After deep thinking, we consulted with Abu Fatouma, the ironer who, besides ironing, was a realtor. You would later meet his white, thin, green-eyed wife Umm Fatouma who collected, distributed laundry and ironed clothes of the quarter's residents. She also collected information about empty apartments and rooms required to be rented in return of a commission for he who would bring a new tenant.

Abu Fatouma lifted the hot iron off primus stove, wiped it on a wet rug to remove soot from it, and then replaced it with another one which cooled. He continued manual ironing while steam was rising from the clothes put for ironing, so you smelled a burnt scent as he was telling us, "There is a respectable family who's going through hard time, so they were forced to rent two rooms of their apartment. One room is rented by a student in medicine faculty, and the other one was emptied by the tenant yesterday. Come along. I will show you it."

We went up with Abu Fatouma by the elevator that looked like a cage inside a rusty iron cage ascending and descending in an open stairwell. A fifty-old-year man welcomed us at the door with a smile on his tired face. He was of medium height and wheatish. His left ear was cut and his teeth were black and decayed... The man welcomed us and showed us first a clean kitchen the space of which was about nine meters, and then preceded us into a polished white marble bathroom. You smelled fly spray scent that you didn't like though here they put to get rid of red American roaches that went out from every hole swaggering, self-confident. You felt disgusted from the smell of their reddish-brown wings and could do nothing but to crash them with your shoe or use pesticides!

You noticed that the rooms here were more spacious, cleaner, tidier, and better than the kitchen and bathroom in Umm Arabi's apartment. Then he proceeded to a big clean room with two single beds. The man opened the window and you were mesmerized by its view. The window was opening onto the Mediterranean Sea! You rejoiced over the vast sea! Whispers and tunes of Fairouz run in your mind, then, "Alexandria beach, O Alexandria beach...!" While Abu Gerges was saying as standing in the room, "Its rent costs twenty-five guineas

a month, and with five guineas discount as an appreciation for Abu Fatouma, it will be twenty. You can live together here, and each one of you will have to pay ten guineas. It is free."

Mohammad Mohammad took you aside and whispered to you, saying, "Ten, ten, then ten each one of us. Here, ten is less expensive than the fifteen in the dark alley there!" Immediately we decided to accept, so you informed Umm Arabi who didn't approve of our leaving as that would make her lose the rents of two rooms from her furnished apartment at once. The woman tried to please us and win our sympathy by saying, "I loved you like Arabi and Nadia, I swear to God!"

Mohammad whispered to you mockingly, "Which one of us is Arabi and which one is Nadia?" You didn't laugh at his unfunny uncalled humor which was not in the right time. Nadia did not care about the news about our leaving as if nothing happened! Maybe she was still surprised at your misbehavior with her the other day.

People who are walking on earth were of green color. A green mosquito and a green fly were playing with a green bee and a green butterfly with excitement as they were flying between the branches of a shady tree; on one of its twig are a green flacon and a green pigeon getting to know each other. And down the tree, green sheep and goats were embracing green lions and tigers with love and easiness! You look at the mirror and you panic for seeing yourself green like them! And when you ask about the traditional children of Adam, they tell you that they became extinct and vanished after they had become corrupt and corrupted the earth with their individualism, greed, and savagery in killing and destruction.

You wake up from a nap terrified by what you dreamt about and saw! You look at your face that is still resisting expiration and laugh at your silly dreams. You try to bury your head in the sand like an ostrich by remembering the bygone past because you are carrying in your memory all students' blocks of apartments and amphitheaters. Still, you don't want to recall the gatherings of male and female students in the engineering drawing-room as much as you remember the subject of society called socialism in that Abu Georges found you revising for that subject, so he asked you," What are you studying, man?"

***

"Socialism." He laughed allowing the rest of his cut ear-lobe to quiver. "An engineer who studies socialism? I don't understand why they are teaching students of engineering university socialism!" You answered him defending your courses, "And why do they teach engineering university students in America the history of American Revolution!? These are the necessary general subjects." He then continued his questions that revealed the rest of his worn-out teeth, "What is socialism for you?"

"Socialism is sufficiency and justice!" He then tested you with his question, "What do sufficiency and justice mean?"

"Sufficiency and justice mean that we have production and enough national data together with justice in distributing them"

He giggled opening the mouth of Said Kishta wide while the rest of his ear-lobe totally shrank, and then said, "No, honey, you're wrong!"

Dr. Mounir, who taught the subject, was not more committed than Abu George's to this socialism intruding the country of farmers, pashas, serfs, and gentlemen. In that amphitheater number one, that could contain one thousand students to welcome all specialties in the first year, the attendance of students was limited and didn't exceed three hundred that Dr. Mounir Al Khuli would say to us," Why are you so shiny today? Students were not as shiny as you are last year. The amphitheater was empty. There were no students." Then he started his lecture heedless for he asked, "Look, what's the first thing you do when you wake up?"

One of the students answered, "Study doctor!"

Dr. Mounir pointed with his hand from the platform, "No!"

Another answered him, "Go to the bathroom, doctor!"

He said, "No!"

"Do ablution and pray doctor!" He rejected his answer, saying, "no!"

"He brushes his teeth"

"Go to university..."

He said, "Also no!"

"He changes his pajamas."

He smiled, saying, "Also no!"

He looks at the neighbor's daughter from the window doctor!"

He laughed, "Naughty boys!"

And when we felt helpless, Dr. Mounir appeared and said wisely, "The first thing one of us does once he wakes up is..." –he remained silent for a while enjoying our curiosity– "eating fava beans, and then he decides to rise or go for a walk on the beach of the Mediterranean Sea or go to university!"

You didn't know why Dr. Khouli was reckless! Was he teaching a subject that he disdained or found useless? Or does he find it easy? Or was he funny by nature and did not want to complicate the subjects? Or was the subject itself ridiculous? Or was the man lazy by nature? You didn't know!

Still, you found most other teachers serious about their sciences. Dr. Mohamad Hanafi, the head of civil department, did not think but about dams, foundations and bridges with traffic turnings and he often said to us with loving mockery, "One starts his days with a bridge project like the beautiful bridge of Al montazah Palace, Al Mamurah better than your sad faces!" He didn't have time to comb his hair at home, so we saw him going into the university coming from some project and ascending the stairs leading up to the amphitheater while he was combing his wavy hair. He removed things tangled in it including dust and remnants of foundations that a student standing on the marble barrier of the stair in the company of another one said, "This Dr. Hanafi is unique. If he lived in the past, they would appoint him the head of the project of building Khufu Pyramid itself!"

The style of Dr. Mohamad Al Risha, the law teacher who enlightened us about rights and duties and the way we did the construction contracts of any civil project we would work on, amused us. He ascended the stairs of the platform of amphitheater number one carrying the same brown cardboard suitcase that was lost at Cairo Airport, but this was as small as a handbag. He put it on the amphitheater's desk, and then took the chalk and wrote on the blackboard his familiar expression, "Good morning!"

One of the naughty underachievers hidden in the midst of six hundred students screamed, asking," Did you buy it for a quarter of guinea, Doctor?

He meant the cheap cardboard case! The Doctor threw his chalk and turned around to face his disobedient students and answered in disdain," Where is the maid's son who said that? "

He looked right and left and continued his insults, "The fault is not yours! It is the fault of the revolution that brought you here! You son of... are supposed to be porters in the harbor now or itinerant laborers who work with sewage or in fields!"

You sat among male and female students, agape because you were neither from unruly students nor from revolution people nor did you know who itinerant laborers were! But after the end of the lecture, Mohammad Mohammad told you, "Did you hear what Dr. Al Risha said to naughty students?

You answered him, embarrassed, "Yes, I did, but I didn't understand what he said!"

He said that it was the fault of the revolution that brought you. It was the revolution that allowed them to enter universities that were once restricted to children of Pashas and the rich. Then Abdel Naser nationalized them and let all those who passed the exam of high school enter them equally, as you know the priority now is for the student with the highest score published on the guarded tablet without mediation or nepotism."

Mohammad walked with you in the paths close to the amphitheater to go back again after the 5-minute break as he continued by saying, " And thus the son of a gatekeeper , that of a poor man as well as the daughter of a porter and that of a janitor entered university.

Hence the university-educated son of an itinerant laborer started to have the right to become an officer in the army, a doctor at university, a doctor at the hospital, and a minister in government while he was once deprived of this and that. A farmer used to be restricted to digging the Suez Canal, as they branded his butt with the diggings of El-Mahmoudia Canal along with that of El Ibrahimiya, not to mention that he was programmed to serve the feudal.

He was a servant who could not breach his class and was a private soldier in the army that he could not go beyond the rank of a sergeant major at his best. He was qualified only to shoot others or be shot by others.. and you don't know who the others were. They might be his fellow farmers wallowing in misery and there was no control over them but through them. The feudal would not say, 'God will handle them,' but rather would say,' let then handle each other.' Hence he set them against each other and sat laughing loud lifting the motto of victory with index and middle fingers and between them there was a long thick Cuban cigar. In the meantime, the son of a bitch lived while enjoying their honey, grains, legume, and fruits! And when he got closer to them in the field you found him disgusted of the smell of the sweat of their work and fetid of the heat of their breaths without which the grape would not ripen or sweeten! "

You asked him as you were entering the drawing-room, "Are the farmers' students the unruly ones in the amphitheater?"

Mohammad Mohammad scratched his back with the long drawing ruler, saying, "No, the farmer doesn't dare to do so, even by nature bred to deride and mock! Why couldn't the indecent be the children of the worn-out aristocratic class who are used to indulgence and derision from others?"

And the conversation about farmers reminded you of that woman farmer selling butter. You were then alone in the apartment of Abu Georges and there was a knock on the door. You opened it and there was a full-fledged farmer girl in the company of her mother displaying butter for sale. The mother in the local black dress said, "This is the butter of local buffalo."

And without consulting Mohammad Mohammad or deep consideration you agreed to buy it, so the white tall plump girl with big breasts rushed —leaving her mother outside the apartment, with her farm green velvet dress embroidered with some drawings and tangled lines fluttering on her bosom like a decorated fence of a balcony looking out from green upstairs— to put butter in the fridge and be paid the twenty piasters. Here in the kitchen, the female, with lips like two ripe figs dripping honey, pounced on you without any preparation or readiness for emotions or drawing your gazes to her or at least a smile or a wink from you or her. She embraced you and kissed you on your mouth a thirsty kiss that made tears sprout in your eyes!

You couldn't understand whether you were an idiot or stupid or ignorant in matters about love, passion, and sex! The farmer woman was taken back, but instead of immersing with her into desire, you went on watching and exploring her full face features that were not colored with any Alexandrian dyes or plucked. You looked at the forbidden hair, white, short, and soft on her cheek and chin sheet that no tweezers could pluck as well as her thick eyebrows and lips that were not painted even with local butter!

In one of the plays you attended, the farmer "Abd Allah Ghaith" asked his wife "Somaya Ayoub", "Do you have some milk?" The farmer woman answered, "No by God!" He asked her again, "Not even cheese?" She said hurt, "I could not afford it!" He added," not even cream?" The farmer woman then hit him on his shoulder with sadness and defeat dissatisfied with her difficult conditions, "If you want to eat cream in this life then what would you eat in the afterlife?"

You felt as scrutinizing her with your gazes that the deprived lips of the girl were full of heat, eroticism, and lust for the lips of a guy who was chaste, and strange to farmers and to all Alexandria. The innocent girl wanted a shield! She didn't want to expose her feminine nakedness dressed in a pile of green velvet clothes covering the whole village and increased as dangling over her hot body bound in chains surrounding her to her big thick feet bridled with a pair of flip-flops, chapped at the heel. But her body was rebellious to all chains!

The girl felt that she was impulsive and reckless. She knew that it wasn't the way things are supposed to be done and that this mean guy was not turned on by her for she made him taste her lust, but he did not savor her desire. She felt you did not respond to her but you were rather watching and scrutinizing her and discovering her status. The suppressed woman did not expect that she would kiss a eunuch, cold and embalmed like a lifeless idol and she didn't enter before an observatory like this one, prepared only for supervision and scrutiny.

Honestly, you were petty and lousy with her. You didn't pity or sympathize with her. You didn't understand or respond to her, either. You rather stayed like the character of ET who lived in the forest and watched from afar that feminine object in front of you. The impulsive farmer was ashamed and felt as if she threw her head in a shallow swimming pool whose depth was no more than five centimeters, thus exploding her head!

You didn't know why you behaved as such with beautiful girls, though you were a human being tense with sex. Also you didn't know if you had motives or deterrents implanted in your genetic map determining your behavior and kept you away from sex which was undoubtedly out of instinct! The woman farmer went out boiling and blurred, without being paid even the price of the butter. You followed her and handed the riyal to her mother. The two women went their way descending the stairs of the building knocking on other residents' houses; perhaps they would sell their goods!

You were standing next to the farmer girl while thinking of your grandmother Aneesa who told you when you were but fifteen years old "Do not give heed to girls. Girls would only tell you, "Give me... give me!" And the one-hundred-and-five-year-old woman told you once," Don't bridle your thing. Try to rein it, and if it disobeys and exposes you for being nervous, be more rigid to discipline it. Hold it and break it because the pain of breaking it would make you forget the eroticism of lust and put an end to your aspirations!"

The old woman could not understand that breaking it would kill it, and ruin its future on which depended the future of its bearer. She meant protecting you against enemies. The grandmother didn't know the romantic feelings that Gibran Khalil Gibran taught you, for you were still learning The Broken Wings novel by heart, "I was eight years old when love opened my eyes with his magic beam and touched myself for the first time with his fiery fingers. Salma Karama was the first woman who awakened my soul by her virtues..."

But your grandmother could not distinguish between romance and custard. Yes, she could cook the green watermelon rind. You told her that day, "Why are you cooking this peel grandma?"

She answered you while wiping oozing saliva off the sides of her lips with a female embroidered handkerchief, that she once told you, was one of the remnants of her box that she left in Akka, "What is the difference between watermelon grind and green bean or zucchini? They are all vegetables!"

You were always such an idiot, standing behind your grandmother, hearing her stories, and being influenced by her. And when you asked your father a piaster to buy something you wanted and he refused on the ground that "waste not, want not" like that boy from Al Khalil who asked his father a shilling and his father told him," What do you need a shilling for? What about two piasters? A piaster is enough. Take this tariff!" The mean father would then say to him, "Do you want me to change for a piaster because of a tariff?!"

And like him, your father used to tell you to save a penny on a rainy day and you replied to him that there was no worse than these days on which he refused to give you a piaster! The answer came in the form of Karabeej Halab one whip, two, three whips from the belt of car fan standing, waiting hung on the wall ready to interfere in case any problem happened. Your grandmother heard you screaming and crying, so she pounced and protected you from whipping cursing your father whom no one but her and God, the Almighty could stop. She hugged you and whispered to you, "I'm hiding for you two piasters under the straw mattress. Go and take them." You rejoiced over the two piasters and kissed your grandmother on her tender cheek. You smelled in the folds of her white hair the scent of the old. Was your refusal to respond to the deprived woman farmer caused by your commitment to the warnings of your tomboyish grandmother? Did you reach the absolute conviction that the only allowed kiss in your life was that of your tender grandmother Aneesa?

A WORLD WITHOUT CHALLENGES

After a nap, Burhan comes in from his celestial room suit, bids you a good evening, and asks you how you are doing. You confide your concerns to him, "I want honestly to ask you about the point of torturing your son Green with this complicated operations whose results might not be guaranteed, God forbid. For this third Man might be hurt by the children of the second Man who would see him as an opponent to them or a danger to their future especially if his green generation will seize control of most of the life outlets in the future that children of Adam and Eve will have no control over the earth. For this reason, the evil will dispose of him and his folk. He's in danger, son!"

"All these dangers are taken into account, father." – he sits on an air chair besides you– "For this reason, we made protection for green mouse, green cat, green sheep, green lion by putting them at the beginning alone and after being reassured we put every two opponents in nature in one luminous room. The cat didn't eat the mouse. Neither did the lion eat the lamb.

After that, we kept them in the same reserve and watched them. No one of them attacked the other but they rather lived in harmony and peace. You saw them relaxing on a sunny rock and watching life around a natural water pool. The hyena is no longer smelly but we rather have a hyena with pine scent, an elephant with oak scent and a laurel-smelling pig. We are living in an amazing world, father. Yet, you are worried about green Canaan from white, black, and yellow man? Challenges are expected for this generation, but we are aspiring to create a world without challenges! We want a green generation living without fear!

Honestly, we want a paradise on earth! If you visited us in the institute, I would take you to Hessen's Forest Reserves where you would see green animals wandering about freely in the woods. Of course under observation, with an iron net preventing the bird from entering the reserves to not ruin the miracle we created! We noticed progress in the behavior of those who started to sit quietly carefree, looking at the sun that feeds them, enjoying it, thinking about collective gatherings, embracing each other happily and romantically, and having sex quietly and with a pleasure that differs from that of the second Man, a pleasure, unaccompanied with worry, fear, and carefulness. They have sex for pleasure not for reproduction that today is achieved through cells. And if we, scientists, do not believe in what we study and implement in the laboratories, how would common people believe in it and how would the universe develop, then?"

You swallow life elixir pill and drink after it a bit of water from the small bottle that is always with you because your saliva throat dries quickly and requires you to moisturize it hundreds of times daily. You tell him," You are comforting me with these daunting thoughts of yours. Yet, I am an old man who feels suspicious and worries about his grandson from annihilation, God forbid!"

"Don't worry; Canaan will be in good hands tomorrow, father. It would not be in the interest of Shanghai Hospital to ruin its scientific and medical reputation because they are scientists and they take their share of responsibility, and any scientific or surgical failure - God forbid - will make their international firm shares plummet and suffer destructive financial losses! Here, taking care of patients is a crucial necessity and the Chinese race is merciless when it comes to management. It is a system that pushes toward development with the force of a rocket. For this reason, we collaborated with them and thus a person from China, another one from Germany and of course I being an Arab became in accord in terms of intellect, behavior, economy, and interest to create a new life!

"Canaan's problem is that he doesn't use a lot of his traditional apparatus like the digestive system and he doesn't use his lungs for breathing, either. And the photosynthesis occurring in his body absorbs Carbon Dioxide and releases oxygen that his body consumes , and thus oxygen is equal to carbon dioxide that's why his lungs are pressing his chest due to lack of contraction and expansion of respiration. But there are no fundamental problems regarding his health make-up because he is a wonderful human being, father. As you know, the smell of his mouth and the purity of his throat are like the scent and purity of stigmas and petals of orange flowers. And since he doesn't breathe, he neither snores nor farts!"

"Hence, you achieved the romantic dream that Gibran brought (Have you bathed in its fragrance and dried yourself in its light?)"

"And who is bathing in fragrance and drying himself in light but green Canaan and his like, father? Romanticism becomes realism. We mingled romanticism with realism that was apposing it and arranged the universe through this green being!"

"Honestly, in the beginning, the experience of implementing your ideas in your children scared me and made me worry about the continuity of family generations because we are people who have customs, traditions and our Arab Palestinian country which we try to preserve, so that its generations would keep running on the earth to the Day of Judgment!"

"I'm aware of those challenges father!"

" I don't understand what's going on in this hospital because these intermingled genetic mappings of living beings are intricate and need millions of universe researchers to work as a complementary team to change the law of life on earth, and then affect the universe that was organized during billions of years. It is something difficult to achieve so fast, if not possible!"

"The world changes so fast. What we discovered in one month is equal to the sciences of a thousand years of those which you count. We are supervising the health of Canaan since his birth. We follow his examinations on the international network, and cooperate with administration doctors in Shanghai. We believe that there is no need for surgery. As for other examinations, we could do via correspondence. Tomorrow a committee of doctors will gather around him and give him a thorough check-up."

"In our days, university study via correspondence was forbidden, so that there would be human social relations inside university campus. And now the time came when correspondence has taken control of all educational tools!"

Burhan takes his leave and goes to see his green son before going to bed. You too get ready for procedures before going to bed! For ten years after the death of your wife Omaima, you have been forced to deal with the robot woman Narjas accompanying you in whatever you do. So, she comes to you with your stuff on the appointed time, "It is time to take your blood pressure pill." she says as she is pampering you. "Here you are a glass of water with the pill."

You drink them while she is praying for your health, well-being, and long life. Whenever you invite her, you find her welcoming you, saying, "Let me reply to Samar's letter on your behalf." And after sending it via cell phone, she adds," I'm going to read your digital mail." She says laughing, "So, pay attention and stay focused to respond to it." And after reading the mail and responding to it she says, "I did the laundry and dried it with the dryer. Next, it came out ironed."

She plays for you the songs of Fairouz that you like, goes with you into the bathroom, prepares your stuff, helps you with taking off your clothes, scrubs your back and then dries your body with the cotton bathrobe. Afterward, she takes you back to your bed saying with tenderness, "Please lie on your bed and let me massage your muscles."

You sigh, "Oh God, I m relaxed, Narjas. All my stresses vanished away."

If it wasn't for this robotic Narjas who when asked she answers you, and when you request something from her ,she would open for you her digital memory on the first volume of One Thousand and One Nights novel reading, "We left off at Badr Basim.

Know, then, O auspicious King, that I am called Julnár the Sea-born and that my father was of the king of the Main. He died and left me and my brother Salah his reign, but one of the other kings arose against us and took the realm from our hands. I fell out with my brother and swore that I would throw myself into the hands of a man of the folk of the land. So, I came forth of the sea and sat down on ashore rock." Narjas told her story as if she was Shahrazad sitting in the presence of King Shahrayar. She continued indulging you with her reading till you fell asleep. So, she sleeps next to you in your bed to soothe your loneliness and to cover you if… You fall asleep and snore and…in her bosom without feeling annoyed or angry at you. Hence, you are convinced that an old man needs this kind of robotic woman!

PANTS

As you are getting ready to go out with Burhan to have breakfast on the ground floor of Guangzhou Hotel, you look from your sky front on the ninetieth floor opening onto the entire sea.. What a bewitching panorama it is! And while waiting for Burhan to get ready to go out with you, memories switch straight away to childhood days. I was terrified of that appalling day! The day when I and Mohammad Mohammad left the apartment of Abu Gerges to enjoy the incredibly peaceful sea!

Exactly like the inhabitants of Alexandria, each farmer of us wore a bathing suit and went out barefooted toward the iron cage that served as an elevator. We met our old neighbor mister Mohammad Ismail Mabrour, a member in the Academy of the Arabic Language. We felt like two stupid swimmers standing embarrassed in front of him in our half nakedness, so you told him, "We are sorry mister Mohammad for stepping out wearing swimming trunks."

The man looked at us and it seemed that he was not thinking about what we were thinking because he immediately objected to the word swimming trunks, saying, "It is not appropriate to say the word swimming trunks, son. The right thing is to replace it with the word pants." You answered him in his language, "When we mention the word pants, the listener doesn't understand whether we mean my grandmother's pants or my father's pants that he wears under his Arab dress or the pants we wear for university or pajama pants or the thin knickers of a teenager girl." Mohammad Mohammad laughed and said mockingly, "They all become pants."

The old man who was wearing a red velvet robe fastened with a belt of the same fabric around his waist upon his striped pajamas didn't know how to answer. Still, you proceeded to say, "You, teachers of the Academy of the Arabic Language are the ones who compel us to say, bikinis, trousers, short, knickers, pants, and pajama bottoms to be able to distinguish all these names from my grandma's pants."

You smiled as you were approaching him saying, "It is you who let the Arabic language down and maimed it, the language about which Tah Hussein said, 'Our beautiful language!' The old man shrank as he was answering you, "It's the fault of our government that deprived us of being the pioneer in technology. If we had created swimming trunks that you mean, invented sciences and arts, and made the modern devices, we would have released for every little peace in TV, pump, car engine, or rocket an Arabic name. It's the fault of Arab League that was born embalmed and failed to achieve the requirements of Arab unity including language in that it doesn't have the budget, or administration or the will to regulate a united Academy of language, the Arabic words of which and even Arabized ones would be imposed legally on all users.

We left the linguist embalmed in the coffin of his Academy and stepped out heading toward the beach sand straight away. We rented a wooden chip called a felucca enough for two persons. We boarded it together as if we were at the back of a donkey with our feet immersing in the loud-roaring sea. We went together into the sea. We pushed water with our paddles; a wing slaughtered the sea while the other came out of its waves. This morning the sea was as tranquil as an endless glass, and the soft breeze was warm and humid. Our amazing experience was going smoothly and our laughter was filling the sea, warming our hearts and making us forget the passage of time.

Therefore, we continued paddling right, left, right, left, right, left till we arrived three centimeters away from Cyprus. You looked at the far horizon and watched the sea sheet opening onto the whole world. The globe and the high skies...! You looked into the bottom of the sea. You were surprised at seeing a giant fish swimming under our feet. You looked very carefully! They were two giant fish, three fish; many audacious long leaden fish were slipping under us. At that time you couldn't know a shark from other fish, but you felt immense terror and fear!

You didn't tell Mohammad about what you saw. You tried to convince yourself that you didn't see anything to say. And you thought that he saw everything, but you controlled yourself and said nothing. The reason might be not bewildering the companion captain riding this shelf vehicle. And the meaning might be in the belly of the poet, the shark might be in the belly of the sea, the sea might be in the shark's belly, we might be in the belly of the sea and the shark might be in our bellies. Hence, you ignored totally the scene.

The truth is that we sometimes behave in an absurd way because in such moments of confusion, your head swings infinitely fast swings to the point that it would be impossible to explain this behavior as there was no time for explaining or arguing or discussing the aspects of the subject. You were thinking only about one thing, which was how you and your friend would run away with your shelf vehicle without being mauled or drowning. You didn't want any discussion or opposition to achieve that, so you asked him, "Can you swim buddy?"

"No." he said it as such and fell silent as cowardice and weakness were obvious in the tone of his voice. Like you, Mohammad realized the fear that was reaching its nails in our eyes! And you couldn't see the stillness of fear in his eyes besieged by blue claws of death by drowning because he was sitting in front of you in the leadership center. But his silence exposed his cowardice and absence of insight in us.

The brain orders and emotional status were silencing the image and sound and ignoring fear as if nothing mattered. It was a silent fear! Frightened Silence! Silent fear! Frightened fear! You tried to smile ignoring the situation, but you didn't feel the response of your face skin with a sophisticated smile! By a mighty power, you turned the rudder of the wafer that was no more than a flat wooden chip to be able to protect the sailors!

Sense of belonging to Alexandria started to overwhelm you, and a fervent desire to reach its shore started to burn inside you.

How beautiful homecoming is! you thought.

In your eyes, Alexandria turned into a far panoramic view, people on the beach, into a modern plastic painting that did not show the details of their bodies. The sea was arching like a pregnant woman's belly affirming the sphericity of the earth, while we were in the lowest part of the surface of the sea trying to climb the earth as if we held a thin thread like that of a spider. We pulled the thread to slip on the watery glass of the globe trying to reach the water near the shore because if the felucca turned upside down, we would swim the remaining two meters, but we could not even swim the two remaining meters if..

In this watershed moments, Abu Arabi, Arabi's grandfather, and all boaters and fishers, who died from drowning, swam around us in this sea that did not hesitate to conspire against its sailors. You saw them with their satin striped waistcoats along with the same blue greasy groupers! And together we were going into this turbulent sea. They gathered around us with their penetrating sardine smell as they were singing with Fairouz "Hela, Hela, O large, Hela, Hela, your boat will be back!" You didn't know whether they were trying to drown us or save us from this plight.

Never mind, because the strongest of erudite sailors drowned and there was no news about them, so how could they return, gather, approach us, and struggle the sea with us? And if that happened with sea beasts, how could we, the ignorant farmers, who would drown in an inch of water, hold on? That's the issue!

It seemed that a complex was driving you away from this sea that drowned Abu Arabi, Arabi's grandfather together with all Arabi's family, and it drowned you before you were born being banished from beautiful Akka shores by its choppy waves!

Here was the sea again banishing you and there was no kidding with the sea.. It's a perfect world that includes life and death, fantasy and reality, innocence and savagery, beauty and ugliness, water and thirst!

Alexandria became an unreachable view, and you felt that it was your refuge and savior and that with those two paddles which were no different from two mice's tails wet with oil, you would come back with your companion to your basis. You saw with your naked eyes a giant fish racing under your feet. You were aware now that you were foolish by going far into the sea and ignoring all warning and supervision devices. And to survive, there should be strict discipline in the path toward staying alive and swimming back to the shore.

The two paddles kept wallowing heavily in the sea whose waves started to stir. Superficial waves set out to race the invasion of an ogress, Gog and Magog, antichrist, and all sea vermin accompanying the procession were leading us. We fell silent realizing our mistake that would be the cause of our death.

Indifference might be useful sometimes. A lot of Arab rulers thought that their indifference about the oppression and enslavement they were inflicting upon their people, was the reason for their survival in this clashing universe!

You shared Mohammad who was paddling in front of you his feeling of terror, and in spite of that, we were moving forward with flexible paddles, with a precision that our familiar chaos was not familiar with. You knew how the trip started, but you didn't know how it would end by arriving safe surrendering to Alexandria Beach! Our fate was to live! And since then we had never brought up the subject or returned to the seashore.

THE GREEN PARTY

You and Burhan go to a Chinese breakfast restaurant in Guangzhou hotel, allowing green Canaan to sleep undisturbed till the scheduled time, and on the way to the hotel, you inhale the spray of insulin inhaler that trusts its nose into yours on every occasion. And when you sit at the table, Burhan tells you, "Praise be to God that Canaan spared himself the trouble of thinking about food, especially that the cost of food in our trip is ten times as much as the cost of staying at the hotel. That's why his chlorophyll body was a way of decreasing expenses and a victory of life that was fading away amid billions of poor who could not find a bite of bread. Not only that, but it also saves lifetime that we spent in producing, distributing and preparing food and its requirements, the time we spend in eating food ending up in wastes polluting the environment that we don't have time to see and enjoy the athletics of the universe and to achieve our goals in life.

You wipe your mouth with food handkerchief, and then you ask him, "Did the German green party play a role in creating the green animal!? He answers you as he is chewing, "I don't know the extent to which the green party adopted our effluent activity and I don't know the extent to which the governmental authorities will cooperate either, because such businesses have their secrets hidden even from us, their scientists!

The green party indeed supports our creation of a green being, and it might be just an emotional supporter for the great project, but we certainly do not allow any authority outside the institute to interfere in the impartiality of this amazing production for one reason which is them not claiming to be the first inventor and not demanding their rights because we and the German green party have one thing in common. We both are an establishment with a pure human insight and both of us refuse the monopoly of genetic genes under the name of intellectual property rights, and we do not aspire to make a profit."

The idea sounds audacious though you are not convinced of its completeness. You tell Burhan, "I wish I could live a little more to see your great accomplishments!" He drinks a little bit of orange juice then says, "May God grant you long life father. This is the century of sciences and long lives. What do you want? A heart!? The farm of human organs will serve it on a silver platter. A kidney? They will give you it under our health insurance! He wiped his mouth with food handkerchief then added, "The human organ farm set up a medical propagation city in Wiesbaden and its activity in laboratories and propagation companies started cloning. They took two cells; one from a man and the other from a woman who were perfectly healthy, intelligent and good looking, and before they multiplied them, they had examined their genetic maps and disposed of each any illness or point of weakness, and then they implanted in them genes fighting all incurable infectious and viral diseases. After the experiment had succeeded, they produced two kids male and female with the same qualifications then took cells from the perfect kids' organs and implanted them, and thus producing several hearts, kidney, arteries, and perfect human organs and implanted as experiments in patients waiting for relief. And when their experiments succeeded they set out to produce them with the purpose of sale."

You stand and head toward the restaurant buffet to bring some fruit and vegetables because you are an old man who cannot eat meat or dairy products or sugars, and then you turn back and sit. You tell him, "I saw such farms and hospitals on the international network. They are building them to produce and sell human meat, and some are saying that they are producing these organs from the cells of amniotic fluid of a perfectly healthy embryo and develop in laboratories."

Burhan says, "They have kinds of arteries that won't close which they implant in patients easily and smoothly."

You shake your head, saying, "Classified secrets of firms to keep what you call the intellectual property rights that were called in the days of socialism monopoly, and thus the ugly monopolization has become by a mighty power a preserved right!"

He drinks a sip from his coffee to wet his chewed food then says, "And worse than that, father, is the rise of firms destroying all principles and customs that do not produce organs but rather produce human beings with specific qualifications to sell them for anyone who can buy."

"Slavery is back again!"

"Some buy a kid because they don't want a cord, or delivery or waning, and some want a companion because they live alone with no companion, while others want to buy themselves a servant. And more dangerous than this and that is that the most modern armies started to buy their soldiers with a martial qualification from these qualified firms.. "

He takes another sip of his coffee then continues by saying, "But that trade is not easy because journalistic, representative and medical battles are heightened, calling for the necessity for stopping this new human enslavement. They revolted in the face of those in charge of these projects crying," How could you sell human beings?" The press secretary answered them on behalf of the farm saying, "It's we who create human clones from cells and we have the right to do with them as we please."

You interrupt his talk saying, "This is out of the question, son. What you're saying is not acceptable, son, because man is born free and no entity has the right to confiscate his life or even his happiness to live his life the way he thinks is right provided that he doesn't hurt anyone!"

"The association of the intellectual property rights of journalists and delegates pleaded, saying, "How do you want us to treat hopeless patients? Do you want us to steal children from the streets like what happened in many world countries, cut their wanted apparatuses, and then implant them secretly in rich patients?

Imagine they called for their rights to use their agricultural product unlike what happened inside our institute with Canaan who was produced to be free without confines because researcher Peter Hainh, who came from that farm and whom our institute committed to research and production, claimed in the beginning property rights, him being the creator of the green kid Canaan and said, "This boy is one of my property rights!" I made a fuss and told him ferociously, "The age of slaves is over Peter Hainh!"

"I asked you that day to remind him of Umar Ib Al-Khatab's statement, "Since when you enslaved people and their mothers had born them free" upon which the principles of human rights in United nations have been built in the eighties of the twenty century!"

"Indeed, I told him, "Your property rights mean enslaving a newborn!" And he answered bragging his arrogance, "He's not a baby, but rather a creature in my laboratory!"

"They were unforgettable black days, son!"

"I told him, "You, Peter Hainh, are still thinking with the mindset of a commercial firm! You forgot that you had a contract with us to produce a free green that cannot be sold or monopolized or what is known as intellectual property rights. You think with the mindset of someone who wants to take us back to a more appalling age than the age of the second man who lives on killing, hunting, and preying on others." Burhan finishes drinking morning coffee, praises God then proceeds to say, "The answer of our institute was severe and it was undoubtedly in our favor and the institute's researchers supported us in that the researcher Hamburg said," Intellectual property rights are increasing and dominating to take us back to the age of slavery, whereas the Bavarian Irish man said," if we create an improved man, then there would be no need to complicate him and gag his mouth from the first day and there would be no need to create him in the first place!" And when I asked him, "What was the response of the press, the public and men of religion to the issue of intellectual property that the commercial farms and firms lead?" He answers, "The men of Christian religion said that no matter what the cell is, it is God's creation. And Mufti of the Islamic center said that any improvement on or into the cell, is no more but taking on an extra passenger in a stationary train in the station and it is God who created the cell, and that the scientists working in this field are but bulls grazing clover and benefiting from God's creatures. Undoubtedly, they are creative explorers and their work is appreciated, but they are not a creator God, and therefore no matter how they claimed creation, God is the best of creators and they don't have the right to own the improved humans. The civil battles continued, courts worked, and churches testified against them, while rivaling scientists envied them and sadly some supported them! This popular support and legal bridled the greed of savage capital firms, supported the activities of our institute, international monetary donations rose and its job accelerated immensely. Still, our institute appreciated the attitude of Peter Hainh, the supervisor over the success of amazing researches and thus it decided to sculpt a bust for him and erect it in the courtyard of the institute along with his creative colleagues who changed the course of history, and was given a big monetary reward that dropped his requests. Also do not forget, father, that Peter cannot act freely beyond the red line because after he has been given orders and realized that he's committed to the institute's laws, he signed a pledge to not call for such forbidden nonsense, while the institution kept protecting its green production. For this reason, you see them restraining us by legally binding contracts. Peter understood the seriousness of the situation and he was content with remaining as an expert in the center and continuing his job in the laboratory as usual instead of getting lost in the darkness of the path!"

We go out of the Chinese restaurant and my dear talkative Burhan is still talking about diverse subjects!

ALEXANDRIA UNIVERSITY

We meet on time with my green grandson in the hotel main hall at the revolving door...and you don't love these revolving doors in hotels, banks, and sedate blocks of apartments despite their benefits that... that's because you don't like beating around the bush but rather get straight to the point.

And outside the door, we get into the hotel car that takes us to Shanghai Hospital. We reach it, but you are surprised at what you saw. Nothing of those lands and spaces is left! Where is Maternity and Children Hospital of El- Shatby affiliated with Alexandria University that was built in our schooling days here to be used as maternity and pediatrics services center, education center, and experimental laboratories by students and professors of the medicine faculty nearby? Where are the engineering university buildings that were sparkling with Pharaonic style along Abu Kir Street?

And where is the ancient university building whose beautiful platonic building arches were taken from the style of Al-Aqsa Mosque that God blessed its surroundings? You compare the building arches with those of Al-Aqsa Mosque and you realize the cause of encroaching upon the two scenes. And since scientists are the heirs of prophets, they encroached upon both: Al-Aqsa Mosque and Alexandria University including blocks of flats and universities!

Could you imagine! All lands and buildings were sold to a foreign entity for twenty billion Chinese Yuan - the price of two blocks of apartments these days - and thus all universities and their university administration that used to shine from Shatby and spread civilization across the country vanished, razed to the ground and sold. Then, they bought themselves Halva with that money! Was it Halva or Vermicelli the one excavation workers used to eat? For you don't know!

You ask the portable device about what happened to the university. The international network tells you, "They moved its ruins to a suite in a remote building in the farm of an agriculture university in Abis Region whose area was estimated to cover about five hundred and fifty acres. Even when they noticed the presence of this pearl farm inside this agriculture clay oyster, they rejoiced over it and said," It's a catch! "Therefore, they sold it at a cheap price. The strategic firm planted it with the towering skyscrapers, then."

The truth is that you don't understand the reason why they inserted the word "strategic" that they use to frighten us, but you know that they joined to one of its vacant buildings an academic museum containing monuments of the landmarks of Scientific Renaissance in the 60s, and stuff from previous universities' assets as an indicator of beginnings showing how amphitheaters developed then disappeared, and how traditional libraries in the era before the computer and storage on the network and CD looked like. Even students don't exist anymore. And at the stroke of a pen, all buildings disappeared from El Muwasat Hospital to the sea and from El Raml to El Ibrahimiya and El Riyatha Regions. All were sold to a Chinese firm to build on them the department of International Shanghai Hospital as well as its projects, international markets, advanced entertainment fields, international auto shows, exhibitions of building materials and frameworks of building models exhibited to give information about their firms and even clothes, catering and Chinese household utensils along with these Chinese hotels adjoining Alexandria Library!

As for education, as we know the student sits in his house or a specialized information center, and connects his brain with computer devices in the same way as a long-playing record or a movie was recorded through computer, and records in it science, religion, literature or engineering.

You start to record the scientific material in your brain cells, and then you stand off from the wires connected to your head because you took the subject and understood it in the same way as the local rooster used to press chicken seizing, and catching its body with its feet's clamp, then pressed it and in few seconds, the chicken shuddered beneath it. This is how school subjects are recorded; they squeeze the brain of students for one minute or more! There is no use of amphitheaters and no students are coming or going or dormitories where they would engage in social life experiences and some witchcraft and talismans before going to bed.

And as Dr. Mohammad Risha who used to teach us international law subject said, watching students leaving the amphitheater quarter of an hour before the lecture was finished as they started to withdraw one by one... And when their leaving became a daily routine, he said mockingly, "O bro, girls are always in a hurry that they don't stand in a ticket line or respect turn even if it was in the line of socialist cooperatives, and here, before the lecture ends, you find them leaving angry and before one of them reaches her room in the dormitory, she takes off her shoes and throws them in the room, God forbid that she takes off something else!" We laughed a lot at "something else!"

The old man was angry at woman. He mentioned to us an example of the concept of cooperation in law, "Marie Curie and her husband discovered the atomic radiation of uranium, and the truth is that it was her husband who discovered uranium, while his wife was doing his laundry, which means in term of laws, cooperation! And thus they said she and her husband." A girl sitting behind us in the amphitheater commented saying, "His wife might be abusing him in the house, so he comes over here to take revenge on us. Alas!"

We enter the Shanghai Hospital, and one of the robots moving behind the reception barrier welcomes us. Burhan shows him the number of his son's file written on his portable device. The man looks at it, welcomes us warmly, and then orders a clinical transport vehicle.

The machine comes very quickly, Canaan lies down on it to take him straight away to the examination room, while I and Burhan remain in the room staring at each other. In the meantime, a robot woman progresses toward us, welcomes us smiling, and invited us to sit in the waiting room. Without any questions, she leaves and come back within minutes carrying in her hands a tray on which there are a kettle of hot Chinese tea and two original Chinese cups adorned with drawings of the blue dragon. The woman bends down putting the tray in front of us on the table, pours tea, serves it with hospitality and politeness, and then she leaves the kettle on the table and turns back.

"This is the genuine Chinese generosity." You say to Burhan. "And this means we're going to wait for too long till checking the results of examinations." Burhan drinks his cup, and then he rises, excuses himself and goes to discuss or inquires about the arrangements made for his son, while you try to ignore the worry overwhelming you about your green grandson by directing your thoughts to bemoan the memories of a people of undergraduates which they wiped out. You thought about your life that passed in the twinkle of an eye. You turn neither the pages of history that are no longer yours nor that of your university students.

Had we continued our way forward without reluctance to achieve our goals, we would have accomplished many things! Had a novelist or researcher continued reading and writing since he learned it to death, he would have achieved twofold of what he did as he was facing death without attaining his goals. You find each one of us crying over spilt milk, "I wasted that chance, and thus I lost that thing. If I bought the piece of land that was offered me at a low price and now costs a fortune, I would have been...

Had I continued my PhD studies, I would have become... But what would you become O...? For you bumped into Dr. Mohammad Hanafy (the father of civil engineering) in one of Dubai's markets and helped him to remember you. He did not remember you of course, and after talking about the days of drawing-room that we used to share with students of architectural engineering and those of mechanical engineering, he knew that you're one of his students so he said to you, "I came here, son, to give a lecture about building metal frameworks."

The great doctor - what a pity- was staying in a low-budget hotel and eating Edfina Canned Food that he brought with him to save every piaster he earned in return for his lectures to buy with his savings a modern computer that he would take with him when going home. When he asked you about your job, you told him, "I'm participating in an engineering office with 50%of profits" He said as he was huffing sadly, "I wish I worked with my first university certificate and did not obtain PhD. I'm forced to theorize continuously, while you, engineers holding Bachelor's degree, always strike while the iron is still hot." Dr. Mohammad got lost and with him his university except for Alexandria University that is opening its mouth for seawater whose level has risen because of high temperature!

AN ALEXANDRIAN QUARREL!

As you are watching comers and leavers from Shanghai Alexandria Hospital in El Shatbi, you get lost in thought and start to visualize the beautiful old days feeling nostalgia pulling you to the martyr Mohammad Mohammad Mohammad , to his behavior and quick-wittedness especially when it comes to irony that used to entertain you and help you forget your life hardships which made you consider him your best friend in your university life. We often joked and laughed, and sometimes we read the same play by the founder of the Arab theater Abu Khalil Al-Ghabani or the same novel by Ghassan Kanfani and learned the thoughts of the scientist Mahmoud Amin. In some evenings, we would go together to El-Raml Station and start our journey with flipping through the newspapers displayed in front of the tram stop and their headlines that read:"

The completion of Al-Azahar Al-Sharif University on the instructions of Mr. president..

*Al-Azhar is turning from a just mosque to a gathering lighthouse of knowledge.

We read that, and then walked in the midst of the crowd where the throng of place at the intersection of Safia Zaghloul Street and that of Saad Zhagloul. And there, among the moving densely-packed crowd, you saw a girl walking arm in arm with a tall young man as thin as a carob seemed to be nervous as he was pressing his arm on her hand imprisoned under it, while they were thrusting themselves in the throng hurrying toward some place. The skirt of the girl was short. It was no more than two inches long, hence it could hardly cover her bottom flowing with feminine features revealing the aesthetics of the calves of her thighs.

We were taken aback by the hand of a guy groping her buttock. The filly bolted, got nervous, and screamed. The young man, mesmerized by his female, became alert to the aggressor to whom he said angrily, "Watch out, man!"

The aggressor apologized from them with a nod of his head, saying, "I'm sorry." Then the girl's companion accepted the assaulter's apology straight away with a jerk of his head, "It's OK!"

Each of them carried on in his crowd! We, the two strange farmers to town, were astonished, so Mohammad said, "This is an Alexandrian quarrel. By God, if this hit took place among farmers, nothing but blood that would sprout from the hand that stretched or the nose of the aggressor could wash it! If this harassment was in Upper Egypt, the aggressor could lose his life in the accident!"

"O God, the gentle!" you told him. So, he asked you, "How would you deal with such problems?"

"Such problems do not happen in the place where I live for one reason which is the absence of crowdedness. Crowdedness is the cause! "

We laughed and went our way toward Metro Cinema as I had already invited him to watch the wonderful journey movie that displayed the idea of downsizing a team of human doctors to go through the patient's skin pores to his coronary artery, then to the heart and remove from their arterial as well as venous path all fat embolism and myocardial infarction. Afterward, they would go out from the pupil. That movie which benefited from the idea of the dwarves and giants of One Thousand and One Nights which the

West imitated later in Gulliver in the Land of Dwarves and Gulliver in the Land of Giants. It was an amazing idea invented by Arabic literature! And today medicine has progressed as they started to send a huge team of robot doctors each one is as small as a head of a pin to the veins of Man and his arteries, so they swam in his blood to clear the fat sediments, treat Atherosclerosis, attack cancerous cells and remove heart infarction, thus bringing youth back to an old man!

Burhan continues his son's examinations and spends a while talking to experts and specialists while you are in the lounge room ruminating your old memories. Now you know your secret of your refusing the sea and swimming in it for you didn't enjoy Alexandria summer or holidaymakers who undressed and set off along with a vast blue horizon of liberation, vibrancy, and love toward washing off the complexities of life and work to soak in salty water taking out of them the blue genie, devils, grudge, envy and all impurities of time.

You opened your room window in the house of Abu Gerges. You didn't look at the sea, but rather kept your eyes roaming above Corniche Street watching the flying birds and that mummy man who was sitting facing coal oven grilling maize and selling to passers-by, and those girls coming back from the sea in bikini molted with the colors of a rainbow.

Suddenly and without warning, you felt delicate fingers stretching from behind you, and coiling softly around your face to close your eyes. You reached your hand to remove darkness from your eyes to figure out that it was the little Titi. Nay, it wasn't little neither you were old for she was seventeen years old and you were eighteen. And without facing you she kissed you at the neck, and then ran away!

You had never thought that one day you would be drowned to your ears in a childish love with Titi who didn't let her love for you grow like a seedling. She knew that Mohammad Mohammad went to university before you, but none of you knew that he did not go to university but rather to Damanhoury restaurant to help Haja Aliya with changing gas cylinder, cleaning the restaurant's utensils and tables and even the floor. He did all the work in return for free breakfast and dinner that he could not afford , so he saved two meals neglecting lunch because fava beans breakfast and fried food dinner would make Ferro-cement in his stomach, and thus protecting him from afternoon hunger. As for you, after many months you could catch him doing the work. You ignored the situation to not embarrass him because you both were convinced that work was   honorable! Or how would Mohammad, son of an electrical worker from Al Mansuriya, pay for merciless university life? His father sent him but...this was not the subject. It was Titi who noticed the absence of Mohammad in the morning and in the evening, so she showed up the next morning holding in her hands her school tie saying, "Can you help me with my tie because I don't know how to fasten it!

Titi moved her face toward yours as you were fastening the tie on her collar. You felt her hot breath as she was approaching her lips being pulled toward you. And the lips of Nefertiti were beyond description that all Arab's storytellers would fail to describe their breathtaking luscious beauty for they were hazel, soft, young, filled with the honey of Beheira and cloned from the lips of Queen Nefertiti. She moved her lips close to yours to breathe her feminine flaming adolescence on your face while you were hesitant because of your stupidity, cowardice and your rejection of the blessings that God bestowed on you! You were not a poet to describe the delicacy and beauty of her face that was stirring in your body spots of foolishness and enflaming you from head to your low extremities proceeding forward with fertility willing to pierce their bonds!

You put the blue tie around her neck and started to tie it under her chin while she was approaching and pressing against you letting your hands stretch over her neck and her wild hard deciduous breasts as you were tidying her necktie to dangle on her light blue dress. You seized in her softness and curve a magnetic torrent that melted all your snows! And her voice stripped of a magical flute took hold of your senses, hence you yielded.

It was the first time you put your hands on the body of a spring lily girl. Here was Nefertiti offering herself to you, you who didn't know a path to love or a road to the sea, hence you were seeking her presence that bewitched both mind and heart!

And Nefertiti was younger, taller, thinner, more beautiful, audacious and naughtier than Nadia. She didn't let you take the initiative to love her or beg you to love her. She didn't take you seriously either when she took initiatives to do all and conquered you in your own room on the pretext of fastening the necktie.

After many visits, you surrendered to her as she pressed you against her chest while your mind was concerned with your living in their house as such behavior was not appropriate with whom you were living with but you yielded to her! Titi took you from yourself and didn't let you a chance to take your breath?! It was the first time you tried the taste of a female and smelled the scent of her luscious hot breasts. And what a female she was! She was Titi! It was a flame transferred from hell, planted with the safety and chastity of a convent, molded from the innocence of a nun looking down from heavens upon you. Then she drowned you in her folds and burned you with her flaming body while you idiot was thinking about Sartre's saying, "If you want to have a love affair, you should stay away from relatives and neighbors!"

And Titi was the closest neighbor to you, but she was not literally a neighbor, but rather one of the mermaids! Sometimes a mermaid would go out of the sea, go into a building or enter a house and identify with the body of a gorgeous girl through whom she would adore a lover, and elate him by loving him, playing with him with her naughtiness, drowning him in her passion, and enflaming his feelings with her swings and movement floating on the bed. Then she might take him with her to her marine areas where she would live with him happily ever after! You were not sure about the identification of the two characters together, Nefertiti and the mermaid!

Was the reason behind your failing to immerse into the love of Titi your fear of her being a real mermaid? And did the mermaid Nefertiti show up while you and Mohammad Mohammad were in the midst of the sea and saved you from a certain drowning?

Here Burhan comes back, hopeful. I can tell that by the look at his cheerful face.

"We passed the test, father?! All examinations confirm the good health of his green body and his outdoing the health of traditional Man. Canaan will be permanently out of the hospital!"

Burhan pats on your back as he is telling you "Imagine the pleasure of life on earth when the sweat of green people and animals would change into transpiration like pure dew, toilets would disappear from houses, sewer leaks would stop flowing and rivers would restore their pure chastity flowing sparkling and spotless. Also, neither Man nor animal would pee and pollute the water because there would be no pee in the first place. The air would not be polluted with gasses destroying life on the earth, hence the trade of air that they started selling us canned would stop and the temperature of the earth would be balanced again as it used to be in the days of environmental purity, clear and relaxing" –Burhan turns around himself– "when religion and Nations failed to implant love among people and cut the fingernails of mauling, killing, destroying and robbing others, we completed the mission. Genetics now is changing the genes of Man and animal, depending on assaulting the other, into genes of loving the other as well as extending the life span of Man and all other living beings to change the philosophy of life and turn conflict into harmony and completeness. We are aspiring to create a paradise on earth. Now the saying that goes as: "If you are not a wolf, wolves would prey on you" would be replaced by the expression," Man is a beautiful creative thinker, a loving artist and a kind creature to his brothers: Man, animals, and plants."

You liven up and hear the beats of your heart throbbing as you are listening to the news of Canaan and those great ambitions. You swallow the pill of the elixir of life and drink a little bit of water, and then ask him," And what would happen to children and farms of human organs?"

"They would be annihilated, of course. It is supposed to finish with the development of our green production that would seize control of the universe like old gone cars that used gas and now works on hydrogen. Our generation, we ex-combatants, would perish, so companies would not produce spare parts for us or artificial organs. We are going to develop the products that would be designated to serve the green generation. How is your artificial kidney that we had transplanted in the Nephrology Department in Bremen working, dad?"

"My artificial kidney is working properly. Without you Burhan, I would have been dead now. Tell me, what is the reason behind your exclusive dealing with this giant Chinese hospital with its departments stretching in different parts of the world?"

"The Chinese are seizing control of the lifeblood of the world economy centers as the international Chinese Shanghai Hospital Company bought the majority of the shares of German Green Medical Man Company and the specialized departments of hospitals spread in main spots in the world. We trust their laboratories, and thus we cooperate with them in researches and experiments that matter to us as well as in treatments for our medical problems. This shrewd yellow Chinese dragon is spreading in the world easily and smoothly, father. They did not fail like the dictators of the Soviet Union who were crashed against the merciless rocks of the West. These have iron forearms but they covered them with soft Chinese satin made with precision and skillfulness!"

"Burhan, history is like a sea wave that crashes against shore rocks, and then withdraws rejected, but it gathers its pieces and attacks the shore again."

A GIANT FISH

Burhan turns back to finish the papers of Canaan to take him with us while you remain seated waiting for relief, and bringing back old memories in Alexandria, as early in the morning you used to come down to study while walking on the wharf of the seashore... The sand, the concrete cubes, rocks, and the sea were at your right side and serried wide wooden doors of small chalets were lined at your left side like a wooden belt around the sea waist of Alexandria. You took notice of a big fish swinging on the water surface and saw getting closer to the shore. It seemed unconscious!

It might be drunk due to excessive drinking tonight in the bars and clubs of Alexandria's sea, hence it couldn't recognize its house in the mid of marine quarters and alleys! It might be sick or hit by sea torpedo with which some fishers explode the sea, so some hit fish that would emerge and float on the water surface. What's a torpedo? You didn't know. That's what Abu Gerges told you as he was eating a fish at the kitchen table...

You put down your book on the sandy shore and reached your hand to hold it. You were the one meant by the proverb that states" The one who holds fish in the sea." It was impossible to hold a fish in the sea, but you tried. You reached your hand with your foot dipped and your shoes sank into seawater, but you were still in control because the fish leaned toward rocks, and then squirmed and tried to go away. After gluey maneuvers, you hold it in your hand and took it out of the sea. You felt that it weighed about three kilograms... You carried it stunned and run to the flat where Abu Gerges was surprised at seeing it. Umm Gerges took it from you feeling it heavy in her hands, and then stretched it next to the kitchen sink. Abu Gerges bombarded you with his questions, staring at your face while you were watching the remains of his cut ear shaking. Investigation went on, "How did you get it? How? When? Why? Who was with you? "A lot of questions followed by opening its gill, looking into its eyes, and then flipped it over from one side to another…and the result was that the fish was a kind of a respected blue fish according to the report of Abu Gerges. Hence, you felt reassured that it was in a good health and that it was in safe hands. Then he told you that you were invited today to eat the blue fish for lunch with the family.

"By God, it's generous of you to invite me, Abu Gerges. Well, what about Mohammad?"

The talkative man gave in laughing," Ok, Mohammad and two of Mohammad too! I leave our matters to God!"

You sat with them in the kitchen to see what's going to happen while Umm Gerges stood up to clean it, add spices to it, and then sliced it. After that she wrapped it with a layer of flour and fried it in oil, and thus it came out roasted and toasted smelling delicious. You and your friend ate with them until you were full. It was the first delicious fish you had ever tasted in your life!

It was no secret that Abu Gerges left the house now and then, and no one knew where he went because since they nationalized his American commercial real estate agency and his happy ranch, he was lost and loose. He left and did not come back, and when at house he would sleep and never would wake up. At his nights, he would drink till he got drunk and start to hallucinate, but what you liked most about him was his laughing too much.

Umm Gerges went out in the company of her little Nousa and her kid Gerges tired of her bitter life while Titi refused to go with them to see her aunt Helen, partly because she did not like her aunt, and partly because of her study. But when she was alone, she left her books saying "Go to hell!" Then she would go into your room like a ball thrown toward the goal out of passion to leap between your arms, smelling your breaths and sucking your nectar with hot kisses! And as time passed, she sat in front of you on your bed to talk to you about terrible things.

"Hush! I discovered a wondrous secret!" she told you shyly, "An incredible secret!"

"Good Lord! And what's this incredible secret? "

"Do you know that my mother is Muslim and from the farmers of Beheira?"

She lowered her gazes shyly as she added," She does not visit her family and they cut ties with her as well. They do not visit us either! "

"It's weird Titi! What else? "

"She fasts the entire Ramadan?!" –she got closer to you– "and this means she is still Muslim!"

"And how are you sure of her being..?

"I saw her birth certificate." She kissed your nose with hers, repeatedly rubbing them teasingly as she was breathing your breaths, and then drown her lips in yours with sweet long slides. After that, she took a deep breath then said," It was written in it, Name: Fatma Mohammad Aziz. Religion: Muslim"

"Why are you watching her?"

"I'm trying to know her, honey. She my mother, isn't she? She confided me that she visited Sheikh Arafat the imam of Sidi Jaber Mosque. Who knows? She might have confessed to him and she might have wept in front of him! I was watching her. When the canon announced the feast of Muslims, she sat crying silently because she was deprived of feast gathering with her mother, father, and brothers about whom I don't know anything. I love my mother, Mashhour, and I love the fact that you are a Muslim in the same way as my father loved my Muslim mother! What about me imitating my father, so I marry you while you're a Muslim and give birth to Muslim children in the same way as my mother gave birth to his Muslim children? Tell me why Christians' children are born Christian and Muslims' children are born Muslim each one of them latched on the religion of his father, and their approaches differ without any excuse."

You couldn't answer her because you were drowning in her lustful desire and feeling high in her femininity tarnishing your innocent body. You did not remember to tell her that "There is no compulsion in religion; truly the right way has become clearly distinct from error."

"It seemed that my father met my mother here in this apartment and had an affair with her! After being involved with him and becoming pregnant with me and his love for her bewitching beauty...! You know, Mashhour, my mother was a queen of beauty. Can't you see that she is white, tall, and very beautiful even after she grew old? That might be the reason why my father was in love with her while he was brown, short and..., and for this reason , I often hear him singing for her teasingly, 'The girl is fair, fair, fair! The girl is fair what shall I do? '

But his strong love for her when she was young, her fear of scandal and revengeful killing to wash off the shame as farmers of Beheira say, forced him to marry her and she was forced to run away from her family house and hide from them forever by living in this retreat house. You noticed that his ear was cut. He said he fought with... farmers and the truth is that those–whom he said were thieves– are my uncles who engaged in a wrangle with him and one of them attacked him and ate his ear?! They would have killed him if he didn't run away and hide. They didn't know the location of our apartment. They only knew the manor that he sold cheap lest they would return for revenge."

After deep thinking, you asked her, "Is it for this reason why you find him insulting and defaming farmers?

"Farmers had revolted against their dire condition in the manor, uncle."

"Why are calling me uncle, while you're one year my junior?"

"My father and my mother forced us, I and my sister Nousa, to call those who live in our house uncle to not have an affair with them."

"You're a great actress Titi!"

"I'm indeed acting when it comes to the word uncle, but I'm honest about my love for you without any acting."

"Was your mother a field worker in his manor, and he seduced her or assaulted her? Or was she who surrendered herself to him as a submissive lover?"

"I don't know the truth. All that she told me was that they used to harvest wheat, but they used to sleep hungry being denied ardeb of wheat that was all their food and that they owned nothing but what they stole. When a spy he placed among them, ratted on them, things turned upside down and whipping went on!

The whips of khedive set off to work, but farmers revolted and their chief said, 'We endured hunger, but our dignity doesn't accept beating!' Then he cried out,' O men, hit him hard. Dignity is over humiliation.' Here, farmers attacked and bit him that he was about to die. Things got worse, and one of them bit his ear and pulled it. The farmer was hungry and craving meat, so he cut it and chewed it, and then..."

"You said that it was your uncles who cut it, and then say that one of the farmers ate it with his teeth!"

"I don't know the truth," she answered you mumbling, "Each tells his story as imagined. My uncles might be the ones who did that and it might be the farmers, and maybe my uncles were the farmers working for him, they and their daughter or they and their sister who is my mother!"

"It might not be a battle of hunger, robbery, and beat as much as it is a battle of honor!" you added this analysis from your own perspective. "Maybe the farmer found out about the secret of the relationship that got his daughter involved with the farm owner, so he and his folk decided to take revenge for their gone honor! This explains the reason for the loss of the fifty acres that the revolution left for your father, so he sold them to escape from Abu Kir region not to be killed. He could have sold them to pay for the expenses of drinking and gambling with friends! Anyway, the matter was no more than a fight between farmers and a seigneur!

THE MONK OF THE CONVENT

You shift restlessly in your chair, as you are waiting for the dawn of Canaan eagerly. Praise be to God who created you in the best form. Be patient my heart till the emergence of the green twig. You try to be patient until meeting your cherished hope and you have nothing but Alexandria's beautiful memories...

For when living in the house of Abu Gerges, you used to go to the convent, there next to Sidi Jaber Mosque where you studied all your subjects . There was a reverent monk who welcomed students at the entrance of the convent smilingly. He gave you a private room in the middle of which there was a decent wood drafting table big enough for your civil drawing, a large board on the wall, colored chalks, and a rubber. He offered you his help that he brought you upon your request from the convent library all drawing tools that wanted.

The reassuring thing was that he did not ask you whether you were Muslim or Christian or a blue genie. He did not ask you about your identity, either. Time didn't allow him to know your personality at all. Many of neighborhood students came to study in the public convent library. The private room was for those who came early while the public room was given for other students. The convent offered its services free to all students including city dwellers, farmers, Upper Egyptians, Bahri, and Arab students equally. They were all equal like comb teeth!

The master of people is the one who serves. After finishing your study, you went to Sidi Jaber Al Ansari Mosque to perform isha duties.

Why isn't there in this great mosque a public library like that of the convent serving the readers of the neighbor, though the first word in our wise book is read? And why does this modern convent read, and they don't?

Today there are no teeth of comb because they shave our heads bald! The forty-old-year stout monk of the convent ran here and there with his white milk clothes as he was thinking all the time about more service! He ran bringing a microscope for this student, and then came back with a dictionary for that one or a drawing ruler and engineering tools for that female student.

You went back to the house of Abu Georges who opened the door asking, "Where were you?"

You answered him as you were lifting your head, "I was studying in the convent."

"If you keep living with us, we will baptize you a Christian like us!"

He said this, while his eyes were fixed on a sitting nun visiting them. Then he whispered in your ears saying in the sham dialect, "And I am talking to you!"

After she went out, you asked him, "Is this nun a relative of you?"

He answered you disgustedly, "Praise be to God! She is neither a relative nor a non-relative. She is a boring visitor!" he grumbled, saying, "What a bore!"

You were taken aback by his words, so you asked him, "How could you talk about her like that, her being an example of chastity, innocence, sacrifice, and giving?"

His grumbling got worse. He said, "It's neither sacrifice nor shit! She comes by to explore news and then transfers them from one house to another house. She's talkative, hypocrite exposing the secrets of families and transmits them like contagious diseases!"– he laughed– "hush, I screwed up! I gave her the news as I like not as desired by blamers!" He stopped talking and started dancing and singing a song by Farid Al Atrash "How much he told me and I told him. O blamers boil with anger! O blamers boil with anger!"

The man was drunk as he was dancing in front of you!

They were beautiful days of beautiful interaction and religious tolerance. Today if you go to the restroom, they would record your name, and take your identity. And the racial, religious, doctrinal, tribal, sectarian, clannish, and color discrimination emerged too ... as for class disparity, dear! Tell me about it! How did those dreamy quarters and alleys change into a stressed entertainment city turning everything upside down! Time changed everything as the song of Umm Kolthum says:"

"Time will make you taste in absence my fire,

Time that will avenge me,

Time has always changed things!"

Here time took revenge on us that you, lady, changed. We grew old and venerable, and then withered, we, the teenagers of Alexandria!

FITEER MISHELTIT

Every minute spent in waiting Canaan sounds like a lifetime! You don't know why your resistance withered and why you failed to be patient while waiting for the end of examinations. Burhan told you that they were successful and that the green raceme was blooming!

You go back to your memories with Mohammad Mohammad when the paper seller in El-Raml station was crying out, "Nasser is opening Ak-Ahram building, the most modern technological paper in the world…Ak-Ahram paper releases the first edition with natural colors…Haikel is gelding an administrative meeting with the managers of Al-Ahram on the phone while he was alone in his office."

You invited Mohammad Mohammad to see War and Peace movie based on the novel of Tolstoy that was shown for the first time simultaneously in Moscow and the Rialto Movie House in Alexandria. We were amazed by seeing the great artist Mahmoud Morsy and the old painter Saif Waili, the long—haired artist of Alexandria, in the company of the captain of Soviet fleet visiting Alexandria Harbor. They were talking and laughing with a person who seemed to be the mayor of Alexandria, their host.

Then we went in the darkness, and the hall worker lighted our way with the faint light of his torch to show us our footsteps, so you gave him a tariff.

"Give him a piaster not a tariff", your friend warned you saying, "By God, without those piasters that people pay, I and my alike would not be able to go to university! My father who works as a collector in El-Mansura for seventeen peanuts that he was paid after this long age by electricity authority can barely provide us with bread. But people give him for every bill a piaster and some of them whom God blessed with his bounty, pay him two extra pilasters. From theses pilasters, Mashhour, my father saves my university expenditures, and thus you see me hanging around with you, going to the cinema, and drinking a soft drink that my father did not drink unless one of the rich clients treated him to one once in a year. Hence I would feel I'm keeping up with people of my generation and understand life in the same way as they understand it and do not suffer from any psychological complexes while I'm living among them without a soft drink for example! "

After the half-yearly vacation, Mohammad Mohammad came back from Al-Mansura loaded with Fiteer misheltit, two pigeons stuffed with rice as he was saying, "My mother Nathla sent them, one for you and one for me. She is saying to you, 'These presents are on the occasion of our settlement in the new apartment that the social housing gave us.' Such flats give money to workers of governmental firms and factories provided that each one of them pays its cost in installments."

You, happy, asked about the news, "Are you going to pay its cost without bank interest!?"

He said, "No interests and not even partial payment!"

"What's this?" you asked him again.

"That's for workers."

"What about the lodging of farmers?"

He said lifting head confidently, "Every farmer, given a piece of land from the project of agriculture reform, can draw a loan from Agricultural Credit Association to build on it a house for himself."

Mohammad ate while laughing and telling you about his neighbor's child in El-Mansuura Mohammad Alyan Mutawaly who was his school mate in secondary school, but he failed and could not go to university. And on the night Mohammad was leaving, his neighbor came to bid him goodbye. While he was drinking tea, he told my father, 'Could you imagine that your son is drinking Spiro Spathis in Alexandria, uncle?"

Mohammad wiped the last rice grain off his plate, saying, "And the idiot Alyan imagined that my father did not know about these tricks, but my father Knew that Spiro Spathis is an Egyptian drink alternative to cola, so he accepted the joke and pretended that he fell for the trick of the idiot Alyan, and exploded with anger, "Is that true son? You drank Spiro Spathis behind my back when I'm saving every piaster and depriving your siblings to provide you with two piasters for your education, but you spent them on drinking Spiro ,O boy Alyan!'

I smiled and my father broke loose from his acting with laughter that I saw for the first time his jugular veins protruded. He said mockingly, 'Instead of making fun of people, you should have passed the exam of high school, Alyan son of Mitwaly.'

The son of Mitwaly stood up with his face pale, and then went out dispirited without bidding me farewell or even saying Salam Alaikom!"

We ate the two pigeons and we felt full. We had then fiteer Misheltit sweetened by honey for dessert. You understood the situation and you knew the score, so you rewarded him generously. The price sometimes rose to reach two piasters and the ticket price rose from fifteen piasters to reach twenty five that you weren't enjoying the movies, but rather started thinking about the unreasonable rise in prices, and therefore you were forced to a less expensive class in the camp shire or in El-ibrahimiya where an expensive ticket was no more than twelve piasters.

You took with you your neighbor living on the first floor, Mohammad Yusuf from Ismailiya. The student in engineering university and you sat with families in Odeon Cinema Theatre. Lights were turned off and the show of a French movie featured by the famous actress Jane Moro started. And upon starting the display of animated cartoons Mickey mouse, Tom and Jerry and the advertisement of movies coming soon, you were surprised by a loud voice coming from one audience member dissipating the silence accompanying the scenes, screaming, "Your father sits on gas can, pretending to be a funnel !"

The audience consisting of families laughed at the triviality of this funny tramp. Another answered him loud, "Your mother wears panties with shoehorn!" The audience laughed. A third cried belching out a bad word, "Your mother wakes up to find (....) crushed!" The audience laughed at that dirty word!" Then a fourth troublemaker yelled saying, "Isn't there among you someone.... who could insult me?" Someone in the far corner answered him with a bad insult," (..) your mother (..) your mother (..) your mother! (*)

Here the security cinema worker came and lighted with his electric lamp here and there and you didn't know how the childish comments and rudeness would finish. The audience males and females hushed and followed the appalling dramatic movie events that started with a hand reaching eggs in a bird's nest on which there were dark spots affirming that the eggs were about to hatch and birdies would come out. Suddenly, the hand was stretched out to hold the eggs and feel their warmth. The hand thought a while, and then fisted its killing fingertips and with a sudden press, it broke all eggs at once. Like this crush! Then the hand opened dipped in flowing gluey blood!

The movie showed the story of a teacher at a village's children school in her late thirties suffering from sexual suppression being unmarried. Hence she woke up in the dark night all alone ,worried and stressed that she went out to the village farms, and every time she took out her anger on them by committing a secret crime. One night she poisoned the well water basin from which the cows of the village drank, and therefore all cows coming there died wholesale.

Another night she set fire to the threshing floors of farmers. And every time the farmers thought that the doer was a stranger they knew. He was a man in his forties working as a carpenter in the woods of the village .He was a strong widower. And every time he rushed to take part in putting out the blazing fire or stood by their side in any problem facing them, some of them would say, "The criminal must go back to the scene of the crime to savor his results in front of the inflicted, and that's why the stranger must be the doer!"

And one night the spinster teacher went out to the woods and met the stranger who worked as a tree cutter and they had sex with the cruelty of the deprived. They rolled over the grass and thorns, and thus she returned from his woods only at dawn, while the men of the village were looking for her worried that something bad might have happened to her or that the stranger might have attacked her. When they met her coming back from there and saw her clothes torn and blood bleeding from her body that was soothed and numbed with the intoxicating desire, they asked her, "He too who..!" She answered recklessly," Yes, he is who..! "

While the woman, elated, went home to sleep peacefully, the men of the village progressed together toward the woods in the direction of the fooled carpenter and without asking him or waiting for an answer; they attacked him with their axes and cut him to pieces..!We do not watch these great cultural intellectual French movies anymore and nothing was left for us but American movies, tak,tak,tak that generalized terrorism and terror in the world!

And in return for your invitation to watch a movie, Mohammad Yusuf Ismaili invited you to visit them in their first–floor apartment. You thanked him reluctantly, so he argued gently, "Yes, man, you, people living on the upper floor don't bother to visit those living downstairs!" So you answered him embarrassingly," You know Mohammad Yusuf that I wish to visit you but the system of my familial lodging doesn't allow us to invite my colleagues in the family apartment."

"Come and visit us, man, and there is no need for me to visit you in your apartment. It is enough to meet at the university and sometimes we go to the cinema!"

You didn't decline his request, and therefore you visited him a week later after that cinematic party. He welcomed you with his colleague Mohammad Ibrahim. We sat, got to know each other, and laughed at everything. Then he told us a joke, saying, "A fisher looked for bait but found none, so he put a paper on which written bait and he attached to the hook, and then threw it in the sea. After half an hour, he lifted the hook. It turned out that he fished a paper on which written a fish!" We laughed at the innocent joke and before Mohammad Yusuf brought the tea from the kitchen, the doorbell rang. His fellow student Mohammad Ibrahim opened the door and a thin woman carrying some clothes on her arm peeked out.

Mohammed welcomed her as she was coming in. She peered at us with her blue eyes, greeted us from a distance, walked into the kitchen, and then returned. She had prepared tea instead of Mohammad Yusuf and bent down when she served us it. You watched the white young woman who was wearing a colorful common dress! The woman was covered, praise be to God. You felt at ease, then.

Whores are different images of the devil, you thought. If you had to decide about them, you would have burned them and relieved people from their vices. I seek refuge in God, how could a woman sell her honor! And how could she sleep with this and that? How could she contaminate this and that, transmit germs, transfer the diseases of Syphilis, and gonorrhea from this to that, and then transmits to her husband if she had a husband? —back then Aids disease and others were not familiar— how did she get paid the price of her flesh chewed under men's merciless wheels? Those women look like the city mice moving in every direction and go in here and there and thus they transmit diseases from this to that!"

All this nonsense went on in your mind as you were watching this strange woman. You knew that the two students Mohammad Yusuf and Mohamed Ibrahim were strange to Alexandria and that they were coming from Ismailia, so that the first would study engineering while the other would study laws. They had no relatives or families attached to them in this apartment, that's why you were suspicious, so you asked Mohammad Yusuf, "Who is the woman?"

"She is Umm Fatouma," he answered you, laughing, "The wife of Abu Fatouma, the ironer, man!"

"But it's night. Does Umm Fatouma collect and deliver clothes to be ironed at night? She is a mother, a wife, and a housewife? "

He tried to cover himself, being investigated, "She visits us at any time and without appointments. It means she's not strange to us!"

"The woman is beautiful." Mohammad Ibrahim added," Tell us, did you like her? "

"You said she is the wife of Abu Fatouma! Even if I like her! There is no doubt that she is good-looking."–she bent down as she was pouring us tea like a deer drinking from a stream– "and as you are saying, she just dropped by!"

Mohammad Yusuf laughed, saying," If you like her, what about wrapping her for you in cellophane? And if you didn't like cellophane, I will wrap her for you in satin! Enjoy yourself, man!"

"What do you mean by your wrapping her for me?"

"I mean if you desire her, she is ready and this is the bedroom. Come..! "

"I seek refuge in God! Is this woman one of those...?

"She is not one of those..." Mohammad explained her work."She is a respectful woman, but she loves us, brother .God's creation is wonderfully diverse!"

"She loves you and sleeps with you. How would she then sleep with me if she doesn't know me?

"O brother, this is a laundry woman, but she is a full automatic laundry woman. I mean she is really nice!"

"Full automatic, she collects laundry from the quarter's inhabitants and sleeps with...! What job is this?"

Mohammed tried to soften your stubbornness and simplify the subject to you, "You can say, doing the laundry and ironing job! All!"

You couldn't stand it anymore, so you got your back up and took heart like Popeye who ate spinach that his muscles would augment and his powers would increase and explode in a great job! And you could not control yourself, so you thought of saving these two innocent guys from this whore. You thought a lot about saving operation and then decided on your own. Without consulting with them, you found yourself saying boldly, "Go out from here quickly!"

The two guys were stunned and the woman stood bewildered! But she looked at you silently smiling, saying nothing. The two neighbors did not talk, still respecting their hospitality to you.

They all exchanged gazes and felt the immensity of the rudeness of this guest and the seriousness of the loss! But a guest was a guest and he had to be respected! And they both did not forget that this bore was a stranger and he visited them for the first time, so they didn't say anything. The woman understood the situation, so she went out rejected. Still, she gave a cunning smile as she was leaving.

You were surprised at the woman's behavior and thought that she lacked dignity and reticence as she smiled after all this cruel treatment, so you drank tea slowly and took your leave before the party started.

The two guys did not object to your leaving before the start of the party, but rather rose and bid you farewell at the apartment door and no one of them told you at least," Visit us again."

You felt relieved for saving these two innocent men from ruining themselves as if you said to your grandmother Aneesa, "Did you see your grand child's shrewdness? I'm implementing your instructions carefully! "Whoever amongst you sees an evil; he must change it with his hand; if he is unable to do so, then with his tongue."

The next day you met Mohammad Yusuf under the giant marble pillar lifting high the glamour of engineering university building that looked like the palace of Pharaoh Hatshepsut in her time.

"Good morning, Mohammad."

"Alaikom Assalam, Mashhour."

"How are things?"

He answered you briefly, and solemnly," fine."

"I'm sorry about what happened yesterday, but I should do something and make a difference even with my tongue."

He answered mockingly, "Why with your tongue, Mashhour? Do you still use your tongue?"

"What happened with the woman Umm Fatouma? Did she come back after I had left?"

"The truth is that she came back straight away after you had gone out!"

You ignored the shock and asked him, "And did you..?"

He answered you embarrassing as he was looking at the marble pillar, "Yes. Do...!"

"What did she say about me? I ask you by God to tell me the truth!"

"Since you're asking me by God, she said, "The client seems to be effeminate. He is in trouble and came here for you and feared that I would take his share!"

"I seek refuge in God from the evil of this woman who...!" you answered, astonished. "Is she who said that?"

"It seemed that things were not as simple as you imagined, Mashhour. It seemed that the tongue doesn't work in such situations!

RASHIDI FESIKH

Are they the ones coming from the end of the hospital corridor? It seems that your poor eyesight could not distinguish Cannan from others! "Patience is good, buddy, and the talk of people..." Focus on the talk of old people, old man! Stay with your friend Mohammad Mohammad when you came back to El Raml Station from your movie as the evening newspaper seller was crying out, "A plan to implement the project of a tourist city around Katara Lake will be supplied with Mediterranean water to generate electricity to lighten Egypt...the suggested Katara City will compete with Alexandria in its tourist activities."

You went home late paying no heed to the instructions of Abu Gerges who said to you with firmness ," It was prohibited to stay out late after midnight and that the one who would be late, must sleep where..."

You boarded the last tram that moved before midnight and after which the ones going home had to take a taxi paying a lot of money, and you both did not have a piaster apart from your student subscription card. On the way, you were attracted by the voice of driver Mohammad Al-Mirghani famous in all Victoria lines for his melodious singing as he was driving his locomotive in standing position and stomping his foot. The rings of the tram would rattle as if it told the pedestrians, "Keep out of my way, man!" And tonight, he was entertaining us with a song for Mohamad Kindil (Amid two shores and water, my eyes adored you, O dear to my heart, O folk of Alexandria, O folk of Alexandria!)

Many passengers gathered around the singer driver and some of them went off from the second floor of the locomotive just to enjoy a cherished song. They all were repeating what he was saying.

When the train arrived, we got off at Cleopatra Hamamat station. And before the tram moved to continue its journey, we were taken aback by a shabby-looking young man jumping behind the locomotive. He seemed to be a drunken thief. He behaved foolishly pulling the tram electricity rope whose end touched the air electricity wires, and thus the tram stopped working. The driver's helper went off to find out the cause of the breakdown and you pointed him to the running boy who was laughing, cursing, and stumbling in his running. Hence, the assistant reconnected the rope pulley with air wire as he was returning the naughty boy's rudeness with greater rudeness while we were shocked by such kids' naughtiness.

Every afternoon you went back from university and stopped by a respectable restaurant called Hati El-Ibrahimiya. There, the waiter Mohammad Murad would welcome you, offering you the dish of the day unlike the song of Tholathy Adwa'a El Masrah in which they said, "And here is today dish, chocolate with garlic! Here you are today dish consisting of vegetables, rice, veal, an orange or a banana. You paid eighteen piasters for it besides two piasters as tip. You left and when arrived home, you went into your room and took your nap. And before sunset, you went out from the building to walk as a reader on the sidewalk of the shore and watch people of God.

In May as it got hotter, the heat started crawling on the sand, umbrellas started to be implanted here and there, the number of holidaymakers got bigger and stripping off heavy clothes increased showing bikinis. Tennis game was active again and cups of tea and soft drinks were distributed among families. Some daughters plunged into the water with their clothes or covering trousers and a family composed of a mother, her four daughters and a little child were eating salty Rashidi Fesikh, Domiati cheese and Tantawi onion with the

Alexandrian bread of Beheira, that you smelled the odor of Rashidi Fesikh and onion reaching your nose. Today there was no Rashidi Fesikh left, not even Rashidi City itself that was wolfed by the hot sea together with its deltas because of environmental pollution that killed the earth.

And in the closed chalets, covered with fabric curtains— as the law forbade closing them unless they were utterly empty -you heard conversations and sometimes you were stirred by brash voices! A seller passed by with his huge basket while screaming:" Simit, egg, and Rumi cheese ..eggs, simit, and cottage cheese..", a girl was fighting with three young men claiming that they were harassing her, a handsome man, who resembled Abdel Halim Hafeth, was flirting with a brunette that seemed to play hard to get, kids were hitting an octopus against the shore rocks to… a fishing boat was approaching the shore with its fishers in their Alexandrian waistcoats and hats… and a guy was walking swaggering while joking with his friend mockingly in a feminine playful voice, "Help me, may God help you!"

The problem was that you did not see anyone of those reading a book or flipping through a newspaper unlike holidaymakers of the West who read in their free time even if they were lying down on the beach naked!

You looked ahead of you and you saw stairs going up from beach pier to Corniche Street, so you climbed the stairs quickly and crossed the highway coming back home. You encountered Abu Gerges, so you asked him why you always found him in the kitchen fully dressed, instead of relaxing in the living room. He told you that he would rather sit in the kitchen than sit in the narrow living room at the entrance divided among all rooms because you found anyone who entered or went out and anyone who wanted to go to the bathroom passing through the living room. Hence he would say Asalam Alaikum if he was Muslim like Mohammad Mohammad, and if he was a Christian like Dr. Rida living in that corner, he would tell you good morning or good evening and either way, you found each one of them violating the privacy of the one sitting here!

He took a sip of his glass, and then he proceeded to say," For this reason, you find me preferring sitting alone in the kitchen and here I drink two glasses of brandy and become elated!"

Indeed, you went into the kitchen and found him sitting singing and telling stories from the East and sent it to the West and from the North to …"I am a reliable man!" he told you as he was pointing with his forefinger."I was American CMC car dealer, son. But sons of … nationalized it and the government of …took responsibility for importing them or at least importing the necessary spare parts. Who knows? Import might stop, unless God blessed a person with a car that he, personally brought from America itself."

Then he stood swaggering singing while stretching out the sounds of drunk words, "IIIIIIII waaasted myyyyy liiife loving you !"

You took notice that he was crying this time, saying, "I went to college (Farouk the first) in 1944, but unfortunately for me, they changed its name, and thus I graduated from Alexandria university in 1948, the year of Palestinian Nakba. I got married in 1950 and unfortunately for me, the revolution broke out in1952 and I had Noussa in 1956 and unfortunately for me, the Swiss War was declared and Gerges was born in 1962, and the same year, unfortunately for Gerges, they nationalized CMC agency. And when my beautiful daughter Titi turned fourteen years old in 1964, they nationalized my farm as me being feudal, so you can say that they are all occasions of setbacks! Hence I ended up broke.

The drunk kept weeping, saying, "But I didn't leave a door without knocking on it, bro Mashhour, or a friend of God without visiting him from Al-mursy Abu Al-abbas to Said Al-badawi seeking healing and help. I told him, 'Help me Sayid Al-badawi, heeelp!' but they denied me help, sons of a …and then the wealth in which I was wallowing dissipated, the wealth I appreciated only after I lost ..it's true that health is a crown on the head of a well person that only a sick person can see, and now I'm sick, I rejoice on a piaster, while I swear on your honor, I used to light the cigarette of a whore with an English pound not Egyptian!" You laughed at him as he was swearing on your honor.

"Look at me, look how I ended up!" –he wiped his tears with his palms, and then said smiling," I used to be fond of women .Once I was walking behind a woman, who seemed beautiful from her back ,so I told her flirting, 'O beauty resembling that of Prophet Mohammad!' but the woman did not turn. I approached her saying, 'O beauty reminiscent of that of Isah!' Still, she didn't turn! I got closer to her and said to her,' O beauty of Muses! 'She turned and I was taken aback by an ugly face that I screamed, 'O Jamal Abdel Nasser!'"

You didn't laugh at the silly joke while the drunken man continued narrating his life story, "I waited for a year, two years and three because God might change a situation to another but he did not."

He poured his eleventh glass in his head, saying, "The situation got worse and my manor in Abu Kir was confiscated. They said it is about one hundred acres, and thus they took half of it and gave it to farmers, sons of …and we, though intelligent, are lost! A few animals who don't know what way to take became landowners! He said, 'By God you wear trousers, so how would you pee, then?' Telephones now are in the houses of dregs of society! He told him, 'O father!' He told him, 'Yeah!' He told him, "If one talks on the phone and the wire is cut, what would happen?' He told him, 'Words would fall from wire, son!'"

You laughed at his silly jokes. Today in the mid twenty-first century, there was no wire or even a telephone because the mobile attached on your ring finger does all calls that you want...

Abu Gerges proceeded to say, "I used to have a villa looking like a mermaid sitting by the beach. It's so breathtaking, boy Mashhour. It has two floors and an attic. The ground floor consists of a living room, a guest room, and a wide French kitchen while the second one consists of four bedrooms and the attic consists of an office for me, a snack bar, and a small kitchen. I can stay only in the attic. I was like Muslims of your heaven, living in the highest place! From there, you could watch the sea (He's talking to a brick wall) I used to drink a box of beer when sitting in the attic while farmers and animals were plowing, planting, picking, and eating half of the crop behind my back!" —he raised his hands to pray, "May their food be poisonous, God willing! Milk, cheese, and local ghee were abundant Mashhour! Not to mention eggs, local chickens, turkeys, ducks, and geese! I used to have two pigeon towers, and every day I got two barbecued squabs or ones being fried in local ghee. They're so delicious. You will enjoy eating them …I swear by this blessing!"

He swore as he was lifting the glass of brandy that was in his hand and you laughed at his blessing! The tired man took a pull at his worn-out cigarette to fill his lungs with the deadly blessing ,and then exhaled the smoke of an old train that was still working .His voice cracked when he was singing maiming the genuine art as he was wailing ," Everyone who fell in love was crashed. I am alone me wept!" Then he wailed crying, "They dashed us sons of a …they confiscated the villa and your life, and then forced you to recruit!" H

e was both crying and laughing while his tears were falling down his face, saying, "He said nationalize it, he said so, and then my villa became the property of the nation! And what would the nation do in it? Hhh! They decided about it by surrendering it to be a residence for the Socialist Union Branch in Abu Kir! And they stole from my land 50 acres and distributed them to farmers who once were my servants! Servants have become neighbors and colleagues! Well, who would work for me after the situation has changed? Could you imagine, boy Mashhour, that one of the animals that the acres were distributed to, looked at me, and told me, 'Who do you think I am? Don't underestimate me! My late grandfather was the director-general of the greatest urinal in Cairo! ' It puzzles me that one of the bastards of the socialist union would sit in the attic and drink the cognac of Napoleon! Napoleon the Emperor on your honor! I am a connoisseur of cognac, Mashhour! It was not this Diesel that we drink. It is rather Mr. Napoleon itself, the best cognac in the world. I swear by our prophet that Napoleon with his greatness was delivered to me in boxes from France without taxes or bills! It was a unique gift from Madeline and his friend Isabel.

"They used to take grapes from my farm and my stupid supervisor used to collect for them the grapes of the farms of my friends and acquaintances in the region to make prestigious French wine. Here in the land of the farm, we dug for them wide clay catacombs open onto the sea air as if the sea air passed through them with fans, the degree of its temperature set between ten degrees and thirteen degrees Celsius. Then they started to store in them the wine, fine wine, son! The wine of Madeline was white and bitter, while Isabel's wine was red like a ruby! As for pink wine, we called it Alexandria rose.

"We used to sell wine to day of wine, O boy! Do you know what the truth is Mashhour? Christians made wine and sell it while Muslims drink it! Hhh! It means a sort of collaboration between religions!" he said, laughing a lot that the remnants of his decayed black teeth appeared! The man was not so happy, but rather so angry because they drove him out of the highest place in paradise."

YOUR WISH IS MY COMMAND, CHIEF!

On the eve of the veracity of the bitter defeat that his moody military leadership brought upon him, President Jamal Abdel Nasser announced his resignation as president and that was on the eight o'clock evening news bulletin. And within five minutes from the end of the abdication speech, you started to hear the voices of the people roaring in the street and the crowd was chanting. You went out to the street and you saw the Nile inundation that you read about in the ancient Pharaonic fruit days! You didn't know where these people came from. Hundreds of thousands of men and women demonstrators, coming from Victoria and Bakos, his birthplace, through Sidi Gaber and from all sides, were walking in close-knit groups like a roaring torrent and the torrent was still gathering, cotton balls were inflating and numbers of people walking were increasing to the area of Cleopatra and El Ibrahimiya. You walked with them, and chanted their chant:

"Who freed the canal but you Jamal !"

"The high dam, Jamal…the workers, O Jamal."

"Education…O Jamal…dignity, O Jamal."

"The farmers…O Jamal..factories, O Jamal."

"Agriculture…O Jamal… a loaf of bread, O Jamal."

The roaring people met in El Raml Station and gathered in El-Manshiya. About millions of men and women were exclaiming against the resignation of the president! Abu Gerges was scrutinizing and watching demonstrations shouting in anger, "We don't want anyone but Jamal. We don't want anyone but Jamal!"

Demonstrators continued with such chants for several successive days with people sleeping on the streets. One gathering to refuse the defeat stretched from Al-Manshiya Square to El Raml Station. You found them lying on the ground around Abu- al Abass - Al-Mursi Mosque and at the Unknown Soldier Memorial and sitting in public spaces, and more than that happened in Freedom Square in Cairo and other cities till the president yearned to his people's will and resumed his responsibilities. And here Abu Georges surprised you as he was standing in his glorious kitchen and said to you, "Did you hear what happened after midnight last night?"

"What worse would happen than we heard and witnessed?"

"What happened should neither be read nor written, sir!" –he said ,laughing, opening Said kishta's mouth wide– "what happened was that the ladies of Alexandria's nightclubs and cabarets took part in massive demonstrations chanting with one voice, 'Ahha! Ahha! Do not abdicate!' And in response to the call of women, Mr. President decided to resume his responsibility as president of Egypt, the mother of the world! "

Mohammad Mohammad came in, and hearing this nonsense, he lost his temper and pulled you, telling you, "The man is insane, drunk and of course angry because government nationalized his cars agency, thus going broke. He thought that time came for revenge and gloat over enemies! But no, we will fight again and again and again and we'll join the resistance, Mashhour .The end of the occupier is known!"

In the university canteen, a Sudanese young man, who seemed to be a leader student and knew what he's doing, stood speaking gently to a crowd of students who gathered to understand what happened and what would happen. We were in the midst of June 1967, and students' exams ended quickly, but the university did not generally close its door.

"If there was inside each one of us Jamal Abdel Nasser, the nation would be much better." the man who was relatively older compared with the age of the students said. "It is true that the man was hasty in his last war and haste is waste, not to mention that centers of powers that were sailing the ship against the wish of the chief might have tricked him. And if these great efforts, focused on the union with Syria, on Yemen War along with Palestine Liberation War, are directed at bringing Egypt and Sudan together instead - as they used to be when he took them from the king of Egypt and Sudan- he would have created a great state like Iran or India or Turkey. And from the state of the Nile River, he could set off to realize an Arab Union and that would be achieved through education, understanding, and caution.

"Arab League could start to unite economy and Arabic currency besides opening the doors for the labor force and intraregional trade inside Arab markets without any confines, and then an Arab united representative council would decide a united path for Arabs which doesn't contradict rulers remaining each in his position.

Every Arab president or king would remain is in power without usurps or massacres overruling thrones provided that real democratic elections for delegates and the Prime Minister will be held. Also, the number and colors of ministers will be defined according to their parties' weight or the strength of their unions in parliamentary elections, municipal councils as well as professional and student associations. And there would be no need for the expression 'Your wish is my command, chief!' to lead a battle."

The audience was listening carefully to the man, while the Sudanese added saying, "If this revolutionary young experience had been adopted to reduce the complexity and weakness of general administrative not to chase thinkers even if they were from the opposition party and to achieve planning to provide Arab food security... Sudan alone, brothers, is feeding with its bounties and waters all people of the Arab World for the coming wars are wars over water.

"As for liberation battles, nothing would be better than the approach of Vietnamese people's resistance to attain Arab rights , not with military power because of the advanced technology that enemies surrounding us from all over the world are using, while we are militarily powerless!" The Sudanese man did not finish his talk for three men came and led him to an unknown place. And when I inquired about him the next day, they told me they deported him and he didn't return!

***

Titi told you all family secrets. She didn't know that secrets should not be exposed outside family. This time she visited you telling you new information in the form of an embarrassing scandal, "I want to tell you a secret!"

And you didn't mind hearing secrets."Tell me! "So, she told you, "My father sleeps with my mother every Tuesday!" You felt shy, but you listened!

"You witch! How did you know that?"

"When we were kids– I and my sister Nousa,–my father used to rent three rooms to students and in the fourth room we all sleep together."

"Did your father own this apartment the time he owned the villa of Abu Kir Beach?"

"He had bought it and furnished it himself to be seclusion for him where he stayed with his friends and girlfriends. This is what I heard from my mother once as she was very angry at him. She said to him, ' I was doomed to get involved with you in this damned

~ 196 ~

apartment! Were it not for my plight, I would not accept to marry a bad man like you!' I told my mother, 'What was your plight mum?' She rebuked me saying 'Shut up!' So, I shut up. But after that I understood everything."

But Titi uncovering the secret stirred your curiosity, so you asked her, "And how did you know that they were sleeping with each other on Tuesday not on Thursday for example as the song of Shadya says, 'Do you know that every Thursday…?'"

She smiled shyly, saying, "As the eldest daughter, I was spying on them to understand what was going on under the blankets."

She turned her head with shyness, bit her full lower lip, and then said, "One night, I woke up because I heard strange sounds! I heard him panting and moaning loud. I thought in the beginning that they were fighting in bed, but my mother was asking for more! I woke up, but kept eavesdropping over them feigning sleep!

"I did not understand the details of what happened that night, so the next day I mentioned that to my friend Nouha. She said, 'Let us ask my aunt's eldest daughter Sousou. She is in high school and knows everything.' We asked her and she laughed. She explained to us everything and told us an obscene joke saying, 'One night, I asked my mother, 'How did you bring me into the world?' My mother said, 'We bought a melon, cut it, and found you inside of it, so we took you out, and I breastfed you and took care of you until you grew up. And here you are as you can see!' I asked my mother laughing ironically, 'Why was all that trouble for? Wasn't … known in those days?' My mother blushed and asked me to leave carrying a kitchen broom to beat me with it.'"

Titi laughed and proceeded to say, "Since then, I started to stay up every Tuesday. I rather feigned sleeping and paid full attention to any move coming from them. And almost at midnight, whispers, groans and give and take started that the hair of my flesh stood up, and my neck stretched to hear what's going on there, honey! I used to see my mother as a symbol of innocence and shyness, but I was shocked at her having this soul loving... And this is what made me sexually mature before my other classmates.

"In the beginning, I started to look for sexual information, tried to read medical magazines, talked to female students older than me about it, and then asked old women. And upon my inquiry, one day, one of them tried to tempt me to see an open operation of this kind. I was frightened when I knew that she was a whore and wanted to get me involved with her. I refused and ran back home!"

All this crossed your mind. "If Burhan and Albina had followed the way of watermelon to produce their green son Canaan, their way would have been gentler than his coming out of a merciless experiment tube," you said to yourself mockingly.

BAHRI GIRLS

The cultural committee of university students had invited poet Ahmed Fouad Najm and singer Sheikh Imam to a concert held in the college theatre that was called during daytime "auditorium number one, but the concert was canceled few minutes before it started. They said that the cancellation was due to security reasons. In retaliation for cancellation, Souhir Elmahalwi, an activist, quoted poet Ahmed Fouad Najm, saying, "What is this government and security that fears a blind man who walks on the side of the road leaning on whoever backs him? Was it to this extent government armed with... feared those poor who could not find the bread of their day? Is our government too weak to this point that a man suffering from anemia could turn it upside down, toppled it, and then sat on the sidewalk, sniffing himself?"

Still, the cultural committee did not yield, and Souhir El-Mahalawi, Fayza Rashid, Abdel Massih Atta Allah together with Noha..., I can't remember her family name, organized a concert that was held in Egypt Café opposite train station. We went there, I, Mohammad Mohammad and of course friends, and in the café whose most chairs were on the sidewalk , many people gathered with no enough space available for them. There, poet Ahmed Fouad Najm stood reciting his beautiful Alexandrian poem,

Alexandria, El –Mahrousa…

The fishermen and fish of Marsa,

Wherever you go, you bump into people...

O Mursy, give something for the sake of God, O Abu Al-Abbas,

People from Upper Egypt and people from Bahri,

With the heart looking upon Bahri

Melting in the charm of girls from Bahri..

And love under a parasol,

O how beautiful you are, Alexandria!

People are in and outside the sea,

In Alexandria are the wonders of towns and the coastal city, O Abu Alexandar,

In it, there are quarters in Almaskin and a paradise in Ras El Tin,

In the afternoon she is a tilapia fish and the forenoon, soft and playful,

And the night is your groom, O bride,

Life is a jungle and a park!

And upon the ending of the wonderful poem, the audience was agitated and excited, whistling and cheering. One of them cried out," O great Ahmed!" Hence the big crowd was encouraged and cried at once saying, "Look what Najem can do! Look what Najem can do!"

And before the end of the stunning Alexandrian poem, they had brought "the blind" man who resembled the dean of Arab literature, walking leaned with his thin hand on the shoulder of one of the committee's young men, accompanied with a thin flutist wearing local dress, a drummer, as big as a mule, and an innocent boy who seemed to be the violinist. They sat him down on a wicker chair like that of Umm Khalthoum. Once the noise had calmed down, the singer stood with his companions and sang out Guevara 's song, while the audience was clapping and repeating after him like a choir,

The latest breaking news on the radio!

In churches, streets, and bars! Guevara died,

And the thread of chat and comments has been extended!

The ideal hero died! O it's a big loss to men!

The hero died atop his cannon in the woods!

With no fawners cheering or advertisements!

Guevara died like a man!

O swanky, O polished, O old-fashioned!

The people's singer did not finish his song for a bunch of guards of honor approached him. I'm sorry I mean security men, and took the man with his band and the poet to an unknown place! The crowd burst into mixed feelings.

The next day you stood nearby several male and female students who were the nucleus of 68 demonstrations gathering around the student activist Souhir El-Mahalawi. This asked her and that commented while she was answering," They were put in a prison camp."Another asked her," Why were they arrested? You heard the answer, "Things are going suspiciously!" A third person would cry out, "It seems that something was going on behind scenes" And a tenth person would scream enraged," We don't know what crime they had committed!"

This committee composed of ten students of both sex did not quit national social activity for at the beginning of the first semester after the defeat, the student Fayza Rashid stood in front of students crowded at the door of amphitheater number one and took off a simple gold necklace that was in her chest and said, "No more ornaments for us unless our dignity returns victorious."

They all said in one voice: "We'll fight.. We'll fight…We'll fight!"

Faiza Rashid finished her speech by asking all girls loving their countries to take off their rings, bracelets, and gold necklaces to be confiscated and registered accurately by competent witnesses from the national student committee and to donate their price to the wounded and the injured in the battles of June 67.

Souhir El-Mahalawi urged the committee to go out to the markets, shops, mosques, churches, and every place to raise money under the supervision of the committee to be given later to the men of Egyptian resistance who were running the war of attrition.

You noticed that the girls of the university were tougher than men in the congregation and civil mobilization in the aftermath of the defeat as female students proceeded to support the war of attrition, motivate and mobilize for another inevitable war that was on the horizon.

Hence you saw them standing in hundreds at the forefront of 68 protests shouting inside the university campus and the streets, "We're going to fight. We're going to fight. We're going to fight. We're going to fight!"

Three Palestinians and a Transjordanian student convened in the cafeteria of engineering university and decided to go back to the Jordanian Palestinian valleys to join the resistance. A year after their absence, you heard that they led the Fedayeen resistance with the support of the brave Jordanian army, invaded the enemy, and won the battle of Karameh.

You and Mohamed discussed the issue of volunteering in the resistance as he told you," Volunteering in the battle could not be arbitrary. Everything has its own time, and the time of the battle is after our graduation. Today we focus on our study and tomorrow we will go to war!" And truly —what a pity for his mother—the hero Mohammad Mohammad was martyred in the battle of liberation that hadn't ended yet!

ARABS ARE EGYPTIANS!

O idiot, you spent five university years without going into a bar or a night club! And after all these university ages you asked Abu Gerges, "How does a night club look like from inside? What are they doing there?"

The man of medium height like the imported wooden barrel of Fisikh would tell you as he was putting his hands in the pockets of the shirt of his blue and white striped cotton pajamas that he did not change inside his home, maybe to make you feel he was tall, "I can't believe that you are still naive at this age and you haven't entered a night club or a bar yet ! Go brother to the night club and sit there and thus you see everything in it. The story is over!"

You felt ashamed of yourself for this ignorance, so you answered him shrinking, "But I don't drink alcohol, Abu Gerges. So, what shall I tell him if the Waiter comes and asks me?" The deceased man laughed, saying mockingly, "What shall I say if he comes and asks me? By God, I mistook you for Najet Asaghira! Tell him I want a fizzy drink and he would bring you a fizzy drink! Enjoy it, watch happily and go home safe! The story is over!"

Abu Gerges was moody and drunken. At one night, I and Mohammad heard a naughty voice coming from the kitchen, so we entered. On his table, there was an empty bottle on which written Cognac for which he was singing:

"Bring me the bottle,

And sat to entertain me,

This beautiful is fresh,

And I'm happy!

Bring me the bottle, son of a bitch!"

The late Abu Gerges was a funny humorist and a clown with a loud voice that compensated for his medium height!

We sat with him in the kitchen and felt that the man was drunk as he was listening to the news bulletin of Voice of the Arabs that announced the suicide of the Field Marshal in a mysterious way! He looked at us and laughed a lot, and then told us a joke,

"When the funeral of the field marshal reach the cemetery," – he interrupted it with a resounding laughter; he did not interrupt the funeral but rather the silly joke with the usual laughter of Said Ishta - "when the funeral of the field marshal reach the cemetery, the dead would rise from their graves to greet and welcome the chief and all would cry cheering,

We want but Jamel!

We want but Jamel!

You were surprised at this spiteful joke, so we didn't laugh but rather felt humiliated and disgusted! The man broke loose bubbling over with his usual viewpoint!

You sat watching for you were at the age of receiving not theorizing, and you were not in the position of accepting or objecting either. Also, you were living in the house of the man, hence you could not argue with him in public. The Arab ruler is a dictator, and so is the Arab citizen. Abu Gerges was a dictator and as they said at university the doctor is a dictator! But Mohammad Mohammad did not care about this and that, hence the gentleman engaged wholly in discussing and arguing with him ardently, telling him, "If Abdel Nasser had lived for himself, he would have acted differently at the end of the fifties when the American administration paid him three million dollars to spend secretly on his security. He instead put the amount of money in the hands of people council as it was and suggested building Cairo Tower as a symbol of national dignity." –his voice tone rose as he was attacking the landlord–"One of man's achievements is nationalizing the Suez Canal that would achieve the strategic center for Egypt and realize billions of dollars yearly for the benefit of the treasure and billions of guineas as revenues of Egyptian employment and trade linked to the canal."

Abu Gerges hit the empty bottle against the table saying, "The decision of nationalizing the canal was one of the most senseless actions that we are familiar with!"

"How could we then liberate our canal from the claws of colonization that is seizing control of the heart of Egypt?" Mohammad asked him.

The man answered him insistently, "Security Council, international legitimacy, and the decisions of United Unions are the sole route."

"Now I understand the statement of actor Tawifik Adaan ,'Hello nations! ' He meant the United Nations?! Palestine has been occupied since 1948 and all decisions of the United Nations were futile. It was rather the decisions of the United Nations that created the Zionist entity and acknowledged it as a state, and the more the occupation extends the more the United Nations support the colonizers! Honestly, you're defending the bygone epoch, Abu Gerges!"

"I'm not defending the epoch of Said Khedive or Ismail Khedive" –Abu Gerges laughed with his hands inside the pockets of his white striped pajamas– "and I've never meant to be prejudiced against Jamel Abdel Nasser Khedive. I'm just saying that they are all

Khedives. The difference is that is a civil Khedive and this is a military Khedive, but the civil Khedive is less harmful than the military one! Abdel Nasser would tell you, "Arabism and what will explain to you what Arabism is? What does Arabism have to do with us? We are pharaohs and not Arabs!", he said mockingly.

"If our mother Hajer, who traveled forth and back from Safa and Marwa and we still travel froth and back like her, is Egyptian, and if Ismail, the son of Egyptians, is the father of Arabs , then all Arab Egyptian women 's children are Egyptian or to put it more accurately, all Egyptians are all Arabs. Say it as you like!"

Abu Gerges was surprised by this piece of information, so he fell silent defeated while Mohammad pulled you saying, "It seems that the man doesn't only rent his two rooms, but also rents his brain to the devil"

He took you inside our rooms, saying, "The man is hallucinating. If Abdel Nasser built public housing for farmers, they would say, 'The agricultural lands were violated." and if he built factories they would say, 'He destroyed the environment.' And here it is the West ruining the entire universe with its scary factories' fumes and chemical wastes and no one could object! Egyptian cotton and wool, Mashhour, used to go to Britain almost for free in return for Britain protecting the security of Egypt as if we could not protect our country knowing that the fox is guarding the hen–house! And the protection was only for a limited number of seigneurs who were actively serving the colonizer to plunder the riches of the country. Today our giant factories started to manufacture our Egyptian products and export. Our religion at Al-Azahar University has become under the guidance of Abdel Nasser - whom they shot in Al-Man's hiya - the religion of science, work, literature, and arts. World students from Indonesia, Malaysia, and the Philippines would learn the principles of religion and all modern sciences there. The high dam generated electricity and thus we connected it to all Egypt factories and villages that were watching Aladdin's lamp, so Egyptian man would say to Egyptian, "Light be upon you! Hence there was no more darkness in rural areas for thieves and bandits! As for corruption and nepotism stretching in the dark, they are worldwide for there are thieves in all countries, and Abdel Nasser could not sterilize the country all alone!"

Mohammad said this, and then drew Al-Ahram paper from his books and went back to the kitchen. You followed him to prevent the eruption of a personal fight. You saw him saying to Abu Gerges, "Read what media is publishing about the effect of Abdel Nasser that you don't like." he read when Abu Gerges didn't want to, "Because of attrition war, New York Harbor's workers were refusing to empty the Egyptian ship, Cleopatra, under the pressure of Zionist lobby…in response to the boycott, Abdel Nasser asked Arab workers to not empty any American ships in Arab harbors…the workers in Arab harbors obeyed the president, so the American army was forced to empty immediately the cargo of Cleopatra ship in New York Harbor!

"That's the leader who shook the world with his speech!" Mohammad cried out angrily." Not the demonstrations of the dead that you are dreaming about, you alone!"

"Come Mohammad!"–you dragged him out of the kitchen–"the man is drunk, and your blood is boiling in this ferocious defense of you!"

"These are interests, buddy," he answered you confidently, "I'm the child of an electricity worker defending my working interests while Abu Gerges has his own interests in the return of feudal and colonizer, so we would borrow with billions of dollars cola drinks and burger meat and forget yummy Mango juice, delicious sugarcane, and pink veal! They want to drown us in their food and drinks that deteriorate health and government budget!"

O Alexandrians, here comes today the green peaceful generation of Canaan that doesn't drink cola or eat a burger and not even pink veal! If the experiment of Canaan succeeds, colonization will collapse in the entire world and stop plundering the riches! This idea of greening is amazing! I am astounded at this idea of the green animal!

***

The next day after interest battle, Titi came to you seizing the opportunity of the fact that there was no one in the house and you were the only one practicing regularly your engineering drawings. Even Mohammad was wandering about or going regularly to El-Damanhouri Restaurant. She interrupted your seclusion to find you indifferent to love and childishness, though you, wicked, desired her presence, so you got ready to welcome her. She approached you and you met her with open arms. You inhaled her flaming orgy feminine breaths that you stepped out of the earthly world toward that of numbness. You sucked her flowers' nectar that you couldn't compare that desire running through your body to honey or to whatever life pleasures God has bestowed upon Man!

Here was Titi, an angel visiting you in your waking dreams. She mingled with you, melted her soft body with its overwhelming ecstasy into your arms, and sucked from you what drove you crazy. She unveiled all her charms and treasures to you as she was hugging you. Then you imagined your grandmother Aneesa in front of you repeating her statements "The path of girls is thorny." So, you pulled away, but Titi pulled you toward her with her nails, crying out, "Get closer to me, coward, get closer to me, rascal!"

You knew that you were not a coward or a rascal but rather a man of principles! It seemed that your grandmother Aneesa could uproot from you the fattiness of your sexual desire, and therefore you grew up as a man compressed with sex, but suspended! Still, Titi did not let you think and made you forget your grandmother and all your family. Hence your bodies changed into two forms of energy and disappeared from the universe.

THE BREAD WE BROKE WITH EACH OTHER

Your leaving Alexandria didn't differ from Adam going out of heaven after which Adam suffered from a chaos of senses or blurring in vision or psychological complexes. And this happened to you that you couldn't handle yourself. Your first goal after the setback was to return to your folk in Palestine that became all colonized. But returning to it became forbidden with the power of weapon!

"God's chosen people" allowed Palestinians to go out of heaven, but returning to it was forbidden! So, your temporary concern was to find a job opportunity to provide for yourself while Mohammad Mohammad went to recruitment and war of attrition. He and his comrades were involved in getting ready to breach the Bar-Lev Line. Jamal Abdel Nasser died mysteriously. Then those gloating over his death rushed to look for his savings, but found nothing in his fridge but one kilogram of veal…

Canaan's green generation that objects to the consumption of veal hadn't come yet and if you had generalized the idea of Cannan that time, his widow (Mrs. Tahiya Khathem) wouldn't have even found a kilogram of veal in her wounded house…They looked in all Egyptian and Arab banks, but they did not find any bank account in his name. All his accounts were in the pockets of poor and oppressed Egyptian people. And these in their infinite roles gave up all his accounts and good deeds to his afterlife ("The Day whereon neither wealth nor sons will avail, "But only he (will prosper) that brings to Allah a sound heart!)

All the oppressed in the Arab world wept over him and Nixon ordered to halt the training of the sixth fleet in the Mediterranean Sea saying that there was no need for training after the death of Nasser.

Your brother applied for an entry visa for you to enter Dubai. Then you entered it and worked as an engineer in its municipality and from there you and one of the citizens agreed to open a common engineering office for construction.

And because of bread, you broke with him and Feteer Misheltit, and because of your becoming a business owner, you decided to make engineer Mohammad Mohammad a partner in your civil projects for, after the clearance of dust of war 1973 that dimmed visions, you noticed that you didn't hear any news about him anymore, so you tried to contact him to be surprised at him being martyred in the battle of crossing! You were shocked by the news that you cut your ties with Alexandria, Al-Mansoura , and everything in them!

You started to attract hundreds of Egyptian qualified engineers to your construction projects, provide them with job opportunities, and sympathize with them. It seemed that you were grateful for the halva, still remembering its taste!

After ten years of rupture, you never gave up thinking about returning the favor and it crossed your mind to call the house of Abu Georges. You had forgotten their number, so you asked from Alexandria directory enquiries the phone number of Markes Georges Mitri living in Cleopatra Hammamat. You called the number and it was the voice of Umm Gerges who was surprised by your call. After greeting, longings, and informing her about your life, you asked her how life was treating her and how Abu Gerges, Gerges, Teati and Nousa were doing.

"Our situation would not please a friend." She cried on the phone, telling you, "Abu Gerges died five years ago! And I took the responsibility after his death, so we rented the three rooms to live from their revenues. Titi spent five years in France. She worked there and came back a year ago. Nousa works as a music teacher. Gerges is a student at engineering university. And the situation is the way God planned! "

You were shocked at the death news of the man, so you offered her your condolence on his death even if it was late," May God have mercy upon him. Who's there at this moment with you to talk to?

She answered, "I have Titi. Here is she. Talk to her." You talked to Titi and thus she stirred sorrows of your memory as she was saying, "How come that we crossed your mind after ages, Mashhour?"

You answered her, eager to hear her voice, "You were not absent from my mind Titi to remember you once again."

You told her about your works in Dubai and did not ask her if she got married, because if she did, she would have mentioned that to you or talked about her husband children but it seemed that she was.. You asked her, "Do you work, Titi? Or let me ask you how do you spend these days?

She answered you frustrated," I work as a secretary in a French office. "

You could not forget the fact that you were married when talking to her, but you asked her about the specialty of Gerges in engineering, the main concern of your phone call, so she answered you with the eagerness of someone who was chasing a job opportunity for him, "Like you, Gorges specializes in civil engineering, and he will graduate this summer. He's polite, well-mannered and kind. He deserves from you all attention! I know your personality Mashhour, I mean Bash muhandis Mashhour." It seem that her mother standing next to her bucked her for calling your name without the expression" Bashmohandes", so she corrected herself and proceeded to say, "Gerges would be the best assistant if you find him a work contract in Emirates."

"That's great! I suggest that you and your mother should find out how much he is eager to immigrate to Dubai to work with me in my civil engineering projects?"

Bubbled with happiness, she said enthusiastically," You became a top-class contractor, O chief engineer! May God protect you!"

"My personality has changed, Titi, for I became a professional man"–you told her laughing–" but I'm still naive in matters of love as you know me!"

Indeed you arranged for him a work visa and welcomed him with open arms at Dubai airport.

"By God, you grow up dear Georges and became an engineer, the best of engineers!"

"That's thanks to you, Bashmohandes Mashhour," he answered you with extreme politeness.

"Please call me by my profession, engineer Mashhour, without this pasha for I'm not a pasha. Besides, Abdel Nasser may God bless him put an end to the age of pashas!"

"But the title of pasha is back now worse than it used to be in the time of King Farouk!" Gerges answered laughing, "After it was confined to pashas, now the security policeman becomes a pasha, and so do the plumber and the sugarcane juice seller. The title of Pasha is everywhere! Anyway, I am at your disposal, Bashmohandes."

You took him to your house and straight away you found him an annex in a calm remote house consisting of a room with a hall and its house wares isolated from neighbors in that its door opened from outside. You included him in your work cadre, trained him, supervised, and gave him the opportunity for drawing, working, and monitoring.

Indeed, Gerges became the right engineer in the right place and could be your assistant and your right arm at work. Then he moved to a better lodging to welcome his new bride.

After many years, the respectable man didn't hide from you the fact that he gained back the fifty acres his father once sold by purchasing them and that he filed a lawsuit to restore the fifty acres that the country nationalized and gave to farmers, and thus he restored them. He told you that during the last juridical stages of restoring the confiscated villa in Abu Kir, he was surprised at gaining back what his father had lost.

And after his wife had given birth to his two sons and two girls, he left you and returned to where he came from mentioning to you that he would restore American cars agency that had been nationalized and confiscated from his father.

GUESS WHAT IS IT?

Here Canaan come with his father from the basement of the hospital...the green boy jumps over you, gives you a hug and kisses your face elated with his accomplishments, while Burhan brings you the good news about the success of examinations. We embrace each other and shout rejoicing over the result that Burhan had predicted.

And what makes you more astonished is seeing a green girl with her transparent clothes like Canaan, holding a beautiful cat with green fur and eyes. It seems that she comes out of their genetic laboratories. She is standing next to a serious woman with European countenance. Burhan takes notice of that and says, "I introduce you to German woman Elza and her daughter Monica who came with the green group undergoing medical examinations in Shanghai Hospital like Canaan."

You notice how hospitable Canaan is toward his girlfriend Monica with green grass hair cascading like a green pony tail on her naked back. Burhan tells you that a large group of green boys and girls came together to be examined in this International Hospital and then would go on a tour around the beautiful Alexandria. Like us, they are staying at Guangzhou Hotel, and thus he would have friends and companions in Alexandria with whom he could spend his time having fun and learning about culture.

We go out from hospital together and you are thinking of giving a party to celebrate his cheerful health results. Canaan takes your permission to invite his girlfriend Monica and her mother to the party and you consent. You know that the Europeans are bewitched by the landmarks of the East.

It's a chance to visit tourist Cleopatra that the sea had swollen that tourists had to dive to look for it in bottom.

You notice that the time is evening, so you say, "What about going on an amazing tour tomorrow?" They rejoice and say yes.

In this happy evening hotel in which the walls of skyscrapers are glowing with luminous light that the reinforced fish paper stored from the sun all day long, and then release to the city all night turning the night of Alexandria to a day, and thus there is no room for darkness to dwell, so it leaves rejected to the quarters of poor areas whose traditional houses are still dark and blind even in the middle of the day.

You press button two on the portable device and the restaurant manager answers you that today's dinner is seafood. You inform Burhan about that and then take him out together with the German Eliza to dinner while the two kids Canaan and his friend Monica are playing together in the room of the two Germans.

This restaurant is occupying a whole floor of the hotel. You can say it is a city of seafood and not like the orphaned bluefish of Abu Gerges. Here, you see all that souls crave. But in front of this luscious German woman, you don't feel like eating for a human being even when growing old, sex remains his third moving force toward creativity, activity and healthy thinking.

The host takes you to the seafood displayed and says to you," This caviar is good for... and this is Salmon. It is a source of Omega 3 preventing oxidation and this and this. There are thousands of types and types of seafood dishes, this is smoky and this is grilled, this is fried, this is cooked, this is boiled and this is Fesikh, varied in its kinds, ingredients, and oil. This is eaten uncooked, so pick what pleases you."

They eat their plates, but you don't feel like eating. You lost your appetite unlike your open appetite in front of the grilled bluefish in the kitchen of Abu Gerges.

You think about your being alone like an uprooted tree, with no wife soothing your loneliness! You feel useless and hopeless at this age as you cannot marry. The sad thing is your being on the edge of a hole... as the actor, Abdel Warith Ossr said, "One would be able to know everything only upon graduation!

Burhan and Elza are eating avidly, while you are bringing in your imagination all these experiences, and life is nothing but a series of experiences and thus it leads you to a total conviction that time is over and the time guardian tells you in the same way as the phone operator tells you, "You have one minute to end this call." You, expired old man, have one station. So let's take you to your last station in Akka!

In the restaurant, you announce your decision to Burhan like this at once, "I'm going back to Akka, Borhan! There, I can live in the bosom of the family of your sister Samar and spend a pleasant time in the parts of the homeland with my grandchildren who are now active men, great traders, and professionals in Akka.

The reassuring thing is that my extension now in Palestine yielded more than twenty-four gold carats. I mean fourteen boys and girls if I counted the grandchildren of my daughter Samar, and there, I can travel with them every holiday to Haifa or Jaffa or Al-Qudus or Gaza, and from Upper Galilee Mountain, Rosh Hanikra and Hadar Hacarmel, we can watch the sun coming down and plunging into the sea. I will play again with my children exactly as my grandfather and grandmother used to play with us in our old childhood days and ask them to solve the riddle of my grandma Aneesa she used to ask us about as she was playing with us (Make a guess! In the sea, she is a diver. Her inner is made of gold and outer is made of lead! What is it?), and one of them would tell me as I used to tell her, 'The sun!' We all would laugh, then! You know I grew tired of life expenses, Burhan.

I want to take a rest and to relieve others."

Burhan and Elza, who cannot understand your Arabic language, look at you and he is midway between happiness and sadness, but he does not comment on your feelings as you are talking to him about the duty of return rather than the right to return to it!

In the morning of the third day, we leave early for a walk in the yards that the Chinese industrial complex bought, destroyed it, and then rebuilt in its special way in that Safiya Zaghloul was cleared, and Saad Zaghloul was wiped from the ground and they got rid of their parts. Some buildings were destroyed, and thus the sea of El Raml Station open onto the famous Romanian auditorium which was agreed to be given for free to remain a witness to the age.

We, the three, walk together with the two greens. Canaan and Monica walk behind us with the arm of each surrounding the neck of the other... You tell Burhan the story of Cleopatra with Caesar Antonio who colonized her country and made love to her in Alexandria. Then he translates it into Elza's language.

We reach the Romanian auditorium that resisted being cleared by globalization and went on an excursion to the Chinese city of commercial shows, adjoining bars and movie homes. In this region, they set up theaters and opera house next to Said Darwish Theater that stayed alive, the glorious history of which was displayed by the pictures of Yusuf Wahbi, the dean of Arab theater, in his wonderful plays with Amina Rizk and even the childish gestures of Safa Abu Asououd in musical performances and others.

In the cultural room of Yusuf Wahbi, a large computer screen on the wall displays his beautiful old plays when he was standing talking to Amina Rizk with his polished harsh voice. "Oh, my God, you let me down. O Amina!"

She answers him shocked with her hand on her chest, "Me! I'm a dead loss! No, by God! It even...!"

And in the open space, we see giant theme park games for grown-ups and children similar to Disney games but in a modern Chinese way, the large yards of which were surrounded by modern glass towers buildings designated for businessmen crowned by skyscrapers with the twin Chinese towers (Tianjin) that look like two infinite rockets penetrating the sky.

We go sightseeing and we see commercial malls, administrative offices, cafés, amusement parks, entertainments rooms, financial markets, and intercontinental firms. A big Chinese commercial industrial foyer extends on a large space on the east side the street that was once the street of Saad Zaghloul, and when we are passing through the crowded yards, we see a display of models for international Chinese projects to market their civilization.

In the meantime, a guy who snatches an old woman's handbag in the public square draws our attention. The old woman is walking holding the arm of a robot as if she leaned against him.

The robot walking next to her, was telling her things seemed to be funny jokes for the old woman was giggling silently raising her head to the sky as stretching her other arm carrying her bag far, laughing. And as the robot was busy cheering the one hundred-year-old woman up whose appearance shows that she is rich, the thief jumped all of a sudden, snatched the bag of the embalmed woman to a moving form, and launched running away in the square.

The robot releases the arm of his old companion and launches behind the thief as fast as the flash... And after chasings between hydrogen-powered cars, under air vehicles that were proceeding silently above and between buildings, jumping over walls and running through barriers the robot catches the thief...

We stand stunned as we see the thief turning back shrank with the robot to the old woman in the same way as a rabbit shrinks between the claws of a wild eagle, while the robot is nailing his claws in the nerves of the thief's wrist. The wrist is dripping blood and the thief is crying loud in pain which halts the movement of all who are in the luminous square. Police proceed forward, put handcuffs around the wrists of the thief and arrest him. Afterward they accompany them somewhere–it might be the police station– and then they disappear out of sight.

The walk continues. You say to Burhan, "In the olden days, here in the tram station, we used to arrive by tram coming from Cleopatra Region. We watched the displayed goods of the Street of Safia Zaghloul starting from books of Almaraef House till we reached Brazilian coffee beans. We sat and ordered Turkish coffee. I used to prefer yellow, so the old brown barista Abdu Assaidi would grind the Brazilian coffee beans for us. He took them from his large cylindrical roaster as if there was a ton of beans in it as it was whirling in front of us giving off its fogy smoky scent that filled noses with its delicious smell that my friend the martyr Mohammad would say, 'We call the one who enjoys smelling the scent a sniffer.' I answered him, ' Now I understand the origin of the word 'ala al–riha' because a gourmet drinks the scent!'

"A lot of nonsense was filling our time as we were sitting watching this beautiful woman coming in and this old man, whose black hair dye exposed that white layer growing under the ash, acting younger than his age leaning against the barrier, along with that effeminate beetle and that arrogant guy who was watching with eagle eyes two girls sitting with total innocence and modesty!

"And before the Upper Egyptian man had ground the coffee beans, he asked us, "With cardamom or without?" And we both ordered coffee without cardamom. The Upper Egyptian expert on coffee would say then," It seems that both of you are connoisseurs of coffee and a coffee connoisseur doesn't accept to mix it with cardamom!" He took a yellow-reddish copper coffee pot in the size of a coffee cup and we watched him filling it with water, and then putting it on fire. He asked us," With a lot of sugar, with a little bit of sugar or black?" So, I answered him with all respect and appreciation for his precision, 'Medium sugar.' Mohammad told him, "Tahiya Carioca said, 'Safety lies in the middle course!'"

The old man laughed and served it us, saying, 'A coffee made specifically for gentlemen!' We felt comfortable with his loving way of getting along with customers. We drank it and the coffee smell was cheering our chests up. Mohammad asked me surprised, 'Why is that Brazilian coffee beans are very common here not the Adenese coffee beans?" I answered him feeling unhappy about the Arab humiliation, 'Because the land area of the country of Marab Dam is sufficient only for growing khat that makes them feel high and forget to think about life as a whole!'

"We stepped out from the Brazilian coffee beans, and wandered for a while in the street of Safiya Zaghloul, looked at the last exhibits of shoes and clothes from behind the window of commercial shops, just looking because none of us owned the price of a pair of shoes to buy. And what's wrong with the shoes we were wearing? It was true they were not perfect but they were still walking on the ground!"

Burhan listens to your story silently as if he recorded these documents as a kind of oral chronicling. You seize the opportunity that someone is listening and recording and you say, "We didn't have TV those days. Cinema was the solution to learn about what was going on in the world of thoughts and arts and enjoy its data. For this reason, I and Mohammed Mohammed tended to explore the new week cinema, so we arrived at Plaza Movie Theatre, then Metro, and after it, Amir and we did not forget to stop by Rivoli Movie Theatre and that of Rialto that were all in these squares that...while the philosopher Mohammad was telling you a silly joke.

"We laughed at anything. We just laughed. They were youth days when we laughed at anything, Burhan. But today my face doesn't smile even at a hot loaf of bread. That's because the acidity of my old body prevents me from eating bread!

We went and roamed the streets as we were singing tasteless and meaningless songs of crazy people loud together teasing the melodies of the Said Darwish, the people's artist. So we said instead of "My country, my country, my country",

Plaza, Plaza, Plaza,

In you there is a very sweet movie,

Plaza, you're the best of cinemas,

in you, I found my goal and my quest,

And toward Metro, turn, so stay safe, O plaza!

And on the way to Metro movie theatre, Mohammad Mohammad told me, "In spite of victory, the Yemen War exhausted us, Mashhour. The flow of oil in Arabia Pennsylvania made the west support powers protecting the flow of cheap oil toward it, and this in return enflamed the jealousy of the Arab liberation movements that arose in the gulf to stand against plundering the oil riches of the Arab nation. And this is what made Abdel Nasser support the liberation movement there. But as you can see, the danger overtook us as we were moving from Yemen to Sinai toward Palestine with a victorious army, but it is tired at least because of dense moving from one country to another. And without any advanced strategic planning, it seemed that we were being dragged forcefully to an expected, ill-timed war! And here we are calling for withdrawing the international forces from the strait of Tiran, which means war with the Zionist entity. And after fifty-six, comes sixty-seven, ten years of quick successes. Would we end up with the great victory, the victory over Israel? The last adventure scares the hell out of me! I'm so scared, Mashhour! And this field Marshal…

"Could you imagine that during the Falklands War between Argentine and Britain in 1982, I remembered the words of the martyr Mohammad Mohammad, Burhan ? I imagined while I was back then in Dubai that if the battle of the Suez Canal occurred in the days of

Thatcher, Britain would eat Egypt with its teeth. How would Britain, that didn't give in an inch of Gibraltar to the Spanish or to the Moroccans and that denied Argentina the Falkland Islands, allow the heart of Arabism to seize control of strategic Suez Canal?"

We take notice that we isolated ourselves from our guest Eliza through our conversation, so we apologize from her, and Burhan translates it into her language, but the woman doesn't show any distress about that, but rather smiles, saying "I'm enjoying watching these beautiful Alexandria landmarks."

THE SEA IS DEVOURING ALEXANDRIA LIBRARY!

We are approaching Qaitbay Citadel that looks small like a dot next to the tower of the lighthouse of Alexandria, the skyscraper. At the thresh of the gate of Cleopatra City sparkling underwater, Canaan progresses toward us, saying, "What about going to the tower of the lighthouse, while I and Monica go with green friends –who gather there – to the sinking Cleopatra city?

You wait to hear the opinion of Burhan, who doesn't object to his request regardless of the tight supervision over his green son and thorough care he receives. He whispers to you," It seems that all members of the green team coming from the green city in Hessen had planned with their associate teacher a group trip to the drowning city of the last Pharaohs, so it is natural that they get to know each other and go for a walk and thus enjoying their luxurious life."

We reach the gate of Cleopatra Beach being recently opened in the Eastern Harbor. We pay entrance fees and you go with Burhan and Elza to see the landmarks of the highest skyscraper in the world crowned with Alexandria lighthouse that has been recently lately, so that its construction stones would appear similar to the old ones though they are artificial Chinese fibers both very strong and light to be carried by a building hung in the sky.

"In 297 Ptolemy II built an immense tower for the lighthouse in this place," the tourist guide tells the tourists gathering around him, "And its reaching a height of one hundred and twenty meters made it one of the Seven Wonders of the World. And now the tower was rebuilt, so that the beacon of Alexandria would be at its summit but of standard height." The tourist guide laughs, saying," And as you can see, the Chinese firm had rebuilt the monument of Cleopatra City to be the only drowning city in the world, and then bought the franchise administration."

We climb the ancient spiral staircase that is enclosing the beacon to the second floor on foot to feel the scent of history. The guide says, "As you can see the tourist ascent and descent between the first and second floor from the beacon is done through an outer spiral staircase exactly as in the past, but now the Chinese firm designed the tower in an advanced and modern way after they had become experts in building the highest towers in the world."

We ride the elevator with a group of tourists to the restaurant situated on the top of the beacon on the one –hundred–and–fifth floor that we can see the Montazah Palace, Al Mamura, and Abu Kir from the east and even El Alamein and tourist Qattara Depression from the west. The entire world around you is sparkling and bathing on the azure beach that made you feel as if you were in a spaceship launching high in the sky and the lantern, the source of light in the lighthouse is fixed on the top, and therefore we see a giant mirror reflecting the beam allowing faraway ships to reach their destination safely.

We sit at the revolving restaurant in the summit of the lighthouse tower to have some sandwiches and warm drinks. We see water flooding Corniche Street and the sea proceeding to eat Alexandria library that was rebuilt at the end of the twentieth century. Hence, Elza says regretting the loss of this planet from our hands, "They are killing the earth and what upon it like someone who is smoking avidly to kill his lungs that give him life oxygen! They don't deserve this amazing planet with its wonders, complementarily, tenderness, and affection toward its living beings!" She eats her sandwich and adds with extreme agitation reflected through her nervous eyes and brows, " I'm sad because world forests and freshwater have been witnessing a scary decrease. The icebergs of the arctic are drowning in the waters of oceans. Plants are disappearing due to the excess of demographic expansion and what is more disastrous is using it as biofuel."

Burhan supports her by saying," And here comes the genetic engineering to solve the problem of the universe and that is by producing the green animal that doesn't violate nature."

"I am worried that our green children," –Eliza shivers– "whom we produced from our flesh and blood would be destroyed by the greed of capital because the commercial genetic engineering opposing you, is posing threats that might be more appalling than the law of the jungle."

After Burhan translated what the lady said, you say backing her up, "If the genes of the genetic makeup of conventional people are fixed without a radical change of the natural human traits that would be better!"

Elza says," And for this reason, we need a collective action to bridle the craziness of companies and hamper the craziness of extracting biofuel from plants that will eradicate the last source of freshwater, damage the inventory of plants and spread hunger in every place where crops being cultivated are not designated for hungry mouths."

CLEOPATRA SPARKLES UNDER THE SEA

We go back to the gate of the tourist city where we sit waiting for the two greens in the lounge.

Here they are withdrawing from their green group, which attracted the attention of tourists, and then run toward us on time. They Kiss and greet us before they sit with us. Though Monica with a green waterfall cascading on her well-shaped body, is aware of your inability to understand German, she explains in her language what happened only to her mother and Canaan's father, while green is laughing telling you childishly when you ask him," Hey! How was your green trip?"

"They were watching us with amazement and asked us to board a tourist submarine to go sightseeing with white tourists in the quarters and alleys of the city descending in the sea bottom, so I and our green group decided to cross our way diving in the sea like fish. It was then when the watchers went mad seeing us walking freely under the sea surface and descending to sea bottom dauntless without oxygen cylinder or even artificial swim fins. Robot life savers whistled, female robot security was alert and tourists from old generations were stunned when they saw us outside their submarines as they didn't know that we don't breathe air.

We were walking amazed at what we saw in Cleopatra kingdom. We walked on stone-paved roads and watched a stunning royal galley made of gold, the sails of which were woven of silver. The blows of its oars made of a whale's tail, were fluttering with bewitching sounds of guitar and flute music. Inside the galley, sparkled queen Cleopatra in her shelter the threads of which were woven of gold, looking like the Queen of Sheba in her precious convoy, and on each side of the boat ten boys were paddling as if they were scattered pearls, that you didn't know whether they were human beings or jinn. As for her virgin waiting maids and odalisques, they were like mermaids and angels of mercy moving here and there and ordering boys to direct the boat with their paddles right and left. As for the ropes of the boat, they were woven of sedge which amazed everyone."

Monica laughs shyly that the aesthetics of her fresh green body comes to sight, continuing her talk in German, while you are amazed at what you heard of Canaan's imaginary talk. Burhan tells you, taking pride in them," They are forming a green revolution which is changing life concepts on globe surface."

Canaan adds as if he performed a play-act, "And when Cleopatra's galley arrived to her palace entrance the sides of which were lighted along with streets with scorching torches lifted on high pillars, and once it was docked, Antonio who was waiting for her, approached it, hold her hand helping her debark from her royal boat with love overwhelming her heart, led her into the palace hall lighted with a chandelier of pearls sparkling with light, the pearls of which were brought by pharaohs sailors coming from the land of Maya peoples.

Cleopatra accompanied her Caesar in his great royal parade being surrounded by a retinue, ministers, maids-in-waiting, boys, odalisques, each in the center of his or her location, while he was rejoicing over her company and the sweetness of her talk tune cheering up the greatest man."– Canaan sits on the edge of your seat and embraces you– "We enjoyed seeing the royal quarter crowned by Cleopatra palace, and the high buildings surrounding it. It's not far from the sea.

"As for Alexandria library, we saw the harbor workers retaining the books of ships docked in the city, so manuscripts were copied, and then the originals were returned to their owners inside the ship. While we were walking on its stony streets, a destructive earthquake hit the city and the whole island fell apart, marble pillars fell and roofs collapsed landing at a low place under the sea and thus its old beaches were drowned."

Canaan finishes narrating his wondrous story, so you ask him amazed at his narrative art," Tell me, gentleman, how did you watch all this, while you were absent for just two hours and a half?" Canaan laughs happily as you almost fell for his trick. He said, "No, by God, grandpa! We saw all that among the arts of modern sound and light shows prepared to make tourists feel as if they had lived the bygone historical events and to link place with time."

You feel amazed and thankful for the art done to rewrite history in this magical city which tempts you, Burhan and Elza to visit it the next day, but via a submarine that we ride with tourist comers like us. It carries us down to the bottom of the sea of the city where we marvel at the early computer scenes of the facades of the renovated and newly-built monuments as if they occurred now in front of us in four dimensions and in life-size!

You visualize your presence inside the drowning city as if you were two characters from One Thousand and One Nights wandering among the tribes of sea people and an idea crosses your mind, so you share with Burhan.

"Since green creatures succeeded in touring this marine city without using submarines and without polluting the environment with their useful greenness, green Man can extend building his cities in the sea and live there, commuting between the sea and land after being spread everywhere and taking control of the earth, and thus the sea cities would ease the burdens of land without causing any environmental pollution."

"Your viewpoint is stunning. I think it was not included in the program of our big human project, father. I will keep for myself a record of your environmental scoop, and I will register it as the theory of Mashhour for marine housing."

And as we are going back to our hotel, you see a world of young green women and men debarking from a giant cruise ship on Alexandria shore running joyfully, and with each one of them there is a green animal. Their number is more than three thousand green people that you start to think that many things have changed in the bewitching Alexandria, the city that fought all history challenges and remained sparkling, bewitching, and spotless.

THE BOX

Things go well in Dubai; you finish your business and return to old Akka. Your grandchildren and their children welcome you. Samar's grandchildren gather round you, excited to meet their grandpa. You enter the city renouncing worldly life at the sacredness of its entourage like a worn-out impious man entering an altar at a monastery surrendering himself to God and repenting of all his evil deeds and sins thanks to Him...

You kiss the giant wooden gate of Akka strengthened with antique metals and walk with them in its quarters and alleys. You step out of your personality's stillness and stiffness and start to play and run with your offspring in those quarters and alleys that Thaher Al-Umar used to protect their dignity with power and placed on their heads laurel wreath. You walk delighted in their company and sit with them facing the shore to tell them about the history of your grandfather who disappeared behind the fog. You watch the remnants of fishing boats that are still gathering and scattering along sea waves looking at you in their turn as if they winked at you.

You approach that sea mermaid, she runs from you, but you chase her down. You dive in the sea swimming after her. She attacks you that you are about to drown. Fish, whales, and all sea creatures push you to get you out of the place angry at your determination to search again, while laughing dolphins are playing with you and tiny sardines flowing around you like black clouds darkening sea bottom as you are looking for your lost grandfather. Perhaps, he stays here under a boat, fixing or hammering or talking to fish jumping here and there but you forget that they had fished him!

No, no, they did not fish him because if they did, he would have been among fish spread on the deck of the ship. You look for him, but you find nothing but seashells. You sit with your children decorating the wedding treasure chest of your grandmother Aneesa that your grandfather bought for her from the Levant.

He brought for her from there the most beautiful chest to put in it her embroidered Akaai dresses, secret pants, necklaces, bundles, henna, and wool balls of which she made socks and sweaters for family.

You sit with your children to mend the old chest by decorating it with Akka seashells. But where is your grandfather to give him the chest? Your grandfather was lost. Your grandfather was here! They might have chopped up him and canned him with white Tuna for no one here supervised Tuna fish that changed into red color. You look for your grandfather to give him the chest. The chest immerses into sea waves sounds. The sounds of a chorus and a singer, Abu Lamaa and Ghawaja Khristou as they were singing with him: They stole the chest, O Abu Lamaa. Abu Lamaa would say, then:

But I have the key.

-the chest!

-the chest!

-the chest,

-subsequent rings,

-smooth!

(with hearts believing in God, squeezed with grief, we mourn the late engineer Mashhour Shahir Alshahri aged one hundred and two years he spent in the activities he mentioned above. After preying on him in Thaher Alomar Mosque, he was buried in the cemetery of

New Akka in the presence of his children, grandchildren, and great-grandsons together with the reverent Akka residents on 25-9-2051 after he had finished his novel.)

(The Private Intelligence Agency)

ABOUT THE NOVEL:

Titi took you from yourself and did not leave you a chance to take your breath! It's the first time you tried a female taste and smelled her luscious hot breaths…What a female Titi was! She was a flame transferred straight from hell, looking down from gardens of delight upon you…engulfing you in her folds and burning you with her blazing body!

It is said that a mermaid sometimes would go out of the sea and enter a house. She would immerse into the body of a charming woman, fall for a man, make him feel euphoric with her love, and then take him with her to the sea where she would live with him happily ever after! I'm not sure about the immersion of the two characters, Titi and the mermaid together!

When the green man takes control of the universe and all world animals become green, no waste would be discharged, the sweat of green people and animals would change into pure transpiration and dew, toilets would disappear off houses, sewers would stop flowing and rivers would restore their pure virginity flowing sparkling and pristine. Air would never be polluted with gas destructive to the universe, and earth and temperature would return to equilibrium!

Our goal is to change the human brain and get rid of the idea of conflict in it so that man would not harbor ill will against his fellow man, the beasts and living organisms' attack against each other would stop, and nations would cease invading other nations, killing their citizens as well as plundering their riches! Peace will rule the entire world …and if neither religions nor "divided" nations succeed in spreading love among people, we will accomplish that mission. We endeavor to create a paradise on earth.

9 798330 595105